# SOUL RIDER

Kalna squirmed under the hands that held him as the mask was brought down upon his face. He opened his eyes to darkness and moments later felt the presence of the Yorrga's spirit like a cloying syrupy wetness; it entered through his nostrils and swirled down into his mouth. He choked and gagged, trying to spit it out, but it only moved faster. He tried to call up his inner fire, preferring to burn himself to death rather than allow this nightmare to take him over, but even that was denied him. He could do nothing but retreat before its snakelike coils, flinching as its slimy tendrils caught hold...

By Marcia J. Bennett
*Published by Ballantine Books:*

WHERE THE NI-LACH

SHADOW SINGER

BEYOND THE DRAAK'S TEETH

YARIL'S CHILDREN

# YARIL'S CHILDREN

## Marcia J. Bennett

A Del Rey Book

BALLANTINE BOOKS • NEW YORK

This one is for Richie,
In loving memory.

# NOTE FROM THE AUTHOR

I would like to thank Dr. Richard Hosbach for his patience with my questions and his help in making this story medically correct.

My thanks also goes to my agent, Gail Hochman, who has proved her worth and her friendship over and over again.

And a very special thank you to Shelly Shapiro, Editor at Del Rey Books, who has corrected my mistakes, offered thought-provoking suggestions, and improved all of my stories thus far.

And last but never least, I wish to thank my mother, Reatha, who is my number-one proofreader and critic.

Every writer needs such friends as these, and I thought it was about time I thanked them publicly.

Who writes the rhymes that form the lines
       of puppets and puppeteers?
Who pulls the strings of lifelike things,
       the laughter and the tears?
   Who sings the songs that take so long
       and echo through the years?
Ponder not such mighty thoughts.
   Ponder this instead.
       If man be born with fur and wings,
           and the winds obey him when he sings,
               is he less a man? Or more?
                       First verse of "Yaril's Song"
                       from the *Book of the El-ar-kil*

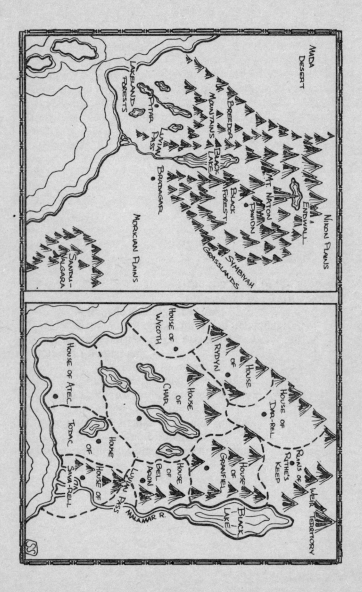

# CHAPTER 1

Late summer had come to the heavily forested Lecarian Mountains. The days were still and warm, the nights cool and clear. Flanked by the Breedor Mountains and Mada Desert to the west and the Morican Plains to the east, the Lecarian Mountains were home to the weirfolk, a race of people who had claimed a portion of the continent of Va-naar over five hundred years before.

Bree, Morican, and Urst also claimed a piece of Va-naar, and all the tribes of men chose to avoid the weirfolk whenever possible for, to them, weir were lesser men, not to be trusted, their strangeness challenging the truths men had so carefully built their beliefs upon.

Kalna cared nothing about men or their sacred truths as he sat quietly in the dappled sunlight, his dark, amber-flecked eyes intent upon his mother as she mixed the ingredients of her special cure-all, a tart potion that warmed the stomach as it worked to revitalize the rest of the body. His thoughts weren't on man's ignorance but rather on the task that lay ahead of him, a task he'd been preparing for for some time.

He knew Graya wouldn't be angry with him if he failed; Kalna would be angry enough for both of them. He didn't like to fail at anything, but as childhood slipped away, he was finding the challenges in life harder to meet, and failure, it seemed, was itself a challenge to be conquered.

Graya stood next to a small stone altar that was sheltered by an overhanging cliff of gray-green stone. She finished her mixing and turned, signaling that she was ready.

Kalna stood and approached the altar, unconsciously wiping sweaty palms against naked thighs.

Graya took his hands and smiled, her amber eyes sparkling with pride. "Kalna, son of Dari," she said softly, "I sense power in you, power you are yet too young to understand. May Yaril guide me to teach you well."

As she turned to stand beside him, one hand slipped down across his back, searching for the telltale bumps that would change her son from weirling to darkling.

Kalna looked into his mother's eyes and instantly knew the meaning behind her touch. It has to happen soon, he thought, or not at all. Male darklings were rare among the weirfolk now, so rare that there was only one known male darkling living at that time. His name was Ek-nar, the Strong One, Lord of the Nikon Plains weir. Some said that darklings were dying out. Was it true? he wondered. In years to come, would darklings be just another legend, a fantasy that only children believed in?

Graya pushed a lock of dark hair from his forehead. "What's wrong, Ka?"

"Nothing. Just thinking."

How tall he's getting, she thought. Soon it will be time for his Naming. She leaned forward and kissed him. "Nervous?"

He nodded and tried to quell the sudden flutter under his ribs. The talent for pyrokinesis wasn't reserved for darklings, and not all darklings possessed the talent, but it was found more often than not among darkling offspring. This was only the third time he'd called up fire and though he understood the basic technique, there was always the chance that something could go wrong. The completion of the healing potion required a very special kind of fire, one without the taint of woodsmoke. That Graya was allowing him to help her with the potion meant that she no longer looked upon him as a child.

He took a deep breath and released it slowly, concentrating on the words that would tap the inner fire that was within every form of life. He heard the soft rustle of his mother's wings and felt their silken touch against his back. That tender caress relaxed and filled him with confidence.

He laid his hands on top of the altar to either side of the clay mixing bowl, palms cupped toward the bowl. All that was needed was a single spark.

*Ki camber anodhal.* He repeated the words over and over in his mind, melding them with his mental image of fire. He felt the energy gather within his body; it was a tingling sensation that coursed up and down his spine like a trapped nalcra. He held it a moment. There was a feeling of euphoria and limitless strength. He held it a second longer then loosed it with a thought, pushing the energy outward through his hands. There was an audible snapping sound as twin lines of power arced from his hands and met over the center of the bowl, igniting the fumes coming from the potion.

The smoke was pungent, and Kalna began to back away. Graya caught his arm and whispered urgently in his ear. He drew a deep breath and concentrated once more and instantly the power drew back into his body.

Graya steadied him as weakness washed over him. "Well done, Ka. Go and sit down now. Rest while I finish."

Light-headed and unsteady, he did as directed, returning to the bottommost step of a flight of stone stairs leading up and out of the small glade. He breathed deeply while he waited and gradually his strength returned.

Graya let the fire burn for a few minutes, then she covered the bowl with a clay lid, extinguishing the flames. Standing in the morning sun as it filtered down through the leaves and branches overhead, clothed in nothing but a pair of gold-tinted wings that arched up and out from her back, she raised the bowl toward the sky and blessed it in Yaril's name.

Suddenly Kalna saw Graya not just as his mother but as a darkling, radiant, graceful, and lovingly honored by all weirfolk. How beautiful she is, he thought. Why haven't I ever noticed before?

Kalna stood as Graya approached. He smiled at her as she passed and followed her silently up the stone steps. They retrieved their clothes from nearby branches and dressed; Kalna in a short brown kilt, a belt holding his bolo sling and a knife sheath, and a pair of ankle-length, soft leather boots; Graya in sandals, a longer beige kilt, and a loose-fitting, sleeveless blue smock that fastened around the neck and was open in the back to allow for free wing movement.

Kalna held the bowl while Graya caught up her long, dark-red hair into a coil on top of her head. She fastened it in place with beautifully carved bone combs.

"Mother, what were you and Father talking about this morning before he left?" Kalna asked, as they started down the narrow, tree-shaded path leading home.

"So you weren't sleeping when I called you."

"I hadn't been awake very long. I was just lying there thinking." He glanced downtrail and saw the back of their vine-covered cabin. "I heard Father say something about seeing Thekis before anyone could cause trouble. What did he mean?"

Graya gave him a sideways glance and kept walking. "Your father found something that troubled him, something that wants explaining and quickly."

When Graya failed to say anything more, Kalna frowned, feeling that he was certainly old enough to share whatever problems his parents faced. "What did he find?"

Graya took the bowl as they reached the back door to the cabin and passed through the open doorway without answering him.

Kalna followed close behind, unwilling to let the matter drop. "Mother?"

Graya set the bowl on the trestle table in the center of the main room and turned to face him. "Dari found a Yorrga mask, a discard by the look of it. It was split from chin to crown."

Kalna thought back, trying to remember all the stories he'd ever heard about the legendary Yorrga masks. They were cut from living trees and were said to contain a portion of the tree's spirit, usually a benign spirit, but not always. Much was said to depend upon the time of the cutting and the spirit of the cutter.

"What trouble could come from a Yorrga mask?" he asked. "I thought they were only used for healing purposes."

"That's their intended purpose, Ka, but wherever there is power, there are those who would turn it to their own uses. There are three mask cutters among us now, each well known, their masks as distinctive as their own faces. The mask Dari found didn't have the mark of any of the three, which means that someone else has begun to make Yorrga masks, someone who is probably untrained in the precautions necessary to complete a mask safely."

She turned away. There was a faraway look in her eyes as she looked out through the doorway. "There was something unusual about the mask your father found. It's difficult to explain in words; it's more than it's shaping or design, it's just a feeling of wrongness you get while holding it. It's important that we find out just who the cutter was and to what purpose he intended the mask."

Kalna watched his mother's wings move back and forth several times before she primly tucked them tight to her back. He sensed her uneasiness and realized there was something she wasn't telling him, something important.

"Does Father have any idea who might have made the mask?"

"No. That's why he's gone to speak to Thekis."

Thekis was Kalna's uncle, Dari's oldest brother. "What will happen when they find out who . . ."

Graya turned back around. "There's no point in asking more questions. I know nothing more. You'll have to wait for Dari to return. If he learns anything from Thekis, he'll tell us."

She picked up the bowl and handed it to him. "Take this to Rops and tell him to divide it between four meals, two today and two tomorrow. Also tell him that he's to stay in bed. While you're gone, I'll start working in the garden."

"When will Father be home?"

"I wouldn't look for him until after supper. Go now and come right back. I've some things I want you to do for me this afternoon."

Rops's home lay to the west of the shale cliffs next to a small tributary of the Keilian River, which emptied into Black Lake from the east. It didn't take Kalna long to reach the small woodland home; he knew the way by heart. When he arrived, he found the front door slightly ajar and he heard voices coming from within.

He knocked on the door and the voices ceased. A moment later the door swung open and he faced a stranger, a beran like Rops, only younger. The beran was a head taller than Kalna and much heavier in build. But for a pair of horns that sprouted from his temples, the beran's head, chest, and hands were manlike while his back, shoulders, arms, and the lower half of his body were covered with thick gray fur.

"Who is it?" Rops called from inside.

"I don't know him," the beran answered.

Kalna sidled past the beran and into the room. "It's me, Rops."

"Hello, Ka," Rops called from his bed on the other side of the room. "What've you brought me?"

Kalna took the bowl over to the bed table. "Something to make you feel better." He gave Rops the directions for taking the medicine, then sat down on the edge of the bed and turned to look at Rops's other guest.

"This is my second cousin, Runner," Rops said, introducing the younger beran. "He lives west of Mount Naton. Runner, this is Kalna, Dari and Graya's son."

Runner smiled and nodded in greeting, his glance quickly assessing. He saw a thin, near-adult weirling with red-black hair, high cheekbones, and black amber-flecked eyes. "You live nearby?" he asked.

"A half-hour walk south," Kalna replied politely, as his glance drifted from Runner's wide, clawed feet and gray-furred flanks up to the top of his curly gray head and the pair of pointed horns that curved gracefully outward from the temples. They were shiny black, well oiled, and looked to be extremely sharp. They look like they'd make good weapons, Kalna thought absently.

The beran's eyes were black and at that moment they twinkled with mischief. "Like what you see?"

"Yes. I mean—I'm sorry," Kalna stammered. "I was just admiring your horns. They're quite . . . handsome."

"Be careful, Ka," Rops warned with a grin. "Once you compliment a beran, he'll haunt you forever. Runner loves quickly and easily, and you'll never be rid of him if you tell him such lies."

"Quiet, Old One," Runner said, "let the boy say what he feels. There's no harm."

"Harm no, except that you'll fall in love with him and drive him crazy with your teasing. I know you too well, Runner, and I'll not allow it."

"Allow? And who are you to allow me one way or another, you old fossil!"

"Fossil! Why, you young, mouthy, good-for-nothing. Wait until I get my strength back, then we'll see who's the old fossil!"

Kalna stood up. He knew the teasing banter between

the two beran meant nothing; it was only their way, but he didn't have time to stay and hear the argument out.

He caught Runner's glance. "Will you be staying here for a while?" There were very few weir anywhere near his own age in the uplands above Black Lake, and he welcomed the possibility of new blood to their section of the forest.

Runner smiled, showing a mouthful of beautiful white teeth. "Just as long as he'll let me," he said, indicating Rops. "Do you have to go?"

"I promised I'd return as soon as I could, but I'll be back to check on Rops tomorrow."

"There's no need to *check* on me," Rops grumbled. "I'm fine!"

Runner glanced at Rops and smiled, then looked back at Kalna. "We'll look for you tomorrow. Rops is in need of company. He's getting to be too much of a recluse."

"I am not!" Rops snapped.

"Yes, you are. That's why I'm here, and here I stay until you are your old self again."

"If you stay, it won't be on my account! You go when and where you will, and the only one you ever think to please is yourself!"

"Now, cousin, you know that isn't fair," Runner said, trying to placate the older beran. "What harm is there in making a few friends while I'm here?"

"Harm there is," Rops muttered, "whenever there's a rascal like you around."

Kalna moved toward the door. "I'll see you both tomorrow," he said, leaving the two to bicker amicably.

He started back the way he'd come, but after passing the shale cliffs, he decided on a different route home. It would take him a little longer, but he had something he wanted to check on. Earlier that summer he'd discovered a velhund den, and it had been weeks since he'd checked on the pups.

He left the riverbank and plunged into the blue-green depths of pine and bolwayo. A scattering of bigleaf, oddbark, and dyson oak trees brought light to the forest floor, helping him to find the right path.

It was quiet in the forest that day, unusually quiet. He paused every once in a while and stood listening. Suddenly a strange chill skittered down his back. It raised bumps on his arms and made his stomach muscles tighten. Something was wrong somewhere nearby. A stranger's face flashed through his mind; it was followed by a backwash of pain and fear and a silent plea for help.

He turned and faced south, then started running. What his father called premonitions, his mother called sendings, or *lahal*. He had been experiencing brief flashes of lahal for several years now and was assured by his mother that such sendings were not to be feared, that with time his understanding and control of this gift would enhance his standing among the weirfolk. He wasn't fully convinced that such was the case, not after the last time when he'd misread a sending and carried news of a death that hadn't occurred. His embarrassment and the lecture given him by his father had made him cautious about listening to his inner voice.

But this time the sending was clear; the pain and fear were something he couldn't ignore. He raced through the woods, ducking branches and pushing through the underbrush. The sending grew stronger. He leaped a fallen log and came to a shallow stream. He waded across and took the opposite incline in eight running strides. When he reached the top of the rise, he turned left and followed the ridge. He was closing in on the one who called him. The signal was so sharp now that it made his head hurt.

Suddenly the sending was cut off. He slowed his headlong rush but kept going in the same direction. A patch of sunlight shone through the trees ahead. When he reached the open, he paused, his glance falling on something lying in the grass to his right just at the edge of the tree shade. He advanced cautiously, hand to knife. The something was a body, man, not weir, judging from the clothing.

He knelt next to the body and hesitated, then gently turned it over. There was a bloody bandage made from a piece of the man's shirt tied around his upper right leg and there was dried blood on the side of his head. Ash-blond hair framed a clean-shaven face. The man had a straight nose, a square jaw, and a white scar line that cut across his right cheek and ended at his upper lip.

Suddenly the man's eyes opened and the hand that had been limp in the grass came to life, grasping Kalna's arm in a vicelike grip that was painful. "Who are you?" the man growled, blue eyes filled with distrust.

Kalna tried to pull free but the man's grip only tightened. Kalna's right hand closed around the hilt of his knife. "Let me go," he said, trying to keep his voice even.

"So you can kill me?"

Kalna shook his head. "I didn't come to kill. I came to help."

"Help? Why should you..." The man twitched around, a spasm of pain contorting his features.

The pressure on Kalna's hand loosened. He was of half a mind to run to Rops or his mother for help, but something kept him there, some unnameable feeling that was linked to the sending. The man was in pain and afraid; Kalna simply couldn't leave him there alone.

A few moments later the man opened his eyes again. He seemed surprised to find Kalna still there. "What's your name?"

"Kalna. Yours?"

"Ard, of the House of Char." The man glanced around. "Are you alone?"

"Yes."

"How did you find me?"

Kalna knew better than to admit the truth, for it was known that men feared the special talents of the weir-folk. "I was on my way home," he said, using a half-truth.

"Home? You're weir?" The man's glance passed over him, looking for that mark of strangeness that separated man from weir. All he saw was a thin, fine-boned youth with black hair and the most penetrating eyes he'd ever seen.

"Does it matter what I am?" Kalna asked defensively, reading the man's look.

"Only if you're with the bastards who attacked me yesterday!"

Kalna ignored the man's angry response and glanced at the bloody rag around his leg. "What happened?"

"I was with a hunting party. We were jumped by a dozen men—" Ard hesitated "—or weir wearing the ugliest masks I've ever seen." He wiped at the sheen of perspiration on his forehead. "They never gave us a chance."

Kalna stiffened at the word masks. His father had been right! Someone was using Yorrga masks and not for their intended purpose. "How long ago did you say this happened?"

Ard licked at dry lips and closed his eyes. "Yesterday afternoon."

"Where?"

"I don't know. Somewhere to the west of here, I think. They chased me after my mount went down. I thought you were one of them. I thought they'd finally caught up with me."

"What of the others in your party?"

"Dead, I think. I don't know for sure. I saw two go down with arrows in their backs. My uncle was dragged from his mount, then someone sliced my leg with a sword. My loper bolted. Probably saved my life. I don't remember much after that. I think I cracked my head on a branch. I must have hung on for a little while, then fell off. When I woke up, I heard voices in the woods. Some of them must have followed me. I got up...kept going ...but I was lost. I didn't know which way was back. Then night came and I found a place to curl up...not too far from here, I think."

The man was rambling. Kalna touched his forehead. He was burning with fever. "Ard?" Kalna said softly.

The man's pain-filled eyes opened.

"My home isn't far from here. Do you think you could stand and walk with my help?"

Ard answered by holding out a hand.

The return trip to the cabin tested Kalna's strength and determination, for the man leaned more and more heavily upon him as the minutes passed. Twice he slid to the ground and Kalna had to fight to get him back up.

He was trembling with exhaustion by the time he saw the cabin through the trees. "Just a little farther," he urged. "My home is just ahead. You can rest there while I find my mother. She'll tend your wound, and when Father returns, you can tell him about the men who attacked you."

Ard muttered something about demons following him and kept turning to look behind him.

Kalna half dragged, half carried Ard into the cabin and let him down on the bed in his own room. Moments later Kalna was racing down the narrow path that led to the garden, mentally rehearsing the news he carried and hoping that, whatever actions his parents took, this time he wouldn't be left out of anything.

Kalna watched Ard watching his mother as she left the room. There was a look of awe on the man's face, and the blue eyes that turned to him a moment later were filled with wonder.

He leaned over and touched Ard's forehead. Six hours in his mother's care and already the fever was broken. There was also a hint of color returning to Ard's face.

"Feeling better?" he asked.

"Yes," Ard answered. "The pain in my leg is almost gone."

"Not gone, just numbed. Kari weed and wine," Kalna explained.

Ard glanced toward the open doorway leading to the main room.

"She'll be back soon," Kalna said, smiling.

"Am I so transparent?" Ard asked, lowering his voice. "I've never seen a darkling before. Are they all as beautiful as your mother?"

"I don't think so," Kalna said, "but I've not seen them all."

"Is your father darkling?"

"No. Male darklings are very rare these days."

"I didn't know. The stories about your people are so wrapped in mystery that it's difficult to know where the truth lies. It's been years since any of the weirfolk have been seen or guested in the Breedors."

"That's not our fault."

"No, it isn't," Ard admitted fairly. "The terms of the old treaties have left little room for friendly meetings between our two races. By all rights I shouldn't be here now, but when you're running for your life, map-drawn borders don't mean very much."

"You said you were hunting when you were attacked," Kalna said, bringing the subject back to more important matters. "What were you hunting?"

"The Great Whites that nest in the marshlands north of Black Lake. It's neutral territory."

Kalna cast a quick glance at the doorway. A guest's privacy was sacrosanct among the weir, but he burned with curiosity and he just couldn't keep his questions to himself. "How many of the masked men did you see?"

"A dozen, maybe more. I'm not sure now. My uncle, Lord Alfar, was in the lead. I was riding behind him alongside Prince Jurandyr. They were on us so quickly that few of us had time to get our weapons out."

"I've heard of Prince Jurandyr. He's heir to the House of Dar-rel."

"You're well informed."

"My father is a loo woods wachter. It's his business to know who rules the lands that border weir territory. He thought Prince Jurandyr would be a fair man."

"His father was a good man. In another year, Jurandyr would've come of age and been named Lord of the

House of Dar-rel. This was his first try at the Great Whites. He was so excited . . ." Ard's voice trailed off.

"Is there a chance that he might live? You did, and—"

"Kalna!"

Kalna turned to find Graya standing in the doorway. He wilted under her frown. It took no special talents to know she was greatly displeased.

"Come. You have work to do," she said firmly, "and our guest needs his rest."

Kalna cast one apologetic glance at Ard and headed for the doorway under the watchful eyes of his mother.

"The garden," she said, "until I call for you."

An hour passed as Kalna worked steadily up and down the rows of vegetables that would help feed them through the winter. He grumbled to himself as he worked, wishing he'd been more careful in asking his questions. He cast a glance at his mother, who was gathering geevan pods just a short distance away. She caught his look but said nothing as she gathered her basket and started back to the cabin. Doggedly he returned to his weeding.

Late-afternoon shadows had invaded the garden before Graya finally called him in to eat supper. He breathed a sigh of relief and gathered his digging tools. He washed up outside the kitchen door and went inside. The table was set for two.

"Isn't Ard going to eat?" he asked, glancing at the door to his bedroom.

"I've already fed him. Come. Sit down. You can talk to him later."

Kalna took his place at the table. "Father should be back soon, shouldn't he?"

Graya passed him a plate of sliced brown bread. "He should, but you know what happens when he and Thekis get together. Your uncle can outtalk the wind." Graya smiled. "And your father can match him word for word when he wants to."

Kalna smiled, too, relieved to see his mother in a better mood. He helped with the dishes after supper, then went into his bedroom to look in on their guest. He returned moments later. "He's sleeping."

"Best thing for him," Graya said.

He crossed the room and helped Graya finish podding the geevan. "Mother, Ard said that the men who attacked him were wearing masks."

"So I heard."

Kalna blushed at the reminder of his earlier indiscretion, but he went on, too filled with thoughts of the Yorrga to be sidetracked. "If they *were* Yorrga, why would they attack a party of Bree hunters?"

A shadow of worry crossed Graya's face. "I'm afraid that the Yorrga Ard ran into may not be any of our own."

"What do you mean?"

"I mean that someone is making and using Yorrga masks for their own purposes. Considering what your father found and what happened to Ard, I believe that we're dealing with something out of the past."

She reached out and smoothed back a single lock of hair that was forever falling into his eyes. "The spirit masks aren't something to be used lightly. Their power could so easily be used to hurt instead of heal, to confuse instead of enlighten. The spirits captured within the Yorrga masks are as old as time. When housed within a tree, they are patient and serene, loving and healing any who pass near; but when they're cut free, their patience sometimes turns to restlessness and their delight in life to mischievous behavior. He who cuts and carves a Yorrga mask must be strong in order to control the spirit he has freed, and I don't mean physical strength alone."

"What if he isn't strong enough?" Kalna asked.

She turned away, setting her empty basket in a corner. "There's an old saying, Ka: 'He who wears a Yorrga mask wears death while he dances.' "

"I don't understand."

"The Yorrga masks have a power of their own, power to overcome the weak-willed. To wear a Yorrga mask with other than healing or goodness in your heart is to invite Tennebar, the father of all deviltry, to enter the physical world."

"The masks really are alive?"

"Not alive as we know it, Ka, but aware of what goes on around them—and some seem more aware than others. I believe it depends upon the kind of tree from which they're taken."

"Rops has a Yorrga mask. So does Thekis. But they're not the same. I got a tingly feeling when I held Thekis's mask."

"That's because his mask is special in another way. It has a—" Graya stopped speaking and let out a low cry.

Kalna turned and saw her eyes directed to the nearby window. When he saw the ugly, twisted face peering into the room at them, he lunged past her toward the door leading outside.

"No, Ka! Wait!" Graya cried.

# CHAPTER 2

Kalna's brief glimpse of the masked face in the window sent adrenaline coursing through his veins. He grabbed his father's staff from beside the door, wrenched it open, and ran straight into the waiting arms of a Yorrga.

The Yorrga snatched the staff away and violently pushed Kalna back through the open doorway. Kalna hit the floor rolling and came up against his mother's legs. By the time he sat up, five Yorrga stood inside the house. A limp form dangled from the hands of the two nearest the doorway.

"Dari!" Graya's indrawn hiss of anguish brought Kalna to his feet. The Yorrga had captured his father!

The Yorrga wearing the mask with a crooked nose brought his long knife up and touched the point to Kalna's chest. "Stand still and you won't be hurt."

Graya dropped a hand to Kalna's shoulder, drawing him back away from the knifepoint. "What do you want here?" she demanded. "And what have you done to my husband?"

"We met this unfortunate on the trail," another of the

17

Yorrga answered. His mask was painted black; its long protruding tongue and slitted eyes gave it a sleepy look. "We asked him some questions and he chose not to answer. Now it's your turn."

Graya straightened, wings upright as if poised for battle. "Do you know to whom you speak? Take off those masks right now and let me see your faces!"

"Try any of your tricks, darkling, and your husband dies!" Crooked-nose growled. "And your son will be next. Now—we have something you want, and I believe you have something we want. Give us the white-haired one and you can have your husband back."

Graya never moved a muscle, but Kalna couldn't stop himself from glancing toward the open doorway to his room. He looked back at the Yorrga, fear and anger causing his heart to race. These had to be the ones who had attacked Ard earlier. Who were they? They must be weir—only weirfolk used the Yorrga masks. Why were they still after the Bree?

"Release Dari and we'll talk," Graya said, as if to compromise.

Crooked-nose shook his head. "I think not." He snapped his fingers and pointed at the doorway to Kalna's room. "Look in there."

Long-tongue and another wearing a mask with puffed cheeks and pursed lips started for the other side of the room. Graya's hand tightened on Kalna's shoulder as the two approached the doorway with their long knives drawn.

Kalna jumped at the hair-raising cry that preceded Ard out of his room. Ard threw himself straight at the Yorrga to the right of the doorway, his knife driving into Long-tongue's stomach. He wrenched it free as Long-tongue toppled to the floor and turned to meet Puffed-cheeks's attack from the side.

As Crooked-nose swung around to see what was happening behind him, Graya and Kalna moved as one. Graya knocked the knifepoint aside by slapping at Crooked-nose's arm, leaving Kalna free to dart forward, his own knife in hand. Two quick slashes and the weir holding his father released him. Graya stepped in and caught Dari's limp body and backed away under the protection of Kalna's blade.

Crooked-nose recovered and brought his long knife up. "That was a mistake, darkling!"

One of the weir Kalna had cut stood holding his arm and cursing as blood flowed through his fingers; the other weir, having taken less serious a wound, drew his long knife and advanced on Kalna. His twisted mask was painted black on one side, blue on the other and it had a skull-like appearance.

Graya saw Crooked-nose and Skull-face converging upon Kalna and realized that to withhold her power would be to lose all. Darkling fire wasn't meant for battle, for it drained the user too quickly, but now Graya had no choice. She let Dari's body slide to her feet and raised her hands toward the two Yorrga threatening her son. Words were quickly spoken, tonal inflection and timbre instantly opening the channels to the core of energy that was darkling power. A stream of fire arched out from her hands, catching Skull-face in the chest. Crooked-nose leaped away, trying to avoid the flames as Graya turned toward him.

Skull-face screamed and threw himself to the floor and began rolling, trying to put the fire out. Kalna backed away and tripped over his father's legs. He landed on his hands and knees straddling his father's body, his knife slipping out of his hand. One glance at the open, staring eyes of his father and his world began to crumble. "Father!"

Graya heard her son's cry and looked down. When she saw death staring up at her, she knew but a moment of grief, then rage took over. She bent down, caught Kalna by an arm, lifted him, and literally threw him behind her. "Out, Ka! Get out! Run!"

Kalna hesitated, then turned and ran. One of the Yorrga cut him off from the back door. Kalna twisted to one side to avoid the Yorrga's hands and fell as a sharp pain caught him knee high. He hit the floor on his side and rolled over clutching his right knee, searing agony filling his entire being.

Graya turned, saw her son down and the Yorrga standing over him, his sword poised to strike the unprotected neck. Another blast of fire blossomed from her hands. The Yorrga was powerless before it and began backing away.

Ard still grappled with another Yorrga over in one corner. Crooked-nose moved in on Graya's left as she turned to defend her son. Graya didn't see him until too late.

Kalna saw the Yorrga stalking his mother and yelled a warning, but at that same moment Crooked-nose lunged forward, his blade driving into Graya's side.

She cried out as she slumped to the floor, her fire dying. Her pain reverberated through Kalna's body in waves, taking his breath away. Shuddering with the aftershock, he looked on in horror as Crooked-nose roared in triumph and raised his blade for the death stroke.

But Graya wasn't ready to give up life so easily. Her right hand rose and her lips moved silently. Fire lashed upward, engulfing Crooked-nose's head. The Yorrga stumbled backward, batting at the flames while trying to work free of the mask. He fell hard against the table and tipped it over.

Kalna saw what was going to happen but couldn't scramble out of the way fast enough. The table tipped over with the Yorrga's weight, the edge smashing down on Kalna's right foot. The shock of pain pushed him to the brink of unconsciousness.

Crooked-nose rolled over finally free of his burning mask and struggled to his feet. Graya's fire licked at the floorboards beneath his feet as he stumbled half blinded toward the door. The other three surviving Yorrga were quick to follow.

Crooked-nose stopped in the doorway. "Is the prince dead?" he demanded of his companions.

Puffed-cheeks peered back through the smoke and

fire to the bodies lying still on the floor near Kalna's room. "I think so. Want me to make sure?"

"No!" Crooked-nose turned away. "Let's get out of here. Let the bodies burn, all of them!"

"What if he isn't dead?"

"It won't matter in a few minutes. We'll wait outside. If anyone tries to get out, we'll have them!"

Kalna saw the Yorrga through tear-blurred eyes. When they disappeared from the doorway, he turned and found his mother lying just a few steps away. Blood trickled from her mouth; her eyes were open and she was watching him. Her fear for him now outweighed her pain.

"The cellar, Ka," she gasped. "Get out! Hurry!"

Kalna tried to move but a wave of darkness threatened. He sank back to the floor, his stomach churning. "I can't. My foot's caught."

"Try, Ka! Try!" Graya clutched at her side, pain twisting her beautiful face. "Go to Thekis. Tell him . . . a new kind of Yorrga lives, and . . . it is as we feared!"

Something moved through the smoke. Kalna reached for his bolo sling, sure that it was one of the Yorrga returning. Then he saw a head of white hair, and Ard limped past the body of Kalna's father and came to kneel beside Graya. Blood dribbled down his left arm and fell onto Graya's wings as he leaned over her.

Graya spoke to Ard, then her whispered words trailed off. Ard cursed softly and rose. He turned and peered through the smoke that obscured the upper half of the room. He saw Kalna pinned by the table and hurried over.

"My mother?" Kalna asked softly.

Ard didn't reply. He caught the edge of the table with his good arm and lifted, allowing Kalna to pull himself free. As the table thunked down, Kalna began dragging himself toward his mother. He knew she was gone but a part of him wouldn't accept that fact.

Ard grabbed him from behind. "The cellar!" he demanded. "Where is it? We have to get out!"

Kalna knocked his hand away and turned back to his mother.

Ard caught him by the hair. "She's dead! As you will be if you don't show me the way out!"

Kalna was so overcome with grief that he didn't hear. The death of his parents was like a gaping wound that could not be staunched.

"The cellar!" Ard yelled in his face. "Damn it, show me the way to the cellar!"

The anger in Ard's voice pushed at the numbing wall beginning to surround Kalna. He tried to focus on the man's face. A hand smashed across his mouth.

"Kalna! The cellar! Where is the cellar?"

Anger stirred. "My room! A trapdoor in the corner. Now leave me alone!"

"Where does it lead?"

Kalna began coughing; the smoke was growing thicker. "A tunnel to the outside."

"Can you walk?"

"I don't think so." Kalna looked down at his mother again, trying to push Ard from his thoughts. For a moment he was sure he saw her chest rise and fall. He reached out to her, willing death away; but the eyes that had glittered with love and pride were empty now, empty and frightening.

"Kalna, we've got to go!"

When Kalna failed to respond, Ard caught him around the waist and lifted him with his good arm. Flames were licking at the floor and furniture now and the smoke was getting heavier by the second. Ard limped toward the other side of the room keeping as low as possible. He stepped over the body of Long-tongue and passed through the doorway leading into Kalna's room. It took him but a moment to spot the trapdoor. He set Kalna down on the bed, got the trapdoor up, then made a hurried trip back to the main room. He returned carrying one of the Yorrga long knives, which he slid into his belt. Moments later he carried Kalna down through the cellar hatchway.

The air below was fresh. "Where's the way out, Kalna?"

Kalna heard Ard's voice as if from a long way off. Cruel fingernails bit into the flesh of his arm.

"Kalna, wake up! Where is the tunnel?"

"Behind the curtain!" Kalna snapped angrily.

Ard peered into the darkness, then began to limp forward. Kalna felt the man shudder with the effort of carrying an extra burden. "Put me down. I'll find my own way out."

Ard ignored him. "How long is the tunnel?"

"Seventy-five paces. It comes out near the stream."

Ard let Kalna down on his good leg, turned, then pushed his shoulder into Kalna's stomach and hoisted him up onto his shoulder. Kalna clutched for a hold as Ard stepped into the darkness of the tunnel. Ard used the wall for a guide and several minutes later reached the interwoven bramble door that hid the tunnel entrance from the outside.

Kalna closed his eyes as Ard carried him across the stream and into the cover of the trees beyond. His thoughts were on his parents and those who were responsible for their deaths. Where there had been grief now there was anger. He smelled smoke from the burning cabin and opened his eyes. He could see the flicker of fire through the trees.

Suddenly Ard stumbled and fell, slamming Kalna to the ground. Kalna couldn't hold back a cry of agony as his injured leg hit the forest floor. Stomach churning, he rolled into a ball and clenched his jaws tightly, trying to will the pain away.

A hand touched his shoulder. "Let me see, Kalna." The snap of command was gone from Ard's voice.

Kalna took several deep breaths and unrolled slowly, careful to keep his leg off the ground. "It's my knee, it feels as if something's broken or torn. My foot hurts, too. Don't," he gasped, as Ard touched his leg. "It makes me sick to my stomach."

"Both are beginning to swell," Ard said. "We'll need

cold water to get the swelling to stop. I could take you back to the stream but we'd chance running into those black-hearted bastards again and, at the moment, I don't feel in any shape to fight them off. Is there another stream nearby or a place where we would be safe a little while?"

Kalna met Ard's piercing gaze. Under other circumstances, he would never reveal the home of a friend to a stranger, but these were not ordinary circumstances. He was sure Rops would understand.

Ard found Kalna a stout branch to use as a crutch and they set off together, both limping. It was dark by the time they reached Rops's cabin, but the half moon gave them just enough light to see by.

"Odd," Kalna said, "there is no light showing." He looked around and felt a coldness settle in his stomach. "I don't like this. It's too quiet."

"You stay here," Ard said softly. "I'll go take a look."

Ard circled around and approached the front door from the south. He hesitated outside a moment, then cautiously pushed the door open and stepped inside. He wasn't in the cabin very long.

Kalna's heartbeat quickened as Ard returned. "What did you find?" he demanded anxiously.

"A body. A beran, I think. I've never seen one up close."

"Young or old?"

"I don't know, but he was in bed when he was killed."

Rops. Oh, Yaril, why? Kalna felt the pressure of tears and tried to blink them away.

"From the looks of the place—broken chairs, overturned table—I'd say that there was a fight. You said that two were living here?"

"Yes."

"It's possible that our masked friends paid them a visit before coming to your home. Do you have any other friends nearby?"

"Not close, no." Kalna looked down at the small cabin and thought of all the wonderful times he'd spent

with Rops. Such a gentle soul; never tiring of a child's
questions, always ready for a game.

"Kalna, I'm not sure what we should . . ."

The snap of a branch sounded loud in the evening air.
Ard drew his long knife and turned a slow circle. Kalna
followed suit, drawing his bolo sling.

There was a scuffle of leaves then something lunged
out of the bushes toward them. Kalna caught a glimpse
of long white hair and a grinning face mask, then the
Yorrga smashed into him. His teeth clicked together
painfully as an elbow caught him in the mouth. Taloned
fingers jerked him forward and an arm snaked around his
neck. The smell of uncured hide was strong as his captor
pulled him close.

Ard was aware of Kalna's danger but was unable to
help him, for he faced another of the Yorrga. He parried
a slashing stroke and danced away. His opponent, wearing a twisted mask, growled a curse and followed. It was
dark for such fighting and the ground was uneven. The
Yorrga misstepped. Ard took advantage of the fault and
lunged in, his knifepoint slicing flesh just below the
Yorrga's mask. The Yorrga clutched at his throat and
toppled forward, blood spurting from a severed artery.

Ard's triumphant cry gave Kalna strength to fight
back. He tucked his head to one side and clamped his
teeth into the arm around his neck. The Yorrga yelled
and pushed Kalna from him, then Ard was there, moving
into an attack position.

Kalna had one glimpse of Ard before his bad foot
touched the ground, then pain pulled darkness around
him. The last thing he heard was a Bree battle cry.

When Kalna regained consciousness, it took him only
a moment to realize that the pain in his stomach came
from being carried over someone's shoulder. A bubble of
fear caught in his throat. Who had won the battle? Ard
or the Yorrga?

"Ard?"

"About time you woke up. I don't think I could carry you much farther."

Ard's voice dissolved Kalna's fear. "For a moment I thought you were one of the Yorrga," he confessed, as Ard let him down and steadied him with a hand. Ard was breathing heavily.

Kalna looked around them but the moonlight gave him no clues as to where they were or how far Ard had come from Rops's cabin. "Do you know where we are?"

"South of where we started, I think, but I'm not sure."

"The Yorrga?"

"Is that what you call them?"

"Yes."

"Well, whatever their names, they're still behind us."

"Close?"

"I was sure I heard voices awhile back. I'm assuming they belong to the ones who attacked us. I thought the dark might slow them down, but it hasn't seemed to."

"Not the Yorrga."

"What do you mean?" Ard asked.

"The Yorrga aren't bound by the laws of weir or men, Ard. Day or night, light or dark, I don't think time has much meaning for them."

"You speak as if these Yorrga are more than just weir wearing masks."

Kalna hesitated, unsure how much to tell the man, then he recalled what Ard had done for him. "They *are* more, Ard. Yorrga are tree spirits linked with weir; that joining, according to my mother, gives them a special awareness, and coupled with that awareness is a penchant for great mischief, if the spirit is not kept under control."

"I wouldn't call murder mischief," Ard said.

Kalna looked up at the man. The moonlight glinted off his hair and touched the flat planes of his cheeks and forehead. The scar on his face gave him a somewhat roguish look. Kalna sensed anger in the man, anger that he shared. "Neither would I," he said grimly.

"Do you have any idea who these Yorrga are?"

"No. I didn't recognize any of their voices and I can't think of anyone among the weirfolk who would knowingly harm my mother, even under the influence of a Yorrga mask. Did you kill the two who . . ."

Ard suddenly jerked Kalna up against his chest, smothering his next few words; then slowly he sank to the ground carrying Kalna with him.

Kalna started to struggle, but Ard leaned close and whispered in his ear. "Lie still. I heard something."

Kalna froze, hardly daring to breathe. He closed his eyes to better concentrate on the night sounds around them. He listened but heard nothing. Ard lay half on top of him; he could feel the man's heart beating against his own chest. Was Ard frightened, too? he wondered.

He looked up through the tree branches and saw the moon break out from behind the clouds. To move now would be to show themselves to the Yorrga, if it was they Ard heard.

Time passed. The warmth of Ard's body eventually lulled Kalna into a light sleep. Ard, exhausted by his efforts to carry Kalna to safety, finally joined the young weirling in slumber. His last conscious effort to stay awake was no more than a slight lifting of his head before settling back down.

# CHAPTER 3

Kalna glanced up at the sky. It was overcast with rain clouds and growing darker by the moment. Night was fast approaching, which meant that it would be time to stop soon. He was grateful for that because he was tired and hungry but too proud to ask Ard to stop early. Ard had fashioned him a pair of crude crutches, but after four days of steady walking, his underarms were worn raw, and between his arms, his badly bruised foot, and his knee, he was never without pain.

He looked ahead and realized that Ard had stopped, waiting for him to catch up again. As he closed the distance between them he asked, "Do you think they're still following us, Ard?"

Ard turned and looked back at the weirling who had become entangled in his life. If not for his promise to the darkling . . . He left that thought dangling and answered Kalna's question.

"I don't know if they're still following us, but I don't intend to stop and find out. The House of Balaron is south of Black Lake and west of the Saverin River.

There's a fording place near Latthan that we should reach sometime late tomorrow. Once on the other side of the river, we should have no trouble with the Yorrga."

"You have friends at the House of Balaron?"

"Yes. Distant relatives."

And what of me? Kalna thought dismally. Where do I go for safety? Surely not among men!

Ard noted the dark smudges under Kalna's eyes, the droop of his shoulders. "Tired?"

"No."

"Liar. Sit down. We'll rest awhile."

Kalna was too tired to take offense. Gratefully he sank to the ground, carefully positioning his injured leg.

Ard searched his pockets and came up with a small handful of nuts he'd gathered along the way. He divided them and gave half to Kalna. Rocks were used to break the shells. As Kalna chewed the nut meats, he thought about the gray flyer he'd been lucky enough to drop with his bolo sling the day before. The fresh meat had tasted good, but one small flyer divided between two people didn't fill either stomach. If we could only stop for a day and set some snares, he thought, we might catch a real meal.

Ard popped two nuts into his mouth and brought Kalna's thoughts back to more important matters. "Have you thought about where *you* want to go? I mean, if there's somewhere you'd be safe, rather than staying with me, it might be best if..."

Kalna shook his head. The thought of striking out on his own with Yorrga lurking somewhere along their backtrail made him feel ill. And that thought led to thoughts of his home and what he had lost. Grief tightened his throat, nearly choking him. He spat out a mouthful of nuts and wiped at the spittle on his chin; hatred for his parents' killers churned in his stomach.

The Yorrga were of the weirfolk, he reasoned. Yet who among the weir would kill a darkling? That single thought continued to haunt him and made him question the truths behind the legend or the Yorrga. Who were they really? Where did they come from? Yaril was said to have cut the Yorrga spirits from living trees in order to help heal her children. Did that mean that she was responsible for their evil as well as their good? He had always prayed to Yaril for guidance, as his mother had taught him. Had she been wrong in her teachings? Or had he missed something that would help ease the pain he now felt, that would give meaning to the deaths he had witnessed?

Ard was aware of the youth's distress but not certain of its cause. He gave Kalna a guilty pat on the shoulder. "I wasn't trying to get rid of you, Kalna. I just thought you might be safer on your own."

"That's not what you were thinking." Bitterness tinged Kalna's voice. "You were thinking you could travel much faster without me."

Ard's eyes narrowed in suspicion. "I've heard that no thoughts are private among your kind. Do you read all my thoughts, weirling?"

It was in Kalna's mind to stand and walk away, to leave Ard to fend for himself; but that meant that he, too, would be alone, and that was something he couldn't face at that moment. There were other dangers in the mountains besides Yorrga: there were wild velhund and spitter snakes and, more dangerous yet, nalcra, giant felines that saw both men and weir as fair game. Even with the knife Ard had given him, he would not dare stand up against a full-grown nalcra, and climbing a tree with his bad leg would be an impossibility.

Kalna looked at the man and knew he had no choice but to stay with him. He swallowed his pride and answered Ard's question honestly. "No. I can't read your thoughts. I can feel your emotions sometimes, when you're angry or hurt, like the first time I met you, but touching another's thoughts directly takes great concentration and strength I don't possess at this time."

"How did you know what I was thinking then?"

"A good guess. With this leg, I *am* slowing you down."

Ard's frown slowly faded. "I'm sorry, Kalna. I had no right to accuse you of anything. Are you ready to go on?"

"To Latthan?"

"Yes," Ard said, helping him up. "It would be better if we didn't have to cross into Morican territory, but it can't be avoided."

"Why? Do you fear the Morican?"

"They aren't exactly friendly to the Bree. It comes down to the fact that we have what they lack: good land, timber, water, and minerals. They trade with us because they have to, but never with goodwill. They've envied us for a long time, and gradually that envy has turned to hate. One hundred years ago that hate sparked the Vanaar Trade War and ended in the Sister Houses forming an alliance that successfully stopped the Morican from ever again pitting one house against the other."

"Are we in Morican territory now?" Kalna asked.

"Near enough." Ard started walking. Kalna followed, limping along behind. "The Morican claim all the land east of the Saverin River up to and including the foothills of these mountains. As far as I know, there is no eastern border to their lands."

Kalna's knowledge of men's wars and history consisted mostly of those battles or meetings that touched upon the treaties promising peace between the weirfolk and the Bree. As for the Morican, their few attempts to claim land in the Lecarian Mountains had all led to disaster, for the weirfolk had proved more than capable of holding their own. But those skirmishes had been long ago and Kalna wasn't so sure his people could withstand an invasion now. With more of the weirfolk choosing to live farther and farther back in the Black Forest and north on the Nikon Plains, there were few left to watch against invaders, at least in the most southernly sections of the mountains.

Kalna's thoughts on the subject were scattered as something dropped out of the tree onto Ard's shoulders, driving him to the ground. Kalna reached for his knife as the sound of insane laughter filled the air. A second later he launched himself at the back of the Yorrga, his knife-point driving deep into flesh. The Yorrga screamed and arched back, throwing Kalna off to one side.

A stabbing pain in his right leg threatened to overwhelm him, but fear drove the darkness back, and he rolled over and out of the way as the Yorrga lunged toward him.

Kalna saw his death in the mad eyes of the Yorrga. Panic sent him scuttling backward. The Yorrga followed, crawling on his hands and knees, his throaty cackle sending shivers up and down Kalna's spine. He saw his knife sticking out of the Yorrga's back and searched frantically for another weapon—a rock, a stick, anything.

The Yorrga caught him by an arm and pulled himself closer. Kalna twisted around and used his free fist, oblivious to the pain as his knuckles struck the wooden mask.

One of the Yorrga's hands closed around his neck and squeezed. "Die, weirling! You are one witness too many —and that is not as the Master would have it!" The Yorrga's breath rattled in his throat and slowly he collapsed forward.

Kalna pushed himself away as the Yorrga's hand loosened from his throat. It took him a moment to fully realize that the Yorrga was dead. He looked into the eyeholes of the mask and shuddered, thinking how close he had come to death.

His next conscious thought concerned the identity of the weir beneath the mask. He hesitated a moment then tapped the mask lightly. It was loose. Curiosity won out over revulsion, and he carefully lifted the mask up and off the Yorrga's face. Kalna jumped slightly as it slid free and fell face up next to his leg.

He took several deep breaths, giving himself time to gather his courage, then he leaned closer to study the weir's face. High cheekbones, a long straight nose, a dark beard, and dark curly hair cropped short, all unremarkable features. It was the eyes that told the true story, for they were amber in color.

Kalna looked down at the mask, a twisted face; he was heartsick with the knowledge that, for some unknown reason, weir had turned against weir.

He started to turn away but paused when he saw something glimmer near the weir's head; it was a strange grayish-white light that seemed to be seeping out of the weir's mouth, rising like steam from a fresh morning kill. He had heard about death vapor but had never witnessed the phenomenon of a departing spirit. The possibility that what he was seeing was, in fact, the last physical presence of their attacker filled him with relief rather than guilt.

The relief was short-lived, however, for in the next moment he was awash in an emotional turbulence so filled with anger that it all but smothered him. He gasped for air and tried to shield himself by centering his being on a single word, a special word that his mother had taught him. But the word failed this time because with it came memories of Graya; foremost of those memories was a picture of her lying dead on the floor, the hem of her tunic already ablaze.

He squeezed his eyes shut, willing the scene away. All the while the presence of the Yorrga swirled around him, feeding on his pain and gleefully, madly demanding a joining. In that instant Kalna knew he was lost if he didn't break contact. The spirit of the mask was beyond his control; all he could hope to do was shut it out.

He needed a focal point, something upon which he could center his thoughts, something that wouldn't bring memories alive. He opened his eyes and immediately felt the presence of the Yorrga pushing at him, its invisible body as tangible as the ground beneath him.

It spoke to him mind to mind and demanded his submission; its soundless words were like firebrands burning wherever they touched.

*No! Stay back!*

His mental scream slammed into the tree spirit but it

didn't give way, it simply wrapped itself more and more tightly around him. He was frantic with pain and terribly frightened, his mother's words coming back to him: "He who wears a Yorrga mask wears death while he dances."

He looked down and saw the mask lying against his leg. He struck at it, flipping it away; then his hands touched the ground and he was pushing to his feet; his only thought was to flee.

Then inspiration struck and he dropped back to the ground, digging his fingernails into the soil. The ground! It was the focus he needed!

*Strong. Solid. Heavy.* The words came quickly to mind and he added to them, building a wall around himself. *Massive. Safe. Warm. Stable. Solid.* He repeated the words over and over, shutting off all thoughts but one: *I am earth!*

It was full dark when he came out of his self-imposed trance. The moonlight barely penetrated the heavy foliage above. Strangely, he was neither cold nor stiff from sitting so long, and for a few moments he couldn't remember who he was or what he was doing sitting on the ground in the dark.

He reached out and his hand brushed something. He investigated further. Warm flesh touched cold flesh, and like a firespark it all came back: his name, his parents' deaths, the Yorrga. He recoiled from the stiff, lumpy mass and drew himself back away from the dead body.

The soft *whoo*ing of a nightbird broke the stillness and gradually other sounds seeped into his awareness: the wind in the treetops, the rustle of leaves as some small creature scurried about its night feeding, and—heavy breathing? Suddenly he remembered his traveling companion.

"Ard?"

He turned and saw another lump of darkness sprawled nearby. Being careful with his bad leg, he crawled over to the Bree. The man's heartbeat was strong and steady though his breathing sounded labored.

He tapped Ard lightly on the cheek, trying to rouse him. When there was no response, he slapped him harder.

Ard moaned softly but didn't wake up. Kalna searched Ard's small belt pouch and found a metal container of matches. He quickly gathered a few dried leaves and twigs, but hesitated before lighting the fire. He realized that if there were more Yorrga in the area, a fire might draw them, but it was important to check Ard over to make sure he was not hurt seriously. He decided to take a chance.

As the small fire chased the darkness back, he fed it with more twigs then bent to examine Ard more closely. The first thing he found was a lump on the back of Ard's head the size of a bird's egg, but there was no blood; the second thing he found was the Yorrga mask laying between Ard's legs. He picked up one of his crutches and pushed the mask away, unwilling to touch it again.

He realized that there was nothing more to do for Ard but wait and hope he would wake soon. He added some larger branches to the fire, then crawled over to the Yorrga's body. Grimacing, he pulled his knife free, cleaned the blade in the dirt, and returned it to its sheath.

The flickering firelight accented the gruesome lines of the wooden mask that lay nearby. The Yorrga's dead, he thought, there is no reason to fear it now, so why do I sitll feel nervous? Perhaps it isn't dead, he thought. How long can a tree spirit survive without a host? Minutes? Hours? Days? His mother would've known.

He was touched by a pang of grief. He roughly pushed it aside, knowing that it wouldn't help him now.

Suddenly Ard twitched and cried out, then he began to mumble, but his words were unintelligible. Kalna crawled over to him and spoke soothingly and gradually Ard quieted.

Kalna used up all the small branches and twigs he could find nearby and went to find more. The thought of sitting in the darkness with the body of a dead Yorrga was abhorrent.

Minutes later he had a small armful of branches and
was limping back toward the dying fire when he paused,
sure he had heard a voice. He let the branches down
carefully and turned, listening. The voice came again but
the words were indistinct. His heart beat faster as his
mind centered on Yorrga and the possibility that his fire
had drawn them. He limped forward, carefully placing
his crutches before him. He hadn't gone far when another sound came to him; it was the soft *woofi*ng sound
of a taural, a waist-high, shaggy-coated herbivore that
long ago had been hunted for both meat and pelt but now
was domesticated and served both men and weir.

Kalna followed the sounds made by the taural and
soon spotted the light of a campfire. He realized that the
men around the fire were probably Moricanian but at
that moment it didn't seem to matter. Ard was in need of
help and he was in no position to fight off any more
Yorrga. Hoping that he was making the right decision, he
came in downwind of the camp in order not to alert the
velhunds that were sure to be guarding the herd. His
stomach growled softly as the smell of cooked fish
wafted through the air. He and Ard had had little to eat
the past few days and the supper odors were making him
light-headed.

He stopped on the fringe of the herders' camp. There
were three men at the cooking fire: one was short and
fat, the other two were of average size and height. All
had dark hair worn short around neck and face. The light
from the campfire touched the men's faces, turning them
a ruddy gold.

He readjusted his crutches under his arms. It was
time to make his presence known. Slowly he limped a
few steps closer to the fire. Suddenly a large form mate-
rialized out of the darkness.

"Who's there?"

Kalna was startled by the man's size and voice and he
took an involuntary step backward, forgetting his bad
leg. The sharp pain was too much to bear silently and he
cried out as he fell.

The big herder was on him a second later, his wooden staff pushing down across Kalna's chest.

"What've you got, Haley?" one of the herders at the fire demanded.

"A thief, I think." The man spoke with an accent strange to Kalna's ears. He had to be Moricanian.

"I'm no thief!" Kalna protested. "I didn't come to steal! I came for help!"

One of the herders approached carrying a lighted branch. "Jon says to bring him over to the fire, Haley."

The one called Haley caught Kalna by the tunic front and dragged him to his feet. Kalna grabbed at the man's arm for support.

"What's wrong with you?" Haley growled.

"I've hurt my leg."

Haley frowned as he caught Kalna around the waist and carried him to the fire over one hip. He set him down on the ground in front of the heavyset herder.

"What's your name?" the herder demanded.

"Kalna."

The man pushed Kalna's head around so his face was full to the light. "What are you doing out here in the middle of nowhere? Where do you belong?"

Kalna hesitated, instinctively wary. "We come from the hills to the north. We were being chased."

"We?" The fat man turned and looked out into the darkness. "How many more of you are out there?"

"Just one."

Haley knelt and began to unwrap the cloth binding around Kalna's knee. He was thin for his height, had large features and a shock of blond hair. "Who're the men who're chasing you and what do they want you for?"

"We don't know what they want," Kalna answered truthfully, "but they've been following us for four days."

"How many of *them* are there?" another of the herders asked.

"I'm not sure. Four, I think, are dead. Ard killed three, and I killed one just a little while ago."

The fat man looked at Haley. "I don't like the sound of this. It might be better if we don't get involved. We're on the edge of weir territory and if—"

"Leave off, Jon," Haley said. "There's plenty of time to decide what do to. Let's see what's wrong with the boy first."

Kalna winced as Haley drew the cloth wrapping from around his knee. Gentle prodding drew a gasp of pain from Kalna. "Sorry," Haley murmured, as he moved his hands down Kalna's leg to his foot.

"What's wrong with him?" Jon asked.

"His knee is swollen and discolored. His foot, too. Broken bones perhaps; I can't be sure. You'd better take a look."

Jon took Haley's place. "How did this happen, boy?" he asked, as he bent over to inspect both injuries.

"I was trying to get away from one of the men who killed my father. I twisted my leg when I fell."

"And your foot?"

"A table fell on it."

Jon looked up. "You'd better tell us your story from the beginning, I think."

Kalna decided to trust the herders simply because there was no one else to turn to. He told them his story, omitting the fact that he was weir and that those who were chasing them were Yorrga. Sometimes it was safer to understate a problem when seeking help from unknown sources.

Jon was skeptical of Kalna's story, but Haley and Jacque, another of the herders, decided they believed him, and both were willing to investigate. Haley put Kalna up on one of the two pack lopers and led out lighting their way with a torch. Jacque followed behind leading the second loper.

Like the taural, lopers had been brought from the plains hundreds of years ago. Both the Urst and the Moricanians had had a part in taming the fleet-footed, horned creatures and had traded them to Bree and the weirfolk for salt, foodstuffs, and exotic woods not readily available on the plains.

The loper Kalna rode was an old one, its soft gray hide splotched with the white of old age; still it held its head high and pricked its cuplike ears to every sound as it moved along. Both of its curled horns had been filed to bluntness, which was a necessary precaution taken in order to avoid accidents.

The darkness confused Kalna for a short time but soon he located the place where he and Ard had tangled with the Yorrga. While Haley looked Ard over, Jacque crouched by the Yorrga.

"Your friend is still out," Haley announced, "but he's breathing all right and I can't find any blood. There's not much we can do for him now but get some cold compresses on his head and hope that he'll wake up soon. Jacque, what did you find?"

Jacque stood up. "This one's dead and if I'm not mistaken, I think he's weir."

Haley came to look at the body. When he stood up, he turned and looked at Kalna. "You knew he was weir, didn't you?"

Kalna took the accusation without flinching. "Yes, I knew."

"But you didn't bother to tell us," Haley said, walking toward Kalna. "Why?"

Kalna felt Haley's anger and met it with his own. "Because I knew you wouldn't come to help!"

That outburst seemed to stop the big man. He stared at Kalna then slowly nodded. "And you're right. It isn't wise to mix in the affairs of the weirfolk." He turned and looked down at Ard. "But we can't just leave your friend lying there, either. We'll take him with us and hope it doesn't lead to trouble."

"What about this one?" Jacque asked, nudging the Yorrga with his boot.

"We'll take him back to camp and bury him in the morning." Haley spied the Yorrga mask and leaned down to pick it up before Kalna could cry a warning.

Kalna held his breath as the tall man turned it over in his hands studying it.

"Odd-looking thing," Haley mused. He looked at Kalna. "Was the weir wearing it?"

Kalna nodded.

Jacque wrinkled his nose in distaste. "It looks like it's in pain."

"You said there were others chasing you," Haley said. "Did they all wear these things?"

"Yes." Kalna eyed the mask warily. He wished Haley would put it back down.

"Here," Haley said, handing the mask to Kalna, "you carry it. Jon may want to look at it. Jacque, give me a hand. We'll put the dead one over the loper first, then the live one. We'll have to hold them in place."

Kalna held the mask gingerly by its leather strap and watched as the dead weir and Ard were loaded onto the second loper. He turned his mount around when Haley signaled that they were ready to leave. The mask bumped against his knee and flipped upward, its twisted face leering up at him. Kalna quickly turned the mask back over, a cold chill skittering down his spine as words his mother had spoken returned to haunt him.

*He who wears a Yorrga mask wears death while he dances.*

# CHAPTER 4

It was early evening. The moon was still low in the sky. Kalna lay near Ard snuggled under an extra sleeping robe Haley had provided. Three days had passed since their arrival at the herders' camp, days that Kalna had divided between doing odd chores around the camp and keeping an eye on Ard. Ard had him worried, for though he would waken every so often and drink whatever was put to his lips, he never fully regained consciousness.

Someone entered camp. "How is everything?"

Kalna lifted his head at the sound of Haley's voice and watched as he squatted near the campfire. The herders owned two velhunds. The youngest, a black-and-white bitch named Kessa, accompanied Haley. Tame velhunds were slightly larger than their wildland brothers and were much in demand throughout the mountains, for they knew no fear and would attack a full-grown nalcra if occasion warranted.

Jon handed Haley a plateful of food and threw Kessa several meat-covered bones. "All's well here. How about the herd?"

"Settling down. Jacque said he'd stay with them awhile longer." Haley turned and glanced in Kalna's direction. "Has the Bree woken up yet?"

"No. You realize there's a chance he may never wake?"

"I know," Haley said, beginning to eat.

"I'm beginning to think it would've been better if we'd stayed out of the middle of whatever's going on. The Bree won't thank us for what we're doing. They'll probably try to blame us instead."

"The boy said that the man was from the House of Char. It might mean a big reward for his return," Haley said.

"If he lives."

"He'll live, at least for a few more days. Rafe should be back soon with someone willing to claim him."

"You hope," Jon said. He turned and glanced toward the bundled sleepers. "What about the other one?" he said, lowering his voice somewhat.

"Kalna? What about him?"

"He isn't Bree and he isn't Moricanian, you know that as well as I. One good look at his face in the light and I knew what we had!"

Haley ladled a spoonful of thick stew into his mouth and chewed thoughtfully. "So what have we got?" he asked.

"No one lives this side of Black Lake and north of here but weirfolk. He's got to be one of them and from all I ever heard, their kind are better left alone."

"Are you afraid of him?"

Jon shrugged. "A little maybe. The Blue Robes say that the Ancients were wrong to create such beings, that they don't have souls like we do. They're not like normal men, Haley. I've heard that they have power over the winds and that they can burn a man with a look."

Haley shook his head. "Stories, Jon, only meant to frighten children."

"What if they're not just stories? What if all that's said about them is true?"

Haley grinned. "If true, you'd better start being a lot nicer to him."

"Look, I'm serious!"

"You're letting your imagination get the better of you, Jon. Me, I'm beginning to like the boy." Haley patted the velhund. "And Kessa likes him, too. Anyway, Kalna is too young for the things you're talking about even if some of the stories are true."

Kalna had heard of the sect of men known as the Blue Robes. According to his father, they were a select group of Moricanians who had taken it upon themselves to defend and uphold a belief in the Ancients and their wisdom, speaking and praying to them as gods. Their fanaticism was well known, as was their cruelty to those who didn't believe as they did.

"Did you ever hear of Hillstown, Haley?" Jon asked.

"I've heard of it. It was supposed to be located somewhere on the plains near the Alnarian Pass, wasn't it?"

"Nearer the mountains, in the foothills, in fact. Weir territory."

"So?"

"Ever hear what happened to it?"

"It was destroyed by fire, I think."

"So a few would tell you, but my grandfather was there, he saw what really happened. Hillstown was located on the Urst's northern route to the Symbiyah grasslands. It wasn't a very old town, not more than three years old at the most. The weir tolerated the Urst treading their borders because the Urst never stop to build, but with us, building is a natural thing. We like a place, we settle in and build a town. Only this time we made a mistake and took what already belonged to someone else—and they took it back. According to my grandfather, the weir started fires and then called up the winds to fan them. Not many townsfolk survived those fires. The few who did were chased into the grasslands, which in the summer are more desert than anything. If not for a passing Urst caravan, they might well have all died, my grandfather among them."

"You can't blame the boy for that," Haley said. "That happened a long time ago; times are different now. The weirfolk are seldom even seen these days."

"And what's that sleeping over there?" Jon snapped.

"Just a boy, Jon. Weir perhaps, but nothing to worry about. We're not in their territory and we've done nothing but help him and his friend."

"Friend? That bothers me, too. How did the two of them really get together? The boy told us his story, but how do we know if he told the truth? We certainly can't ask the man, can we? I say that from now on we keep a close eye on the weir and that we get rid of him as soon as possible."

Kalna knelt at the edge of the small stream cleaning the morning dishes. His mind was busy with the conversation he'd overheard the night before. He wasn't surprised by Jon's mistrust—it was what he'd been taught to expect from men—but he was sorry it was true because he'd taken a liking to Haley and Jacque and didn't want them thinking ill of him.

He glanced up at the sky as a large flock of birds flew overhead. He knew they were gathering for their yearly migration south across the Morican Plains to the Jenvale Plateau where it was warmer during the winter months and seeds, nuts, and berries were plentiful.

It was said that another tribe of men lived on the plateau, a strange, secretive folk who seldom ventured out of their homeland territory. Rumors had it that these men had somehow managed to hang onto or resurrect some of the Ancients' knowledge, but rumors had a way of exaggerating the truth, and as far as he knew there was no proof of a fourth tribe of men. He remembered hearing his father and Thekis argue about a lost tribe of men once. Thekis was of the opinion that such a tribe did exist and that they were somehow tied to the fanatical Blue Robes, while Dari held the belief that the lost tribe was only a rumor started by men to enchance their own beliefs in their superiority.

The sound of hoofbeats stirred him from his thoughts. He used his crutch to push to his feet and hobbled up the sloping incline to level ground. He paused beside the large oddbark tree that shaded the stream and watched as Haley and Jon stood to greet the approaching riders. He recognized one of the riders; it was Rafe, the herder who had carried the message about Ard to the Bree.

Kalna dismissed the dishes from mind and hurried toward camp as fast as his injured leg would allow. He wanted to hear what Jon and Haley said to the Bree and he wanted one last look at Ard before he was taken away. He entered camp and came up behind Haley, who was speaking to a tall, dark-haired man of medium age. The man wore a wide belt studded with pieces of metal and tall black boots that laced up the outside. A short sword hung from his belt.

The man's glance fell on Kalna. "Is this the boy who was with Prince Ard?"

Haley turned and dropped a hand on Kalna's shoulder, pulling him forward a step. "Yes. Kalna, this is Captain Banner of the Southgate Guard stationed at the House of Balaron. Captain, this is Kalna."

Kalna nodded in greeting. Captain Banner just stared.

"Kalna," Haley said, "tell the captain what you told us about the weir who chased you and Prince Ard."

Kalna glanced over at Ard who, at that moment, was being examined by two of the Bree who accompanied Captain Banner. Ard a prince? He remembered now that one of the Yorrga had called Ard a prince. He'd almost forgotten that.

"Kalna."

Haley's voice brought Kalna back to the present. Briefly he told the captain about finding Ard, and Ard's description of the attack on his hunting party; he went on to tell about the attack on his own home, the deaths of his parents, and how he and Ard had been chased down out of the mountains.

When Kalna had finished telling his story, Haley retrieved the mask from the pile of packs and handed it to the captain. "Ever see anything like this before?"

Captain Banner shook his head. "No, not personally, but I've heard of them. It's called a Yorrga mask, I believe, and has something to do with a weir religious ritual." Captain Banner stepped close to Kalna and lifted his chin. "Isn't that right?" he demanded, gazing into Kalna's eyes.

"No, it isn't," Kalna answered truthfully, realizing that the Bree had guessed the truth. "It's a spirit mask. It's supposed to be used for healing."

"Did you know the weir you killed?" the captain asked.

"No."

"Are you sure?"

Kalna felt the man's suspicion and took a deep breath trying to calm the flutter under his rib cage. "I never saw him before."

Captain Banner looked at Kalna a moment longer then turned to Haley, a grim set to his lips. "Where's the body?"

"We buried him, but we can dig him up again if you want."

"I'd rather not, but I'd better take a look. Lord Drian will want a full accounting of this business including a description of the weir just in case anyone might know him, though I doubt that possibility very much."

Haley touched Kalna's shoulder. "Did you finish the dishes?"

"No."

"Go then and finish them. There's no need for you to be a part of this."

Kalna did as he was told, thankful to be out from under the captain's probing looks. Though he was as much a victim of the Yorrga as Ard was, he couldn't help but feel slightly guilty because the Yorrga were weir.

Before he was out of earshot, he heard Captain Banner ask, "Did you know he was weir?"

"We suspected," Jon answered. "But he's young so we didn't think there would be any danger in him."

Captain Banner snorted. "You're a fool if you think that! But then you're Moricanian and you don't know them as we do. Live next to them awhile and you'll learn the truth."

Kalna finished with the dishes, slipped them into a mesh drying net, and hung them from a nearby tree branch. He was on his way back to camp when he saw that the Bree had finished making a litter for Ard between two horses. By the time Haley and Captain Banner had finished with the body of the Yorrga, the other two Bree had Ard tied in place and ready to travel.

He watched as Captain Banner fastened the Yorrga mask to his saddle horn and mounted. The other Bree followed suit.

Kalna moved forward, touched by a sudden intense desire to see Ard's face one last time. He hobbled quickly over toward the back of the litter and peered inside. Ard's eyes were closed, his face was pale, and perspiration beaded his forehead.

Kalna shifted his crutches to a solid position and reached over to touch Ard's face. "Fare well, friend. May we meet again some day under better circumstances."

Ard's eyes suddenly flew open. One quick move and his hand came back and caught Kalna's wrist. There was a strange, maniacal smile on his face and as Kalna tried to pull free, he became aware of a tingling sensation creeping up his arm. Panic followed recognition of the Yorrga spirit who had once before tried to enter Kalna's mind. The tree spirit hadn't died! It lived in Ard!

There wasn't time to call for help. No one among the Bree or herders would even begin to understand what was happening, or prevent it. Kalna did the only thing he could think of; he closed his eyes, blotting out the terrible look on Ard's face, and called up his inner fire. Within seconds energy had gathered within his body; he sent their coursing down his arm to his fingers as he clasped Ard's arm. A faint snapping sound was followed by a flicker of fire.

The Yorrga that controlled Ard held on a moment or two longer then released Kalna.

The burning sensation in Kalna's fingers reminded him that he wasn't through. Once again he concentrated and the energy withdrew, cutting off the flame that had begun to burn his flesh. He had to clutch the end of the litter as a wave of dizziness engulfed him. He breathed deeply, trying to push the darkness back. Moments later he began to feel the strength returning to his legs.

The attack and Kalna's battle for freedom had happened so quickly that no one among the Bree was even aware it had taken place. Kalna looked down at his fingers. All of them were red and two were blistered. It was one of the consequences of calling up fire. Had he held the fire much longer, he might well have burned himself badly. He stepped back, realizing that he needed cold water to take the heat out of the burns, but before he'd taken a second step a hand dropped onto his shoulder.

"Kalna, did you want to go with Ard?" Haley asked.

Kalna looked up at the tall man, appalled by the suggestion.

Haley misread that look and turned to Captain Banner, who was checking the wood supports of the litter. "What about Kalna?" he asked. "is he to go with you?"

Before Kalna could protest, Captain Banner shook his head. "You may keep him, but knowing what he is, you might be wiser not to. I'm sure someone will come looking for him sooner or later."

Kalna ducked his head, relieved to have so easily escaped the danger of accompanying Ard and the Yorrga spirit anywhere. It was true he felt sorry for Ard, but his fear of the tree spirit far outweighed any guilt he may have felt. He glanced at Ard, whose eyes had closed again, then turned and looked at Haley.

"Captain, what about Kalna's leg?" Haley asked. "It needs tending."

"How does that concern me?" Captain Banner responded.

"Prince Ard might well be dead but for the boy. I think your people owe him something."

Captain Banner frowned in annoyance. "There's a physician in Latthan. Take him there."

"And how do we pay for a physician's services? We won't have any money until the butchering is done."

Captain Banner dug into a small leather pouch at his belt and threw Haley a silver coin. "That should be enough. If not, the man is overcharging you."

Haley dropped an arm over Kalna's shoulder as the Bree turned their mounts around and left camp. "Sorry, boy, I tried."

"Believe me, Haley," Kalna responded fervently, "I had no wish to go anywhere with those men."

"Why not?"

"I feel safer right here," he answered truthfully.

"Is it true that someone will come looking for you?"

"Probably, once I'm missed."

"Well," Haley said, smiling down at him, "until they do come, you're welcome to stay with us. There's always need of another pair of hands with such a large herd, and tomorrow I'll take you to Latthan to see about your leg."

Jon interrupted. "No need of that," he said, plucking the coin from Haley's hand. "His foot is just bruised badly. Soaking it in warm water will help that, and as for his knee, I'll rig a better cast tomorrow. If he keeps his weight off his leg, he'll be fine in a few weeks."

Kalna turned from the greedy look in Jon's face and went to cool his hand in the stream; his thoughts centered on Ard. What would become of him now that he was a Yorrga? The thought that Ard would turn killer saddened him and the fact that he hadn't warned the Bree made him feel guilty. For the hundredth time in the past few days he wished himself back to that day on the trail when he'd first felt Ard's silent call for help. If he hadn't answered that call, he never would have brought

Ard home and perhaps, just perhaps, the Yorrga would not have come to his home to kill.

As he made his way down to the stream, words his mother had spoken came back to him: "The words 'if only' are a road leading nowhere, Ka. You can't change what was, you can only learn to live with it."

# CHAPTER 5

Kalna spent a good part of the morning with Rafe and Jon watching the taural, but as noon approached, they sent him back to camp to help Jacque with the midday meal. He was nearing camp when he heard voices ahead.

Haley, who had been on night duty, was supposed to be sleeping, but Kalna was sure it was Haley's voice he heard arguing loudly with someone.

He gripped his crutches a little tighter and hurried his pace, then cursed softly as his crude wooden cast caught on some grass and almost sent him sprawling. It was bulky and heavy and it made him awkward. Jon told him he'd have to wear it for seven weeks to ensure proper healing. Two weeks down, he thought, five more to go. It seemed a long time to wait, but the thought of tackling a return trip into the mountains wearing such dead weight was pure foolishness. He would just have to be patient, he told himself. There was always the chance, of course, that someone among the weirfolk would come looking for him. Surely a search had begun, unless they believed him dead in the fire.

His thoughts on the subject faded as he came around the last bush obscuring the camp from the narrow trail he followed. He saw three strangers. Two were mounted; the other one was standing to the side of his loper facing Haley. Jacque stood to Haley's left. The grim look on his face bode trouble.

"...can't help you," Haley was saying. "They had their chance and turned it down."

The stranger standing on the ground started to say something but paused when he caught sight of Kalna. His dark eyes narrowed. "Is this the boy?"

"It doesn't matter," Haley snapped. "You've had our answer. Now leave."

"I'm not authorized to offer you anything for the weirling, but perhaps arrangements could be made. I would have to—"

Haley's hand settled on the hilt of his knife. "I said no."

"You're being foolish," the man began, then he stopped, turned, and quickly climbed into his saddle.

When Kalna saw the terrible scowl on Haley's face, he understood why the man moved so fast.

The stranger took up the reins. "This is your last chance. Give him to us and we'll see that you're repaid for the time you've had him—and a little extra besides."

Haley shook his head.

The stranger glanced one last time at Kalna, then turned his mount around and bade the other two men follow.

"Bree?" Kalna asked Haley as the men rode away.

"Yes."

"What did they want with me?"

"Someone at the House of Char seems to have taken an interest in you. I'm not sure why."

Kalna's heartbeat quickened. "Did they say anything about Prince Ard?"

"Not a word."

A chill skittered down Kalna's back as the three riders

disappeared into the forest beyond the camp. It was time to be leaving, cast or no cast. He glanced down at his foot. It wasn't going to be easy traveling, but he'd manage it if he borrowed one of the pack lopers and a few other supplies, without the herders' knowledge, of course.

He looked up and found Haley watching him. "Are you all right, Kalna? You look a bit pale."

"Just thinking about going home," he answered.

"I thought you said that your home had been burned to the ground."

"It was. I meant home to the mountains. I have friends who should be warned about the killer Yorrga."

"You haven't said much about these Yorrga. Is it something you're not supposed to talk about?"

"To be honest, Haley, I don't really know that much about them. All I know is what my mother taught me, that the Yorrga masks are worn by weir who use them to heal—but the Yorrga Ard and I met are different somehow. My mother tried to say something about them before she died." Kalna's glance dropped as he felt the pressure of tears. "I have to go back to the mountains, Haley, and as soon as possible."

"I think it would be better if you stay with us awhile longer, at least until your cast comes off. It should give you time enough to get into the mountains before the cold season sets in and double your chances of reaching your friends."

"What if the Bree come back?"

Haley dropped a hand to Kalna's shoulder. "Are you afraid of them?"

"No," Kalna lied. "I just don't want to go anywhere with them."

"I'll tell you what. You see them coming back, you hide and I'll tell them you left days ago and then I'll send them hunting in the wrong direction. How does that sound?"

Kalna nodded. "It sounds good."

* * *

The sun had set and the night shadows were long as
Kalna went to the stream for water. He knelt at the
stream's edge and pushed the hide flagon under the
water to fill it. Haley and Jon were back in camp talking;
their voices carried clearly on the still night air.

A week had passed since the Bree had come and still
Kalna remained with the herders, his plans for departure
delayed for several reasons; one was the difficulty in pil-
fering from the herders' food supplies, which were managed by Jon; another was that Haley had taken it upon
himself to maintain a watchful eye on Kalna in case the
Bree came back. Just in the last day or so had his vigi-
lance begun to wane.

Kalna was grateful for Haley's concern, but he was
also growing anxious. The nights were getting cooler and
the days shorter, which meant that the Black Forest
would probably be blanketed with snow within a month's
time; he had no choice but to begin the trek north as
soon as possible. He had already planned the route. He
would go straight north along Black Lake, turn east at a
place known as Challon's Outlook, follow the ridge east
two days, and go north again making for Pavion and the
halls of Galen Keep, where many weir spent their
winters and where he was assured of a fair hearing. It
was going to take courage to speak out against the
Yorrga for to most weir they were sacred, but he would
speak out. His parents' deaths would not go unavenged,
no matter who was responsible.

Thoughts of his parents brought a hollow ache to his
chest. He looked up through the layers of leaves, the
bright yellows and golds still visible in the half-light, and
willed his tears away. The time for such things was past.

The flagon weighed heavy in his hand. He brought the
cork out, stoppered the neck, and set the flagon down in
order to retrieve his crutch.

The snap of a twig sounded loud in the stillness. He
turned just as strong arms caught him up. For a moment
he thought it was Haley trying to surprise him, then a

callused hand clamped over his mouth shutting off all protests.

Yorrga! It was his first thought. He kicked and squirmed beneath the arm around his chest as fear-induced adrenaline gave him strength beyond normal. He tried to pull the hand away from his mouth but couldn't get any leverage. Moments later breathing became difficult.

His attacker glided back into the shelter of the nearby trees quickly and quietly. He stopped a few moments later and two men appeared before him. One bent close, peering into Kalna's face.

"Be careful," he hissed, "you're strangling him!"

The hand pressed over Kalna's nose and mouth loosened and air rushed into his lungs. His fear of falling into the Yorrgas' hands vanished as he realized who his attackers were. The Bree had returned to take what Haley wouldn't give.

"You're sure he's the right one?" one of the men asked.

"I'm sure," the other growled. "Let's get out of here before the big herder comes looking for him."

The man shifted Kalna's weight over one hip and started out; the other two followed close behind. When they reached the place where the men had left their mounts, Kalna was gagged, his hands tied before him, then he was put up into a saddle. His attacker mounted behind him.

"Behave yourself and you won't get hurt," the man growled.

The Bree reached the crossing at Latthan two hours later. The river was shallow there and they had no trouble fording the wide expanse of water.

The arms about Kalna tightened as the men rode through the village. The shafts of lamplight that spilled out of windows barely touched the roadway, allowing the Bree to pass unseen; and if anyone did note their passing, what was there to see but shadow lopers carrying shadow riders from ill-lighted streets to the darkness at the edge of town?

Two days of steady riding brought the Bree and their captive through the Luvian Pass and down to the eastern edge of the Lamaric Valley and the beginning of the lands ruled by the House of Char. A day later they reached Naril, the first in a series of towns located on the main road north.

Ganis, leader of the small band, decided they would stay the night in Naril and leave early the following morning. "It should bring us to the Main House around suppertime tomorrow," he said, dismounting at an inn called The Freelander.

Corvan, who was the youngest of the men, took the lopers to the stable in back while Raney, the third man, led Kalna into the inn behind Ganis and stood off to one side with him while Ganis made arrangements for a room.

An open archway to the right led into a noisy dining room which was filled to capacity. The smell of food made Kalna's stomach growl. Meals the last few days had been skimpy.

Raney noticed the direction of his gaze. "Hungry?"

"Yes. We are going to eat, aren't we?"

"We'd better or Ganis will have a mutiny on his hands," Raney replied jokingly.

Kalna hadn't spoken much to any of the three men. The few times he'd asked Ganis a question, he'd been told to be quiet. Raney and Corvan had taken their cues from that and had carefully avoided any long conversations with him.

Kalna looked at Raney and decided to chance a question. Of the three men, Raney seemed to be the most even tempered. He was a man of average height, had dark hair and dark eyes, but unlike the other two, he was clean shaven. "Raney, will you tell me why I'm being taken to the House of Char?"

Raney glanced at Ganis, saw that he was still busy,

and answered, "Orders from Lord Drian, Prince Ard's father."

There was a sinking sensation in the pit of Kalna's stomach. "Does this have to do with Prince Ard?"

Raney nodded. "He's dying and someone seems to think you might be able to help him in some way. Can you?"

Kalna just looked at Raney, appalled by the notion that he had some kind of power to heal Ard. They didn't understand, about either the Yorrga or the powers of the weirfolk. It was possible, of course, that Raney was lying to him, that he had been brought into the Breedors for another reason. What if it wasn't a healer they wanted, but rather someone to blame?

Ganis finished with the innkeeper and beckoned them toward the dining room. "Try anything foolish," Ganis warned as Raney untied Kalna's hands, "and I'll see you regret it. Understood?"

Angry words formed on Kalna's lips but a sudden pressure on his arm cautioned him to be quiet. Ganis glared at him a moment longer then turned and entered the dining room, motioning Raney to follow.

Raney read the silent question in Kalna's eyes. "Why the warning?" he said softly. "Because Ganis has a quick temper and I'd like to see that you get to Lord Drian all in one piece."

They left Naril early the next morning and rode steadily all day, reaching Pitar late in the afternoon. Pitar was the largest of the towns ruled by the House of Char. The two-story, half-timbered dwellings that formed the center of the town were situated at the southern edge of Lake Mataral. Six main streets stretched back from the lake like the spokes of a wheel. Narrow, winding lanes linked the main streets forming a spiderweb pattern that could be seen only from the head of the valley.

Kalna was astounded by the size of the town and more so when Raney told him that, at last count, there were over three thousand men, women, and children living in Pitar, most of them working directly or indirectly for Lord Drian, ruler of the House of Char.

Escape had been uppermost in Kalna's mind since his capture, but the men had remained alert throughout the trip, not once offering him a chance to slip away. The thought of seeing Ard again—or rather, the Yorrga he had become—made him cold inside. There was nothing he could do for Ard. He had to make them understand that.

They left Pitar and took the main road north toward the Main House just a short distance away. The road was lined with oddbark and glimmerleaf trees most of the way, and Lake Mataral lay to the left of the road, the westering sun glinting off its surface. Kalna had heard Thekis speak about the beauty of the Lakeland Forests and now, seeing it for the first time, he understood why the weirfolk had fought hard and long to keep it. But men had conquered in the end, and the weirfolk had been forced to retreat into the Black Forest, which time had finally made theirs.

Kalna's first impression of the House of Char was that of a great stone hill, but as they neared the main gates, he began to discern windows and doorways and open stone porticos. As they passed through the main gates, the lopers' hooves rang against the stone courtyard.

Kalna's eyes widened in wonder at the sight of the seven stone statues depicting men at guard. They were linked one to another by an interlocking stone lintel that separated the outer courtyard from a smaller inner courtyard. There was a raw and massive beauty to the Main House, but as Kalna came into its shadow, he couldn't suppress a shiver of fear, for inside the Yorrga awaited him. He could almost feel its malevolence.

He drew a shaky breath as Ganis dismounted. Stop it, he thought, you can't feel the Yorrga from here! It's all in your mind!

Ganis told Corvan to take the lopers away and turned to Raney, who was helping Kalna down from the saddle.

"Take the weirling inside to the main hall and wait there. I'll go find Lord Drian."

There were a dozen steps leading up to the main doors. Raney assisted Kalna all he could, noticing that he limped worse than he had. "Is your leg bothering you?"

"It's ached all morning," Kalna replied. "I don't think I should be walking on it."

"I'll find you a place to sit down when we get inside."

They passed a pair of guards stationed to the sides of the main doors. Neither man moved or spoke as they passed inside. Raney led the way down a corridor and turned at the first door on his right. There was a large room beyond, its vaulted ceiling almost lost in the darkness of the late-afternoon light. There were cushioned benches along the walls and a series of tall narrow windows to the south and west. The east wall was draped with beautiful tapestries. The center tapestry depicted a battle scene; the two to either side were woodland scenes showing wild velhund on the hunt. A long table stood in front of the tapestries, and behind the table set ten high-backed chairs.

"Sit here," Raney said, pointing to one of the benches along the near wall. "There's no telling how long you'll have to wait."

Kalna grew nervous as the minutes passed. Though it pained him to do so, he stood and limped toward the table. Raney watched him but said nothing.

The rich colors of the tapestries caught and held Kalna's attention, and for a few minutes he was able to put Ard and the Yorrga from his thoughts. He went around behind the table and approached the nearest woodland scene, running his hand over its soft surface. He'd never seen anything like it. How long had it taken to weave and how many hands were responsible? he wondered.

Kalna backed to one of the chairs and sat down, his glance never leaving the woven picture. The scene made him think of his home and of friends who had to be wondering where he was. His glance moved to the gnarled tree in the center of the picture and instantly he was reminded of another facet of the woodlands—the tree spirits. And that brought him back to Ard and the reason he'd been brought there. He shivered. What in Yaril's name was he going to do if they asked him to help Ard?

"Where is he?" Ganis stepped into the room.

Kalna turned to see three strange men standing just within the doorway. Raney pointed in his direction. One man was bent and old. His wispy white hair was brushed back around his ears and he wore a pair of spectacles on the end of his long nose. Another of the men was tall and dark haired. He was a handsome man who wore a neatly trimmed beard and carried himself proudly as he walked at the side of the third man, who was also tall, but heavier than the other. His dark hair was sprinkled with gray and he walked as if one leg bothered him. Raney and Ganis moved aside to let the other three cross the room toward Kalna.

Kalna's heartbeat quickened as the three stopped on the other side of the table forming a barrier of shadows that made him feel trapped.

"Your name is Kalna?" the oldest man asked.

The softness of the voice startled Kalna, and for a few moments he forgot to be afraid. The old man's eyes were so deeply set and his eyebrows so bushy that when he squinted, as he was doing at that moment, his eyes nearly disappeared.

"Answer!" This came from the tall man who stood in the middle. His nose was long and thin, his lips rather stern looking as if he'd not smiled in a long time. He was dressed in a dark-blue shirt and pants; his gray leather vest looked soft and had to be of nalcra hide.

Kalna cleared his throat. "My name is Kalna, yes. Who are you?"

"I'm Lord Drian." He indicated the old man. "This is Duval, my First Advisor. And this is Alfar, Lord of the House of Dar-rel," he finished, inclining his head toward the other man.

Kalna glanced at the tall man standing to Lord Drian's right. He spoke without thinking. "You were with Ard when he was attacked."

"How do you know that?" the man demanded.

"Ard told me. He thought you had died with the others."

"And we were sure Ard was dead until news reached us otherwise. How is it that you came to be with Ard if you had nothing to do with the attack?"

Kalna sensed the aura of hostility emanating from the man and went on the defense. "I found Ard wounded in the forest! I took him to my home! My mother tended him and fed him, then the Yorrga came. They killed both my parents trying to get at Ard and they would have killed me if Ard hadn't helped me escape the burning cabin!"

The three men exchanged looks.

They don't believe me, Kalna thought. They've linked me with the Yorrga because I'm weir. "What do you want with me?" His voice was louder than he had meant it to be. "Why was I brought here?"

The old man moved a step forward. "There's no need to be afraid. No one means you any harm. You were brought here in the hope that you could help us."

"Help you how?" Kalna asked warily.

"We need information on the Yorrga, information only a weir would possess—such as what would drive the Yorrga to attack a Bree hunting party and whether or not they use poison on their blades."

Kalna sensed no hostility in the old man, only a need to know the truth. He licked at dry lips and glanced at Lord Drian, then back at Duval. "I don't know how much help I can be, but I'll try to answer your questions."

Duval nodded and turned to Lord Drian. "I think it would be best if I talked to Kalna alone for a little while."

"We'll wait in Ard's room," Lord Drian said. "Raney,

accompany Duval and the weir and see that nothing happens."

Duval started to object, but Lord Alfar spoke up. "He may be young, Duval, but he's still weir and not to be trusted!"

The warning note in Alfar's voice accompanied a look that sent a chill down Kalna's back. The man hated him, not him personally perhaps, but weirfolk in general.

Raney came around the table and helped Kalna toward the door by giving him the support of his arm. Duval walked to Kalna's left. As they passed through the doorway, Kalna heard Lord Alfar speak to Lord Drian.

"I think it's a mistake, sir. Duval won't get any help from one of *them*!"

"We have to try, Alfar," Lord Drian responded. "Ard's life may well depend upon it."

"But you can't trust them, sir! They're more monster than man. We should have rid the mountains of them long ago and never have signed any treaties with them. If it was up to me, I'd take that one and make an example out of him, and such an example that his friends would think twice, and twice again, about attacking any Bree!"

Kalna heard no more as he passed out of earshot down the hall.

"Lord Alfar has a big mouth," Raney muttered softly, glancing at Kalna.

"He lost Prince Jurandyr the day he and Ard were attacked," Duval said, "and he hasn't been able to forgive himself for that. The boy was young and full of promise. You can't blame Alfar for the way he feels about the weirfolk right now."

"You can't blame all the weirfolk for what a few have done!" Kalna protested loudly. "The Yorrga who attacked Ard are the same ones who killed my parents! And they are not the same as the healing Yorrga. They can't be! My mother..." He choked back the words, unable to go on.

"This has been a bad experience for everyone concerned," Duval said gently, watching Kalna, "but maybe if we sit down and talk we can get to the bottom of things. Raney, go to the kitchens and bring back a pot of tea and some spice bread. I'll take Kalna to my room."

"Lord Drian said that—"

"I know what he said, but you can see that I'm in no danger from this boy. Go now, do as I say. Kalna is safe with me and I with him."

Kalna sat quietly in Duval's cluttered study. The chair he occupied was large and soft and covered by the tawny skin of a nalcra. The head of the nalcra set propped atop the back of the chair; its mouth was open exposing its sharp fangs, and green glass eyes stared out the window into the darkness.

Kalna's glance went to the piles of books stacked in one corner, then moved on to the collection of stuffed birds sitting on makeshift perches around the room. To his right there was another table that appeared to be a writing area with open books, scrolled maps, and an odd collection of metal implements that would've piqued his curiosity under other circumstances. The remains of a meal lay on a tray on the floor nearby.

Duval lounged in a chair near the hearth. Raney sat cross-legged on the floor nearby and poked at the fire with a finely wrought fire iron. The men had been quiet for a long time.

Kalna wasn't sure whether or not they believed his story. He had picked up emanations of sympathy coming from Raney, but the old man's emotions were not so accessible.

Duval looked at Kalna, the quick, birdlike movement of his head belying his true age. "There is nothing more you can tell us about the Yorrga who attacked Prince Ard?"

It was easy to talk to the old man. He had asked a lot of questions about the weirfolk as well as the Yorrga. Kalna realized now that his answers had probably sounded evasive though they weren't meant to be.

"I've told you all I remember and all that Ard told

me," he said, trying to keep the impatience out of his voice.

Raney stopped poking at the fire. "Sir," he said, addressing Duval, "may I ask a question?"

"Certainly."

Raney looked at Kalna. "I'm a simple man with simple tastes," he began. "Some call me blunt. But sometimes bluntness is the best way to get to the heart of a matter." He hesitated. "There's only one question Duval hasn't asked you directly, so I will. Do *you* know what's wrong with Prince Ard?"

There was no meanness in the question, no hate or accusation. Kalna held Raney's glance and neither looked away. Twice Kalna had skirted the subject of Ard's illness, fearing the men would somehow blame him for what happened. He could keep evading, he thought, but eventually that in itself would be an admission that he knew much more than he was telling.

Duval watched him intently, sensing a turning point in their conversation.

Kalna took a deep breath, thought no but said "Yes." He saw Duval's eyes light with victory and cursed himself for a fool.

"Tell us what's wrong with him, then," Raney prompted.

Kalna's glance darted from one man to the other. There was no turning back now. He'd heard enough about men to know that if he didn't volunteer the information they wanted, they'd find a way to make him speak.

"I believe that Prince Ard is possessed by a Yorrga spirit," he said quietly.

Looks of shock and disbelief quickly gave way to frowns. "On what do you base this belief?" Duval demanded.

"On my own experience," Kalna said, and briefly told them of his own battle against the Yorrga spirit while Ard lay unconscious nearby. "When I drove it away from me, it must have entered him. The mask was near him, touching him, in fact."

Duval shook his head, striving to understand. "It sounds incredible. Have you any proof of what you say?"

Kalna shivered. "I have proof, but nothing that I can show you. Before Captain Banner took Ard from the herders' camp, I went to see him one last time. His eyes opened suddenly and he reached back and caught at my hand." He rubbed at his wrist, remembering that moment by the litter; he could still feel the Yorrga spirit trying to take him over. He looked at Raney. "I swear, I could feel the Yorrga spirit in Ard."

"How?" Raney demanded.

"I can't explain. There are no words to make you understand."

Raney cut the air with a hand. "I don't believe any of this!"

"Quiet, Raney," Duval admonished. "Kalna, you are telling us that these Yorrga spirits can dwell in a human being as well as in a mask? And that one now dwells inside Prince Ard?"

"Yes. According to my mother, when a weir wears a healing mask, he becomes a willing host to the Yorrga spirit. In Ard's case, being unconscious, the Yorrga spirit simply took over."

Duval sat back in his chair. "I've heard of soul possession but have always considered it a combination of ignorance and superstition." He rubbed at his eyes with both hands and sighed deeply. "How do we deal with such things if we don't even believe in them?"

Raney was watching Kalna as he answered Duval's question. "Simple," he said. "We find someone who does believe."

# CHAPTER 6

Raney and Kalna stood in the hallway outside the door leading into Prince Ard's quarters. A stern-looking guard was stationed by the door; his glances made Kalna nervous. He turned and looked down the long, dark corridor to the right and wished there were a place to sit down. Though he was using Raney's arm for support, the achy pain in his leg was distracting.

"This isn't going to work," he told Raney softly. "I can't help Prince Ard!"

"You told Duval you'd try," Raney said.

"I'm a fool for saying it! You don't understand, Raney. What I did before was purely defensive. I had to close the Yorrga spirit out and I don't think I can do that for anyone else, especially if the Yorrga spirit is already inside Ard's mind. You need someone more experienced than I, someone stronger, who knows what he's doing!"

"And where do you propose we find such a person?" Raney asked. "I don't know anything about these Yorrga spirits, but I do know a dying man when I see him. If something isn't done for Ard soon, he'll slip away from us. I know he isn't anything to you, but he means much to us, and all we can do is beg for your help. I'll do it because I know Lord Drian won't. Please, try to help Ard."

Suddenly the door opened and Duval stood there beckoning them inside. Kalna's heartbeat quickened as he stepped into the room and saw Lord Drian, Lord Alfar, and several other men over by Ard's bed. The room was large and was lighted by oil lanterns. One side of the room was used for sleeping quarters, the other side contained comfortable sitting chairs and a low table. A fire blazed in the hearth to the left of the door. Opposite the hearth stood a tall mirror. To its left was a long open wardrobe filled with enough garments to clothe three men.

Kalna took it all in as he hobbled past Lord Alfar and Lord Drian. Duval led the way to Ard's bed, motioning another man out of the way.

The man scowled but stepped aside. "I protest this action," he said, as Lord Drian approached. "I've been Ard's physician since he was a child and I can't believe that witchlore will do him any good! In fact, in his present weakened state, it may well be enough to kill him. Please, Lord Drian, send this—"

Lord Drian held up a hand. "I like this no better than you, Caspar, but time is slipping away from us. If the boy can help, I'm willing for him to try whatever is within his power." Lord Drian's glance was on Kalna as he spoke.

Kalna turned away. I can't do this! he thought desperately. It's beyond my strength! He flinched visibly as Raney caught his arm.

"Try," Raney said softly.

"What if I fail?"

"Try. It's all we ask."

All *you* ask, Kalna thought, as he looked at the faces of the other men, but what about them? He freed himself from Raney's hand and hobbled to the bed.

His thoughts had been so centered around himself and

the task they had asked of him that his first glimpse of
Ard was shocking. His face was white and drawn and the
large dark circles under his eyes accented the gauntness
of his cheeks. Even his hair had lost its sheen.

"Ard?"

Duval had moved to the other side of the bed and
stood facing Kalna. "He doesn't respond to anyone's
voice."

Kalna looked at Duval. "Touch him."

Duval frowned, but did as asked and took Ard's hand.

"Do you feel anything? A tingling sensation or a burning?"

"No. Nothing."

Had the Yorrga departed? Kalna wondered. With
Ard's life slowly ebbing away, perhaps the Yorrga had
lost its own hold on life; then again, perhaps it was only
in hiding. There was only one way to tell, and Kalna was
loath to attempt it.

"Everyone is to leave the room," he said, looking at
Duval.

The words were no more out of his mouth than objections began. Lord Alfar's was the loudest. "Leave him
alone with Ard and your son will die!" he yelled, turning
to Lord Drian. "You can't trust one of them for a second!"

Lord Drian looked at Kalna. "Why must we leave the
room?"

"If the Yorrga spirit is in your son," Kalna explained,
trying to keep his voice even, "and I manage to drive it
out and anyone else stands too near, there might be a
chance that it would choose him as it's next host. Stay if
you want, but know that if you do stay, you chance becoming as ill as Ard is right now." Kalna wasn't at all
sure that such a thing was possible, but he wanted the
room cleared.

The men exchanged glances, doubt in their eyes.
Duval moved around to the end of the bed. "Lord Drian,
I advise that we do as he asks."

"No!" Alfar said, advancing on Kalna. "No and no!

You've already taken my stepson! You'll not take Ard, too!"

Raney and Duval moved as one, intercepting Alfar and grabbing him by the arms.

"Alfar! Stop it!" Lord Drian roared as the man began to struggle. "Caspar, help them get him out of here!"

The three men wrestled Alfar from the room and gave him over to the guard at the door, then returned to the room. Caspar glanced uneasily at Kalna. "I know nothing about Yorrga spirits, but I feel that I should stay. I am Ard's physician." The last was said to Lord Drian.

Lord Drian shook his head no.

"I'll stay," Raney offered.

"No. We'll do as the weir asks. But"—Lord Drian looked hard at Kalna—"should Ard die, you will be held accountable."

A coldness settled in Kalna's stomach, for he knew exactly what Lord Drian meant. If Ard died, he would die.

Lord Drian stepped to the side of his son's bed and picked up Ard's right hand, held it gently a moment, then turned and left the room. The others filed out behind him. Duval was the last out the door. He paused and turned.

"Is there anything you require, Kalna?"

Kalna shook his head, not trusting his voice.

"How long should we wait before..."

Kalna cleared his throat. "An hour—perhaps two. I don't know."

Duval nodded. "We'll wait."

Kalna turned back to the bedside. He heard the door close behind him. Instantly his glance went to the window. It was dark outside, dark that would hide him if he could escape the room. He hobbled around the bed and went to the window. The bottom sill was waist high, which gave him a good view of the torchlit courtyard below. He studied the drop, his hopes fading. With his cast on, he'd never make the climb down, and even if he did manage to reach the ground safely, the guards sta-

tioned around the courtyard would have no trouble
catching him.

He turned back to the room and spent the next few
minutes in aimless wandering; he fingered the fabric of
several cloaks hanging in the closet; he touched Ard's
personal things sitting on a bureau top; and he lifted the
lid on a large chest near the bed to see what was inside.
It turned out to hold an assortment of boots, belts,
gloves, a leather vest, and several sheaths. One held a
knife, which Kalna picked up, then put back. He ended
up standing in front of the large wall mirror, its ornate
wooden frame covered with a running motif of wild animals. His glance locked onto his mirror image.

Now what? he asked the image. They expect you to
do something. If you don't, Ard dies. If you do—he still
could die. He took a deep breath and released it slowly.
You're afraid. I can see it in your eyes. Better to fear and
be cautious than to be brave and run blindly to your
death. It's death you're afraid of, isn't it?

His glance shifted to the mirror image of the room
behind him. Truth wasn't always easy to face.

Suddenly something caught his glance. His heart
jumped wildly as he spun around. He peered into the
darkened corner of the room near the hearth. Twisted
features leered back at him; black eyepits glared in pain.

"Damn!" Kalna swore aloud. It was the Yorrga mask.
They'd hung it off the mantel like a trophy. Fools! They
understood nothing of the Yorrga!

It took courage to cross the room and stand before the
mask, and it took even greater courage to reach out and
touch it. Breathing as rapidly as if he'd run a race, he
lifted the mask down, prepared to drop it at the first hint
of life.

Moments passed and nothing happened. His breathing
gradually returned to normal. The Yorrga spirit wasn't
there, which meant that if it still lived, it lived in Ard.

He turned and limped toward the bed and looked
down at the prince. I can do nothing, he thought, setting
the mask down on the bed. A few more days and Ard

will die along with the Yorrga spirit, and that will be the end of it. Then he remembered the look on Lord Drian's face and knew that whether or not he tried to help Ard, he would be held responsible for whatever happened. Which left him no choice at all.

He sat down on the edge of the bed and looked at Ard's face, remembering how excited he'd been the day he'd brought the prince home. And he remembered the Yorrgas' attack upon his home and how Ard had saved him from burning alive.

I owe him, he thought, as he owes me. Minutes passed as he thought about what he was going to do. He had practiced imagery with his mother for as long as he could remember. Like all children, his images had been crude at first, but time had corrected that, and as the years passed his focusing ability had grown stronger. He was still far from achieving perfect control, but he had outwitted the Yorrga spirit once; perhaps he could do it again. But this time the image would have to be different and this time the battleground would be Ard's mind.

I need a wall that protects and hides, he thought, a wall as hard as stone and as hot as fire, a wall the Yorrga can't penetrate.

It took long hours of practice and great concentration to join with another's mind, and such joinings were never done lightly. The only one he had ever mind-shared with was his mother and then only at her invitation and under her control. To enter Ard's mind uninvited was a risk, for there was no telling what kind of a reception he'd be accorded. There was a chance that he wouldn't even be allowed entry, for Ard was a strong man and not one to be taken easily.

He closed his eyes to shut out the outer world and entered a trancelike state that would enable him to center himself for control. Once assured of balance, he set his hand to Ard's forehead and entered darkness. He moved quickly and took on the semblance of a rock pile, extending his awareness slowly around him, prepared for the tingling sensation that would warn him of the Yorrga spirit. When nothing threatened him, he made the rock pile glow softly. His rock pile image lengthened and grew, pushing outward to form a circular wall.

Suddenly there was a probing sensation somewhere along his wall. He braced himself, recognizing the touch of the Yorrga spirit. He shuddered as something lapped at the top of his wall. Maniacal laughter filled his mind as the Yorrga lunged to the top of the wall and peered down into the seething swirl of red and yellow that was Kalna's essence. The Yorrga projected sudden confusion, then anger.

Kalna felt the Yorrga as a clump of blue-green mold that clung to his wall. Its presence was suffocating. He realized that it was time to fight back and drew upon his inner fire, loosing it upward and lighting the darkness with a blinding flare.

The Yorrga screamed and dropped back, fleeing the light as a taural flees a nalcra.

Kalna knew better than to relax his rock-wall image. The Yorrga would be back, he was sure of it. He checked his wall carefully then began pushing its perimeter outward once more, his inner fire banked for later use. It was time to look for Ard—if he still lived.

*Ard? It's Kalna. I've come to help. Where are you? Show yourself if you can, but beware the Yorrga. It's—*

The Yorrga struck again, its speed and strength carrying it to the top of the wall so quickly that Kalna had but a moment to react. Fire blossomed upward, the roar of the eruption like the cry of high winter winds. Again the Yorrga screamed in anger but it held its perch, trying to see past the flames. It had taken on the form of a twisted man-shape, its long arms reaching into the fire, screaming defiance. It was wild with frustration and confusion and demanded a joining, for only in a joining could it understand its enemy.

Kalna fed the fire with more of himself, using precious reservoirs of energy that could not easily be replaced. He felt himself weakening and his fire lost some of its brightness, but still it burned.

The Yorrga dropped off the wall silently, disappearing into the darkness beyond, its howl of anger reverberating through Kalna's mind.

Kalna let his inner fires dwindle, that moment's respite giving him a chance to gather what little was left of his strength. If he didn't find Ard soon . . .

*Ard! Where are you? It's Kalna. I'm here behind the wall. Do you see the wall?*

He pushed his wall outward once again, pausing to listen every few heartbeats; then suddenly his wall touched something that wouldn't yield. He heard a scrabbling noise as if something scratched at his wall; then came a whimper. He hesitated, fearing a Yorrga trick. But what if it wasn't the Yorrga? he thought. What if it was Ard? Slowly he opened a crack in his wall and peered outside, straining to see beyond the light of his own inner fire. There it was! A form curled into a tight ball.

*Ard?* He sent his awareness pushing outward and touched the curled form. It was Ard. He was sure of it! Fearing another attack and unable to change forms without becoming open to the Yorrga, he did the only thing he could think of; he opened the crack in the wall and stretched outward around the still form, drawing it into himself and resealing the crack.

The Yorrga's attack this time was silent. It was on top of the wall looking down, its twisted face glowing with triumph.

*No!* Kalna knew he couldn't hold the image of the wall and call upon his inner fire at the same time, not now, so he dropped the wall, spilling the Yorrga into darkness, then before the Yorrga could recover, he stepped in between the tree spirit and Ard, hands open, his being centered on fire.

The Yorrga screeched as the twin fountains of flame lashed outward, and it turned and fled into the darkness, unable to control its own primordial fear of fire. Filled with elation, Kalna recklessly chased the Yorrga, pushing it relentlessly, leaving it no choice but to leave Ard's mind.

One moment it was there and, as suddenly, it was gone.

Kalna drew his fire back inside. Relief was followed by exhaustion and a terrible burning sensation in his hands. He knew he had held fire too long. As the last glow of firelight left him, it was dark again, a shadow world where self-image ruled.

It seemed he had come far from the place where he'd left Ard, and he wasn't at all sure he could find his way back in the murky gloom. Time lost all meaning as he moved within Ard's mind, touching thoughts and memories not his own and calling for the sleeper to waken.

At last he came upon an aura of yellow light, and within the aura he found Ard just as he had left him, curled into a protective ball. He knelt beside him, his burned hands cradled in front of his chest.

*Ard, the Yorrga is gone now. It's safe. Come, open your eyes and look. You know me. It's Kalna. There's nothing to be afraid of now.*

*Kalna?*

*Yes, Ard, it's Kalna.*

*The thing?*

*It's gone.*

Ever so slowly the body around him relaxed. It was strange to feel the outer body and at the same time look down upon the inner being, which was alike and yet different.

Ard lay on his back and opened his eyes. The light around him grew stronger by the moment. *Where are we?* he asked.

*In your mind.*

*I'm dreaming?*

*No, it isn't a dream. You've been ill. You were host to a Yorrga's spirit—but he's gone now.*

Ard shuddered, the inner being as well as the outer. *I remember. It didn't want me here. I fought to make it go away, but it wouldn't!*

Kalna knew all about Ard's inner battle against the Yorrga. It was as clear to him as if he'd fought the battle himself, the pain, the frustration, the panic that hit when he couldn't rid himself of the malicious spirit who taunted him night and day. It was truly a wonder that Ard had not succumbed to the Yorrga spirit long ago.

Suddenly he was aware of Ard's presence within his own mind and before he could stop him, the man had begun to absorb images and events out of Kalna's past. The images came faster and faster, swirling through his mind in a kaleidoscope of scenes that Kalna couldn't stop. He realized that the joining was slipping out of his control.

*I'm leaving, Ard.*

*No. Stay.* It was a request, not a command.

Kalna had to refuse. *You're home in your own bed, Ard. When you wake up, I'll be there. I promise.*

It was all Kalna could do to summon the willpower to leave Ard's mind, for it clung to him as if afraid to be left alone. When he opened his eyes, he found himself lying across Ard's body. He sat up, using what little strength was left him. Ard was soaked with sweat and his cheeks were flushed with color. When he opened his eyes, there was a look of confusion, then he focused on Kalna. "Ka?"

The name struck Kalna like a knife, and as he gazed down into Ard's eyes he experienced a disconcerting twinge of panic. His mother and father, Thekis, and Rops had been the only ones ever to call him Ka. It meant that the joining had been closer than he had intended.

"How do you feel?" he asked cautiously.

"Tired." Ard's glance touched around the room. "I am home. I don't remember how I got here, but I'm here. And you came, too."

"It's a long story, Ard." He caught something out of the corner of one eye and turned. The Yorrga mask was laying alongside Ard's blanketed legs. "I'll tell you about it all later, but first there's something I have to do."

He pushed off the bed and, being careful not to brush his hands against anything, he knocked the mask off the bed with an elbow, then kicked it toward the fireplace. It hit the grate and bounced back.

"Ka, what are you doing?" Ard asked, his voice sounding tired.

Kalna's legs shook and suddenly the room seemed to go dark. The next thing he knew he was sitting on the floor, holding his red, blistered hands to his chest.

The door to the room opened and men poured in. Kalna paid them no mind as he tried to push the mask into the fireplace with his elbow. Excited voices erupted around him. Someone was trying to help him up. He recognized Raney's voice.

He saw a hand reaching for the mask. "No!" he yelled. "Don't touch it! Kick it into the fire!"

Lord Alfar hesitated, his hand inches from the mask.

"Raney, kick it into the fire!" Kalna cried. "It must be destroyed!"

"He's crazy," Lord Alfar said. "You'd better take him out of here, Raney."

"Raney, do as I tell you!" Kalna yelled. "It almost killed Ard once! Burn it or the Yorrga will live!"

Something in Kalna's voice spurred Raney to action. He released Kalna, stood, and with the toe of his boot, nudged the mask deep into the heart of the fire.

Kalna heard Lord Alfar protesting the action, but his voice seemed to come from a long way off. He closed his eyes, exhaustion winning out. The last thing he heard was a strange popping, sizzling sound as the fire caught at the painted wooden mask.

# CHAPTER 7

Kalna woke to the touch of a warm, wet cloth on his face. He opened his eyes and found Raney bending over him. The man smiled, a slow smile that spread from the lips to the eyes.

"Welcome back."

Kalna slowly took in his surroundings. It was a small room with two, no, three doors, one leading out onto the stone terrace to the left of his bed. There was a chair in one corner, a small table next to the bed, and what appeared to be a closet covered by closed drapes next to the door that opened into another room.

His glance returned to Raney, who answered the unspoken question in his eyes. "You're still in the Main House, two doors down the hall from Prince Ard's rooms. I'm in the room next to yours, through there," he said, indicating the open doorway.

"Is Ard all right?" Kalna asked.

"He grows stronger by the day. He's been in to see you several times each day since he got out of bed. To be truthful, I've been more worried about you than him."

Kalna glanced out the window overlooking the terrace and saw a gray, overcast sky. "How long has it been?"

"Two days past a week. You've been conscious off and on—only for brief periods of time—but you never were really with us, if you know what I mean. This is the first time you've spoken, which I'm taking as a good sign. We've managed to get you to swallow water and a weak meat broth at least once each day. Are you hungry now? Would you like something to eat or drink?"

Kalna heard Raney but his thoughts were elsewhere. Ard is all right, he told himself. I've done what they asked. Now they'll let me go home. Thekis will be surprised to see me. He must think me dead by now.

"Kalna, don't go back to sleep. Keep your eyes open. I'll be right back!"

Kalna watched Raney leave the room through the last door, which led out into the hallway. He tried to sit up and found he had no strength. Even lifting his head was an effort.

Raney wasn't gone long and when he returned, he had someone with him; it was the old man, Duval. A tray of food was brought in a short time later and Raney helped Kalna sit up to eat. Kalna was embarrassed to be spoon fed, but Raney seemed most anxious that he eat all he could, so Kalna swallowed his pride and allowed the man to help him.

Duval settled down in the chair near the bed and remained silent, allowing Kalna to eat in peace. Most of the foods were well cooked, even mushy. Even so, Kalna found that the simple act of chewing quickly became too much. "No more," he said.

Raney glanced at Duval. The old man nodded. "It's a start. See that food and drink are available whenever he wants them."

Duval stood as Raney adjusted Kalna's blankets. "I wanted to be the first to thank you for what you did for Ard," he said. "I'd like to talk to you about it when you're feeling stronger. Raney has volunteered to stay here with you to see to your needs. If you want any-

thing, just call him. He'll be sleeping in the next room."
He reached down and touched Kalna's forehead. "You
gave of yourself unselfishly, Kalna. It will be remembered. Rest now. I'll see you tomorrow."

Ard arrived a short time later. Kalna had his mind on
the rainstorm whipping up outside and didn't hear him
enter the room.

"I was hoping to find you awake, Ka," Ard said
softly.

Kalna turned his head. The gaunt apparition in the
doorway brought a series of pictures flashing through his
mind: Ard lying on the ground the day he'd found him;
Ard attacking the Yorrga who had killed his parents; Ard
bound in the litter, his blue eyes glittering with a Yorrga's
malice.

Ard crossed the room and came to stand next to the
bed. "May I sit?" he asked.

"Please."

Ard could've taken the nearby chair but chose rather
to sit on the bed. He straightened his robe, then glanced
around the room. Seconds passed. He licked at dry lips
and took a deep breath, his glance dropping to his hands,
which twitched nervously.

Kalna was tired, his senses dulled, but it took no special talent to realize that Ard was ill at ease. "You're
thin," Kalna offered, breaking the silence. "How do *you*
feel?"

Ard tried to smile. "Alive—thanks to you. And you?"

"Tired."

"It took a lot out of you—what you did. I'm not really
sure I understand what happened. It all seems like a
dream to me. But—the Yorrga was real, wasn't it?"

"It was real."

"I didn't think it was at first. I thought it was just a
bad dream, but each time I tried to wake up, I couldn't. I
tried to push it away and think of something else, like
you do bad dreams, but it only held on tighter. It was like
being smothered, only worse."

The hurt in Ard's voice vibrated through Kalna. Ard

was a strong and independent man. His battle with the Yorrga had taxed him to the fullest and had found him wanting, at least in his own mind. Kalna sensed all this and knew what Ard needed. It took energy that he didn't have to spare, but he lifted his right hand, which was still bandaged, and let it rest gently on Ard's arm.

"You fought bravely, Ard, and withstood the Yorrga spirit for a long time. Few could have done as well, even among the weirfolk."

There was doubt in Ard's eyes.

"I'm telling you the truth, Ard! You have nothing to be ashamed of."

"Perhaps not, but I feel...so angry inside—and frightened. What if the Yorrga returns? How do I fight against it?"

"That particular Yorrga won't be back. The mask that contained its spirit was burned."

"Other masks can be made! You told me that there were three mask makers among the weir in the Black Forest. What's to prevent them from making hundreds of the filthy things? Ka, it has to be stopped! Those masks are evil!"

They weren't meant for evil, Kalna wanted to say, but the words caught in his throat. Dari and Graya had died at the hands of Yorrga. How could he defend them?

"There is a way to stop them," Kalna said.

"How?" Ard demanded.

"The weir High Council has to know what's been happening. If Runner escaped, there's a chance they already do know. If not, they must be told, because the only way to stop the Yorrga is to stop those who are making the masks. As soon as I'm strong enough, I'll leave for the Black Forest."

"And run right into more Yorrga," Ard added.

"They can't be everywhere, Ard. I'll just have to be careful."

"Being careful may not be enough. I think it would be better if you had an escort back to the mountains."

"That won't be necessary, Ard. All I'll need is a mount and a few supplies and—"

"No argument," Ard said. "If you go, you go with an escort!" He stood up. "I'll let you rest now. I know you're still tired. We can talk about all this tomorrow." Ard leaned down and impulsively kissed Kalna on the forehead, then said good night and quickly left the room.

Kalna watched him to the door. There's something different about him. Was it the joining? he wondered. Or his brush with Yorrga madness?

Kalna's strength was slow to return. It was a week before he was strong enough to sit up and eat by himself and another week before he could stand alone. It taught him a valuable lesson about limits, one he would not soon forget.

Ard was a daily visitor, as was Duval, who never seemed to tire of asking questions about the weirfolk. The others who came to see him were a mixture of the curious and those who were Ard's close friends, such as Royar, a young captain of the guards, and Dolf, an older man who had been Ard's arms instructor.

Lord Drian also put in an appearance. His greeting was cordial and his words of gratitude sounded sincere, but there was something in the man's eyes that made Kalna uncomfortable, a bold look that seemed to challenge him to prove himself further.

Ard, Duval, and Ard's physician, Caspar, arrived at Kalna's room early one morning, surprising Raney, who was busy straightening Kalna's bed.

Raney saw Ard first. "Hello, you're around early this morning." His voice trailed off when he saw Duval and Caspar. "Is something wrong?"

Kalna turned at the sound of Raney's voice. He was standing at the far end of the room near the window, crutches tucked under his arms. His hands were still red and tender but the bandages he'd been wearing for weeks had finally been removed. He would bear several large blotchy scars on his hands for the rest of his life, but it was a small price to pay considering he had defeated the Yorrga.

Ard walked into the room. "Nothing's wrong, Raney. Caspar has come to look at Ka's leg."

Kalna counted the weeks he'd worn the cast as he hobbled toward the bed. Surely his leg had healed in six weeks' time. "Is it time to take the cast off?"

"Not unless you enjoy carrying it around," Caspar said testily as he set his medicine pouch on the foot of the freshly made bed. He was a middle-aged man with a deep receding hairline. His long nose and pointed chin gave him a birdlike appearance, and all that saved him from being really ugly were a pair of striking, light-blue eyes.

Caspar had tended Kalna's burns for several weeks now so Kalna knew the man was more growl than bite. The physician reminded him very much of his old friend, Rops. He shied from the thought, remembering that Rops was another of those yet to be avenged.

Raney helped Kalna up onto the bed while Caspar rummaged around in his pouch. "Sit back and sit still," Caspar said, unrolling his tools next to Kalna's leg.

Kalna watched Caspar begin to cut the bindings on the cast. He looked up to find Ard looking at him. There was a curious look on Ard's face, one he couldn't read. "Something wrong?"

"No," Ard answered, "just wondering how you're feeling."

Ready to go home, he thought. "Restless," he said aloud.

Ard dropped a hand to his shoulder. "That's good, it shows that you're gaining strength. I think it's time that you ate with me in the Great Hall. There are a number of people I want you to meet."

"Tonight?"

"Yes."

The thought of sitting and eating in a room filled with

strange Bree made the hair on Kalna's neck rise. "No, Ard, I'd rather not."

"You've not left this room once since you were brought here, Ka. You can't stay here forever."

"I don't mind eating here, Ard. Really."

"Afraid of crowds?" Ard teased.

"No, it's just that I..." Kalna searched his mind for an excuse, any excuse. Inspiration struck as he glanced down at his tunic and pants. They'd given him several things to wear but none had fit properly. "My clothes, Ard, they're not..."

"That has been taken care of," Ard said, smiling. "Raney show him."

Raney stepped to the small corner closet and pulled back the curtain. "We hung them there while you slept," he said, grinning. "Looks like you eat in the Great Hall this evening."

"Ard, no, please," Kalna said. "I'd feel out of place." Ard's smile faded. "Because you're weir?"

Kalna nodded.

Ard started to say something else but Caspar interrupted. He straightened up, the remains of the crude cast dangling from one hand. "It's not the best job I've ever seen, but I don't know that anyone could've done any better under the circumstances."

He moved to one side so Ard could see Kalna's leg, which was still somewhat swollen around the knee. He took hold of the leg and gently moved it to a different position.

"Any pain?"

"A little," Kalna responded.

Caspar moved the leg again. Kalna's sharp intake of air told him all he needed to know. He moved the leg back to its original position and set it down. Then he probed gently around the kneecap, twice eliciting a gasp from Kalna.

"What's wrong with his leg?" Ard asked, as Capar straightened.

"I'm afraid that it's been damaged beyond repair. The

best I can do is to bind it back up in a position that doesn't bother him and hope that time will heal whatever's torn inside. There's a brilliant physician in Bragadar who might be able to help, but he'd never come here. You'd have to go to him."

"You're speaking of Alanford of New Brunswell?" Duval asked.

"Yes. The man is truly gifted as a healer. Of course, there's no guarantee that even he'd be able to undo the damage here. I've seen this type of injury only a few times during my years of practice. What usually happens is that the knee becomes stiff over a period of time and the bones take that shape." Caspar looked at Kalna. "I'm sorry, Kalna. You will be able to walk on it in time, but you'll always limp, and if you move just right, there will be pain."

Caspar gathered up the old splint and cloth wrapping. "Raney, get some warm water and bathe his leg. I'll find some fresh bandages and something lighter to use as splints. Duval, would you come with me? I'd like to speak to you for a few minutes."

"Of course," Duval responded.

The pressure of tears blurred Kalna's vision as he glared down at his leg. To never walk normally again, to limp instead of run—the prospect was frightening to one who had so many years of life ahead of him.

After Duval and Caspar left the room, Ard sat down next to Kalna and glanced over at Raney, who stood unobtrusively to one side, the grim line of his lips telling Ard how he felt about the situation.

"Raney, go and fetch water, soap, and towels, then find us all something to eat. We'll share breakfast with Ka this morning."

Raney nodded and left quietly.

"It's going to be all right, Ka," Ard said softly. "You'll walk again, even if I have to take you all the way to Bragadar. I promise."

Kalna didn't want to cry in front of Ard, but knew

that if he spoke, his voice would betray him just as quickly as his tears.

Ard saw the shimmer of unshed tears in Kalna's eyes before he lowered his head. He hesitated a moment, then put an arm around Kalna and pulled him close. Kalna stiffened and tried to push away, but Ard wouldn't let go.

So simple a thing, a hug, but at that moment it was precisely what Kalna needed though a part of him fought against it. His tears finally came and slowly his arms crept around Ard's back. He wasn't crying just for himself, but for his parents and Rops, and that led to a release of all the pent-up fears he'd carried with him the past few weeks: fear of the Yorrga; of coming to a strange place where he knew he wasn't welcome; of being alone, truly alone for the first time in his life.

"I gave your mother my word that I'd see you safely back to your people, Ka, and I mean to keep my word," Ard said. "It just may take a little longer than I thought." It was not precisely what he'd promised Graya, but close enough.

A few minutes later Ard released Kalna and stood up. "I believe Raney's become lost. I'll go see what's keeping him."

He left the room quickly, giving Kalna a chance to regain his composure. Ard, too, needed a brief respite, for he was ill at ease in the role of comforter.

When the two men finally did return, they found Kalna lying with his back to the hall door and his blanket pulled up around his shoulders. Ard brought in another two chairs from the room next to Kalna's while Raney set things out on the table.

"Time to eat, Kalna," Raney said, touching Kalna's shoulder.

Kalna didn't respond.

Raney turned to Ard. "I think he's gone back to sleep, sir. Shall I wake him?"

Ard looked at the still form and shook his head. "No, let him sleep. He's been through a lot these past weeks. He can eat when he wakes up."

"Sir, may I ask you something?" Raney said, lowering his voice.

"What?"

"Is there going to be any trouble about Kalna's staying here?"

"What have you heard?"

"Lord Alfar has been rather vocal in his denunciations of weirfolk, and it's been said that he's demanded that Kalna either be imprisoned or put out. He claims he's a spy for the Yorrga."

Ard sat down in one of the chairs. "You've been with him since his arrival. What do *you* think?"

"I think that without him you'd be dead by now," Raney replied candidly.

"You believe Lord Alfar is wrong about him, then? About his being a spy?"

"I suppose it's possible," Raney conceded, "but I think in Kalna's case, Lord Alfar is wrong."

"You like Ka, don't you?"

"Yes, sir. He's a bit guarded with his opinions, and he doesn't say much about his people that's not already known, but he's well mannered and considerate and not at all what I thought a weir would be like." Raney hesitated, then asked, "Sir, is it true that his mother was a darkling?"

"True. She was the most beautiful woman I've ever seen. Kalna has her eyes."

"Did you see any other weirfolk while you were in the Black Forest?"

Ard smiled. "Do I detect in you a certain interest in weirfolk, Raney?"

Raney shrugged. "Just curiosity. Kalna is the first weir I've ever met and since he's not like what I was led to believe, I just wondered what the others were like."

"I wish I could tell you that they're all like Ka and his mother, but I can't, not after my run-in with the Yorrga. We're both too young to remember the last of the Mountain Wars, but those who do remember will tell you that the weirfolk are fierce fighters even without their powers. I don't like the idea of another war against them; neither does my father, but if the Yorrga continue to raid into the Breedors, we may have no choice."

"You have recent news?"

"A messenger arrived from the House of Dar-rel late last night. Kirlyle was attacked by Yorrga two days ago. It was reported that thirty-three were killed, sixty were wounded, and the rest scattered. My father has sent a company of men to reinforce the House of Dar-rel. Lord Alfar leads them. We should hear back in a few days."

"If news of this gets out, and it will, won't Kalna be in danger here?"

"Probably. That's why I've got special guards at his doors. They're loyal to me and won't let anyone in that's not supposed to be here."

"You care for him, too," Raney said quietly.

"Yes, though I know I shouldn't, not with what's happening north of us." Ard glanced at Kalna. "It's something beyond his saving my life, something that makes me feel close to him, as if I've known him for a long time. It's strange; I feel as strongly about him as I do my own brother, but I can't explain why. It bothers me."

Raney glanced at the food. "Would you like to eat, sir? No sense in letting the food go to waste."

"We might just as well. I'll take the chairs back into the other room, you bring the tray. There our talking won't disturb him."

"Shall I close the door?" Raney asked after everything was in the next room.

"No, leave it open. If Ka wakes and wants something, we can hear him."

As the men left the room, Kalna opened his eyes but remained motionless. He had overheard everything the two men had said though his eavesdropping had not been intentional. He had simply not wanted to face Ard upon his return because he was embarrassed by his earlier display of weakness.

The news that Yorrga had struck again made him feel queasy inside, for it condemned all weirfolk in the eyes of the Bree and raised the ominous specter of war. And if that wasn't enough to chill his heart, there was the knowledge that the joining between himself and Ard had been much deeper than he had intended. The last frightened him almost more than the first because it meant that the two of them had touched in such a way that neither might ever be the same again.

# CHAPTER 8

Kalna sat on the edge of the bed and looked down at the splint protecting his injured knee. It was lighter than the one Jon had made for him, but it was just as awkward. A week had passed since Caspar had resplinted his leg, but the achy, gnawing pain that reappeared each time he moved wrong would be with him for some time to come, and the thought that he'd never run again or even walk with a free stride made his hate for the Yorrga grow stronger. They had killed his parents, and Rops, and had successfully managed to cripple him for life. They would pay for it all, he vowed silently. He'd never rest until those responsible were caught and punished.

He reached for his crutches, tucked them under his arms, and swung over toward the terrace door. The window next to the door was uncovered, allowing the last light of evening to filter into the room.

He looked down at the courtyard below. The steps leading from the small outside terrace down to the main floor were covered with a light layer of snow, the first of the season. He thought about the trek back to the Black

Forest and clenched his teeth in frustration. If Ard had his way, his return home would have to be postponed until spring, for Ard wanted to take him to the great physician, Alanford in Bragadar. A trip to the Morican Plains and back again would take several weeks, time he could ill afford to lose if he wanted to beat winter travel in the mountains.

A choice then, he thought: a run for the mountains before the snows prevented travel, or a trip to Bragadar, which might or might not end in his being able to walk again. It was a difficult choice, one he wasn't even sure Ard would allow him to make.

Raney suddenly appeared in the doorway leading into the next room. "Aren't you dressed yet? You're to meet Ard in ten minutes. Come on, hurry."

Kalna glanced at the clothes laid out for him. The shirt was light blue in color and its long sleeves were bloused at the wrists and trimmed with gold thread at the cuffs. The pants and overvest were made of soft, supple taural hide, the brown color contrasting nicely against the shirt. He'd never worn such fine clothes before and wondered if they were truly his to keep when he left. Raney seemed to think so, still . . .

"Here," Raney said, advancing, "let me help you. You don't want to keep Ard waiting."

"I still think this is a mistake," Kalna muttered, allowing Raney to help him with the shirt. "I'd just as soon eat right here in my room. Why antagonize anyone with my presence? I know how everyone here feels about weirfolk."

"Ard has reasons for what he does," Raney responded. "Trust him. He means only good for you."

Ard walked into the room just as Raney and Kalna were ready to leave. He smiled when he saw Kalna, for it was good to see him on his feet once more; he looked less vulnerable and more like the indomitable youth who had sided with him against the Yorrga.

"Ready to eat?" he asked.

"Are you sure this is necessary?" Kalna asked.

"I've let you hide long enough. Now, it's time to dispel a few rumors about your people, Ka. A lot of those living in the Breedors today have never seen a weir and they're curious. I think it's better to introduce them to the truth than to have them believing all kinds of wild stories certain people are spreading around."

Meaning Lord Alfar, thought Kalna. He and Ard had spoken about Lord Alfar at great length because the man was quickly becoming a rallying point for anyone with a grudge against the weirfolk, either real or imagined. He had also gained the ear of Lord Drian, which might mean war against the weirfolk if Alfar was successful in his arguments.

The dining hall was at the head of the west wing of the palace. A series of tall narrow windows flooded the room with light during the day; at night the room was lit by chandeliers filled with ring upon ring of candles.

Supper was already in progress as Ard, Kalna, and Raney entered the noisy, crowded hall. Ard led the way toward the long table at the far end of the hall. He was careful to match his stride to Kalna's pace. Raney fell in behind, keeping a watchful eye out for any signs of trouble.

The room was alive with the noisy chatter of a hundred voices and the clatter of plates, cups, and silverware, but as they made their way past the long trestle tables, voices stilled and the room began to quiet down. Heads turned and whispers followed the trio as they walked to the head table.

Lord Drian looked up and saw his son approaching with the weir. He frowned and glanced past his wife, Lady Fralishi, to her brother, Lord Alfar. Alfar met his glance, his dark eyes flashing anger.

Ard and Kalna stopped before Lord Drian and Ard introduced Kalna to his mother and father formally, then to the five men seated to his mother's left, including Lord Alfar; then to the two women and one man seated to his father's right. Duval sat at the end of the table.

Two chairs were empty to either side of him. Duval gave them a nod and indicated they should join him.

Ard dropped a hand to Kalna's shoulder and raised his voice slightly so all could hear. "To those of you who don't know him, this is my friend, Kalna, a weir from the Black Forest. Without him I wouldn't be standing here today. I've invited him to join our table in order to show him that we do not look upon all weir as our enemies."

As Ard squeezed his shoulder, Kalna took a deep breath and held his right hand out, palm up, as Ard had shown him. "I come here in peace and offer friendship to the House of Char."

Lord Drian glanced at Lord Alfar as he rose to his feet. Kalna saw the savage look on Alfar's face as he looked at him and felt a chill skitter down his back. The aura of hate surrounding the man was like the touch of fire. He's death, thought Kalna, walking death to anyone who opposes him. He glanced at the others seated nearby and marveled at their calmness. Can't they feel his anger? he wondered. Can't they see it in his eyes?

Lord Drian glanced around the room. All was quiet; everyone was watching. He looked down at the proffered hand. His head lifted, as if he would refuse the offer of friendship, then he saw his son's face and the silent plea written there. He hesitated, then slowly reached out and laid his hand palm down on Kalna's. Face grim, he said the ritual words.

"The House of Char accepts you as friend. Sit. Eat, and be welcome."

Kalna turned from the ugly look on Alfar's face and followed Ard to his seat near Duval. Raney found a seat at one of the other nearby tables, keeping close just in case Ard needed him.

Food was quickly placed before them, and Ard signaled Kalna to go ahead and eat. All was silent for a few moments, then people began to talk again. As the noise in the room returned to normal, more than a few people cast covert glances at the head table and the weir within their midst.

Kalna pretended not to notice those glances and went on eating. He was nervous at first and a little overwhelmed by the size of the gathering, for there were more people in the room than he would normally see in an entire year back in the forest.

While they ate, Ard acquainted Kalna with some of those people seated nearest the head table. As Kalna listened to Ard, he watched a group of young men and women moving in and out among the tables refilling empty platters and wine cups, and marveled at the organization of it all. That so many people should eat there twice daily meant that the House of Char was indeed a rich House, for only a rich House could supply such large amounts of food and drink on a steady basis.

Duval and Ard kept up a running conversation throughout the meal and both were careful to see that Kalna didn't feel left out. Toward the end of the meal, five or six people drifted up to the head table, spoke a moment or two with Lord Drian and Lady Fralishi, then moved down to where Kalna sat.

Ard introduced the first pair. "Kalna, this is Commander Bito and his wife, Kata. They're good friends of mine. Bito, Kata, this is Kalna."

Commander Bito offered his hand. "I've heard about you, Kalna." He smiled. "Only good so far. Welcome to the House of Char." He glanced at Ard. "Has he seen our loper herd yet? Or our saddle shop?"

Ard laughed. "You can see where his mind is, Ka. Bito is one of the best riding instructors in all the Breedors. When you feel strong enough, I'm sure he'd be delighted to show you around the stables."

Kalna nodded. "I would like that. The Bree are known for their fine mounts."

Others came after Bito and Kata. Kalna greeted each man or woman cordially and tried to remember names and faces. Ard seemed pleased by the attention he was getting. Not so Lord Alfar, who glowered at him from down the table. Lord Drian was also frowning, though whether in perplexity or dislike, it was difficult to tell.

* * *

Ard and Kalna sat quietly in Duval's cluttered study. Ard had brought Kalna there right after supper, and they'd spent some time talking about some of the people Kalna had met that evening.

The last light of day had left the sky and the room was dark but for the warm glow of firelight in the hearth. Raney entered the room carrying a tray of cups filled with hot tea.

"Mind if I join you?" he asked, setting the tray down on the table behind Kalna.

"Please do," Ard said.

Ard got up, added another small log to the fire, and returned to his seat as Raney passed the cups.

"It went pretty well tonight, don't you think?" Ard asked Raney.

Raney knew Ard was referring to Kalna's appearance in the main hall. "I thought so," he replied honestly, "though I'm not sure you changed anyone's mind about weirfolk, especially Lord Alfar's."

"Your father didn't look any too pleased to see me, either," Kalna offered.

Ard studied the fire. "I've tried to talk to him, but with the news of Yorrga raids increasing, he's beginning to think seriously of an all-out war with the weirfolk."

Kalna sipped at his tea, then set the cup on the nearby table. "Ard, I think it's time I was leaving. If I hurry, I can still beat the snows."

Ard looked up, his blue eyes reflecting the firelight. "What about your leg and the trip to Bragadar?"

"I've thought about it, Ard, but it will have to wait. I've got to return to the Black Forest and find out who's behind these killer Yorrga! It's more important than my leg."

"And if you find out these Yorrga come from your own people? Will you join them against us?"

"They killed my parents, and they would've killed me if they'd caught me! No, I wouldn't join them! Is that

what you're afraid of?" Kalna couldn't keep the anger
out of his voice. He had thought Ard his friend.

Ard raised both hands in a peace gesture. "I'm sorry,
Ka, I didn't mean it to sound the way it came out."

Raney spoke up, trying to smooth things over.
"Kalna, a question. Are these renegades among your
people—anyone who might be trying to stir trouble between the Bree and the weirfolk for some reason?"

Kalna thought about that a moment. "It's possible, I
suppose. I can name one or two wild ones my parents
never approved of, but I doubt even they would kill as
wantonly as those who attacked my home."

He pulled his good leg up into his chair, making himself more comfortable. "My mother and I talked a little
about the Yorrga who attacked Ard. She gave me the
impression she thought they might be strangers to our
section of the forest, weir who use the Yorrga masks
differently than we do."

"Is that possible?" Ard asked. "I mean, don't you all
know each other?"

"Do you know all the Bree in these mountains you
call home?" Kalna asked.

"No, of course not, but the weirfolk couldn't number
more than a thousand or so—at least that's what I've
been told."

"You've been misinformed then. There are over two
thousand weir in the southern half of the Black Forest
alone and twice that many north of the Malamar River;
and that says nothing about those living on the Nikon
Plains north of Mount Naton."

Ard looked surprised. "So many. Duval was sure your
race was beginning to die out."

Kalna shook his head. "We live differently than you
do here in the Breedors, and we're scattered over a large
area, which might make it seem that we're dying out, but
I assure you, we aren't."

Ard turned back to the fire, digesting what Kalna had
said. Moments later he looked up. "It all comes down to
the Yorrga, doesn't it? We've got to find out who's be-

hind them and what their plans are, and there's only one
way to do that. We have to capture one alive."

"And hope the weir beneath the mask is sane enough
to answer questions," Kalna added.

"Sane enough?"

"Have you forgotten your own battle with the Yorrga
so quickly?"

Ard's jaws clenched. "No. That I will never forget!
You're saying that the weir we're fighting may not be in
control any longer?"

"Correct. According to my mother, it takes a very
special person to wear a Yorrga mask and maintain control. To lose control is to die because the tree spirits care
nothing for the bodies they inhabit."

"If the weir who broke into your home had lost control, it might explain why they had no compunction
about killing your mother," Ard said.

"But it doesn't explain why they were so intent upon
killing you. I guess only Yaril knows the answer to that
question."

Ard looked at Kalna curiously. "I've heard you in-
voke that name several times before. Who is Yaril?"

Kalna hesitated before answering, "A woman of your
race—the mother of ours."

"I don't understand. What do you mean?"

"You've never heard of Yaril before?" Kalna asked,
wondering how men could've written their own history
without mentioning Yaril.

Both men shook their heads. "Who was she?" Raney
pressed.

Kalna picked up his cup and drank, savoring the fla-
vor of the tea while he gathered his thoughts. According
to all he'd ever heard and been taught, men knew and
despised Yaril's name, yet both men claimed they'd
never heard of Yaril. She had lived hundreds and
hundreds of years ago; perhaps men didn't keep as accu-
rate records as the weirfolk did, he thought. As he
looked at both men, he wondered how they would take
the truth. There was only one way to find out.

"Yaril was one of the Ancients, one of a group of men and women who came to this world to create new life forms unencumbered by the laws of their home world," he began, repeating the story as he'd heard it from his father and he from his father before him. "They made their home on this continent and named it Va-naar, which means 'Beginning.' A city was built and called Sanduvalgara, Valgara's Dream."

Both men nodded; they had heard of the Ancients and their city.

"Yaril and the other Ancients began their work," Kalna continued, "experimenting with different life forms, often using man as their base. Sometimes their experiments were successful, sometimes not. As the years passed, those children born mentally or physically different were given the name weirfolk. As they grew in number and certain *talents* became observable, some of the Ancients began to fear their own creations, and it was decided that some of the more unusual and dangerous of the weirfolk should be terminated."

Ard and Raney glanced at each other, both frowning.

"What do you mean by dangerous?" Raney asked.

Kalna hesitated, then answered, "The beran were thought to be too strong to control, the leondar too vicious when angered, and the darklings, my mother's people, were considered the most dangerous of all due to their ability to manifest and direct fire; and then there were the more exotic beings among the weirfolk, beings who were created by a man named Varrick who believed strongly in the myths of his ancestors and wanted to prove that such mythological beings had once lived by recreating them. Others among his creations were fauns, sirens, dweorgs, and rare winged centaurs whom we now call kimmerlings, who have the ability to move through time.

"Some among the Ancients believed that Varrick was insane. They claimed his creations did nothing but mock mankind and their own efforts to improve the race. The first of Varrick's weirfolk were just beginning to reach maturity when he died suddenly, and suspiciously, leaving his creations without a defender.

"Yaril, who was a great healer among the Ancients, overheard plans to dispose of certain types of weir and took it upon herself to protect them. So she gathered them together and helped them escape the city, then she led them into the Lakeland Forests, which men now claim as their own, and she gave them the name of the El-ar-kil, which means 'The Forest Children.' A short time later the city was destroyed by a great flood. Those men who survived the flood scattered over a period of time and became the three tribes of men, the Bree, the Urst, and the Morican."

Ard's face mirrored disbelief. "Ka, where did you get this story?"

"It comes from the Book of the El-ar-kil, which was begun by Yaril after the destruction of Sandu-valgara."

"You are telling us that men and weir both descended from the Ancients, not just men."

"Yes, Ard," Kalna answered calmly.

"But we're so different," Raney protested.

"Are we?" Kalna said softly.

Raney started to say something, then didn't. He glanced at Ard as if looking for support.

"If all you say is true, Ka, there should be something in our own history books about all of this, and there isn't," Ard said.

"It's very easy to forget what one doesn't want to remember," Kalna answered, remembering words his mother had once spoken when he'd asked her a similar question. "Shall I go on?"

"Yes," Ard said. "I'd like to hear the rest."

"Like the weirfolk, the men who survived the flood had nothing but themselves left to depend upon. All they had from their home world were memories; all their work, all their machines, all their homes were buried beneath water and mud. It wasn't easy to begin a new civilization; some died, some went insane. Those who did adjust were the strong ones, both weir and man.

"It is written that Yaril tried to help her own people but that they rejected her because they believed she had something to do with the destruction of the city, which she always denied. So she withdrew into the forests with the weirfolk where she lived and worked with us, helping us to build our own society."

Raney shook his head. "I find this all hard to believe."

"I don't," Ard said quietly. "Just look at Ka. If not for his smaller bone structure and the glint of amber in his eyes, he could easily pass for Bree or Morican."

"To be born among the weirfolk doesn't always make one weir," Kalna said. "Every now and then a throwback is born, a child who could happily live among the tribes of men. These children are taught the truth when old enough to understand and given the choice of staying or going. Sometimes their parents make that decision for them. We have weir among each of the tribes of men now. Not many, but enough who pass that we always know what men are doing and how things go with them."

"These weir who are not weir," Raney said. "What happens if they marry one of us and have children and the children are born weir?"

"It happens. If they're lucky, they're sent back to us to be raised weir."

Ard frowned. "And if they aren't lucky, they're just left to die, exposed to the elements. I'll tell you both something, something I've never told anyone else. Years ago when I was a youth, I found a child's body lying in some bushes. My velhund had sniffed it out. It was furred, one of those called a beran, I believe. It hadn't been dead very long and there wasn't a mark on it. It was so small; it couldn't have been more than a few days old." Ard looked down at his hands as if holding the body. "I buried it where I found it and never said anything to anyone about it."

"There's very little we can do about such unfortunates," Kalna murmured. "We have a few foot patrols that slip in and out of the Breedors from time to time, and they're always on the watch for such children, but it's almost impossible to be in the right place at the right time."

Kalna said no more for he sensed Ard's and Raney's struggle to accept the truth, and as they fought to try to understand, he remembered his own bewildered feelings when he'd first learned about the origins of his people; the anger he'd felt at the Ancients for tampering with something beyond their knowledge, the uncertainty of his own worth after learning that he was just an experiment.

Time and loving parents had healed his anger and had taken away most of his doubts, but as he looked at Ard and Raney, deep inside he knew he would always wonder what it was like to be one of the untainted images of the Ancients.

# CHAPTER 9

"Ka, do you feel all right?" Ard asked.

Kalna turned his head. He wasn't feeling at all well, and it showed on his face. He had eaten in the main dining hall every night for the last seven nights and had enjoyed the music and entertainment that followed. But this night, all he wanted was to retire to his room. His head hurt and there was a queasiness in his stomach that wouldn't go away.

He leaned back in his chair, suddenly feeling very light-headed. He concentrated on breathing deeply. It wouldn't do to faint now, he thought.

Ard touched the back of his fingers to the side of Kalna's face. "You're flushed, Ka. Have you got a fever?"

Kalna pushed Ard's hand aside. "I'm fine," he lied, not wanting to call attention to himself.

Lord Alfar leaned forward and looked down the table past Lord Drian to Prince Ard. "He's probably had too much wine," he said. "Their kind aren't used to anything stronger than water."

Ard sent him a withering glance. "I suggest you mind your own business, sir."

"And I suggest you do the same," Alfar snapped back. "What kind of a man are you? You sit there and coddle that creature while his kin are out slaughtering our people! Can't you see what he's doing to you? Another week and he'll have you siding with the weirfolk! Your father and I are tired of—"

"This is not the time or place for this!" Lord Drian growled. "Anyway, the boy will be leaving in a few days and that will end this—"

"It will end nothing!" Lord Alfar stated fiercely. "It will only be the beginning. He's seen a great deal while living here, and he's learned a lot more! The Yorrga will greet him with open arms when he returns to them, and they'll use the information he carries to plan more strikes against us! I say he should be locked up, or better still, executed for the spy he is!"

The raised voices coming from the head table captured the attention of the other occupants of the room and gradually they fell silent.

"You're a fool, Alfar!" Ard said loudly, glowering at the older man. "You don't know what you're talking about! Revenge has blinded you to everything including the truth. Ka has nothing to do with the Yorrga. He's as much a victim as we are!"

"All planned! It's what we're meant to think! You are being used, Ard, by that sweet-faced weirling and by the Yorrga! If you don't—"

"Enough!" Lord Drian roared. "I'll hear no more of this at the table!" He stood up, his glance going around the room. "Finish your suppers." His glance went to Alfar, then to Ard. "All of you. There will be no entertainment tonight."

There were murmurs of disappointment throughout the hall but none so loud that Lord Drian would take offense. He returned to his seat.

"Ard, Alfar, I want to see both of you in my sitting room after supper. Duval, I want you there, too."

Ard and Alfar exchanged ugly looks but said nothing more as everyone continued eating. Gradually the hum of voices and the clatter of utensils on plates filled the room again.

Kalna noticed that the room had become extremely warm and the growing discomfort in his stomach had become a swirling chaos. He licked at dry lips and discovered a peculiar taste; then he swallowed rapidly, trying to keep his supper down. Dreading the thought of embarrassing himself in front of everyone, he pushed his chair back, retrieved his crutches from the floor, and pushed to his feet. A peculiar weakness washed over him and for a moment everything wavered before his eyes. He clutched the back of his chair to steady himself as Ard turned to see why he was leaving the table.

"Please excuse me, Ard," he managed. "I'm going to my room."

He stepped back, passed around behind Duval's chair, and headed for the nearest exit, an open doorway that led through a short stone corridor to the main hallway of the north wing of the palace. His vision seemed to worsen by the second. One of his crutches caught the end of the table and jarred him off balance. Somehow he kept his footing and continued on; his goal was the open doorway just a few steps ahead. Five more steps and he'd reached the archway. He lost his hold on his right crutch and it fell loudly to the floor. When he tried to retrieve it, darkness closed around him. He turned and clung to the wall for support.

Raney was the first to reach him. He caught Kalna around the waist with one arm and lifted Kalna's head. "What's wrong?"

"Leave me alone," Kalna said, attempting to push away.

"Stop. I'm trying to help you."

Another pair of hands caught at him. "Are you all right, Ka?" Ard demanded.

"Sick!" he said through clenched teeth.

Ard elbowed Raney aside. "Go find Caspar, Raney.

Tell him to come to Ka's room. Hurry!" He picked Kalna up in his arms. "Caspar will be with you in just a few minutes, Ka," Ard said, as he hurried down the hall with his burden. "We're almost to your room now. You scared me—the way you were acting. You should've said something if you weren't feeling well." He continued talking but Kalna wasn't paying any attention.

Caspar and Duval arrived a few steps behind Raney. Both had seen Kalna's exit and realized that something was drastically wrong.

Ard had laid Kalna on his bed and had begun to loosen the belt at his waist. Suddenly Kalna groaned, rolled over, and vomited all he'd eaten that evening.

A short time later Raney had Kalna cleaned up and lying flat on his back. His clothes had been replaced by a warm winter sleeping tunic; still he shivered beneath a collection of blankets.

Caspar examined Kalna, but other than a slight fever, he found nothing wrong. "Probably some kind of food that didn't agree with him," he said. "Keep him in bed and give him nothing but water to drink tonight, Raney. He should be all right by tomorrow."

Kalna felt a little better with the queasiness in his stomach gone, but he was having a hard time keeping his eyes open. He heard Ard and Raney talking together quietly on the other side of the room and overheard one or the other mention poison. It made him remember the strange taste on his lips. Had someone tried to poison him? Someone like Alfar, who would like nothing better than to see him dead? He fell asleep with that thought in mind.

Kalna was wakened by a cool draft of air. He snuggled deeper into his covers but the chilly air seemed to follow him, seeping in and around his head and shoulders.

He sat up, holding his covers around him. The moon was waning but was still bright enough to provide a little light to the room. It took but a moment to discover where the cold air was coming from. The door that opened out onto the terrace was slightly ajar.

Raney's getting careless, he thought as he swung his cast off the bed and reached for his crutches. No, not Raney, he thought, remembering the servant who'd brought in a fresh stack of wood that evening. Nights were getting a lot cooler, and a fire was always welcome in the hearth.

Ard had argued with him about staying a few more days to make sure he'd fully recovered from his illness several nights ago, but he knew it was time to go. In the morning he, Ard, Raney, and a small escort would take the main valley road north toward the House of Dar-rel. Due to Lord Alfar's animosity toward weirfolk, they wouldn't stop at the Main House but would veer west toward the House of Granfiel and the head of Black Lake. Ard hadn't said whether or not they would accompany him all the way to Pavion. He knew he would feel safer with the escort, but he wouldn't press them to come because there was no way he could be sure of their reception, as it was forbidden to bring any men into weir territory unless given permission by the weir High Council.

As he scuffed across the floor toward the terrace entrance, he felt the pinch of hunger. He'd been very careful what he ate or drank the last three days, choosing to suffer pangs of hunger rather than be poisoned again. He'd said nothing to Ard or Raney about poison, for he knew they both harbored suspicions of their own and were doing all they could to ensure his safety.

He reached the terrace door and pulled it open and stood looking out into the night. It was a peaceful scene of a world asleep. The trees were fast losing their leaves and the moonlit sky was clear, the stars shining brightly.

He shivered and thought of the warm bed he'd left. After closing the door, he started back to his bed but stopped when he heard a noise near the hearth. He peered into the darkness and listened but the sound wasn't repeated. Mice, he decided, and reached down to pull the covers back.

Suddenly something jumped on him from behind; an arm clamped around his neck. Before he could yell for help, something wet was clapped over his nose and mouth. He kicked and struggled, using elbows, feet, and body, trying to find a weak spot in his attacker's defenses. The arm around his neck tightened. For a few seconds Kalna and his attacker stood like two statues, each straining against the other.

"Breathe!" came a whispered order. "Don't fight me, weirling. You can't win."

That voice! It was Alfar! The grip on his neck relaxed a little and air rushed into his lungs, along with a noxious odor that made him start to gag. He realized his danger and tried not to breathe again. He renewed his struggles and somehow managed to twist halfway around; his head struck something hard, wooden.

"Breathe." Alfar whispered again. "You won't be hurt if you obey me."

Kalna had no choice; he simply couldn't hold his breath any longer. Too late he thought about calling up his inner fire. His mind grew sluggish as the fumes entered his lungs. The numbness that closed over his mind slowly ate into his body. Another breath and he went limp.

Cold...dark...danger...Alfar...don't...breathe. Uncoordinated thoughts flickered through Kalna's mind as he stirred. Each intake of fresh air helped to clear his head of the strange fumes that had overcome him.

He became aware of a swaying motion. He tried to speak but his mouth and tongue wouldn't form the words. Breathing more deeply, he concentrated on moving his hands. His body didn't want to obey even the simplest of commands. He tried again and was rewarded by a tingling sensation in his fingers.

After a minute or two he finally managed to open his

eyes. The shadowed form who carried him was silhouetted against the moonlit sky; head and shoulders were
swathed in a hood.

Kalna began to remember: his cold room, finding the
door open, the attack, and—Alfar's voice! Fear gave
him strength, and he brought his right arm up across his
chest and grabbed hold of Alfar's cloak. The hood fell
back, exposing the mask of a Yorrga, its crooked mouth
and twisted nose leering down at him. Alfar? Wearing a
Yorrga mask? Kalna was stunned.

"Do you waken so soon, weirling?" Alfar said. He
paused and tightened his hold as Kalna began to struggle. "I should kill you now, but someone else wants you
alive. He thinks you'll come in useful in the near future.
Who knows, perhaps you will."

Kalna had believed Alfar hated and despised all weirfolk, that he would kill any weir given a chance; but the
calm way in which he was handling the abduction spoke
not of hate but rather of cunning and well-thought-out
plans. His mind flooded with questions: Who was the
someone Alfar spoke about? What did he want with him?
Where was he being taken? And what had Alfar to do
with the Yorrga?

Kalna's sleeping tunic was not designed to keep him
warm in cold night air, and the chill combined with the
numbness caused by whatever Alfar had used to knock
him out soon had him shivering. He tried to ignore the
cold by concentrating on his surroundings, but the trees,
bushes, and open field to his left could have been any of
a dozen places not too distant from the palace. His so-
journs with Raney had been too few to allow him to recognize where he was.

He tried to speak; his voice sounded like the croaking
of a frog. His second try was little better.

"Don't bother calling for help," Alfar said. "There's
no one out here to hear you."

Alfar walked a little farther, stopped, and whistled
low. Four figures emerged out from behind some nearby
bushes. They were also cloaked and hooded.

Alfar passed Kalna to one of the other men. "He's starting to come around. You'll have to keep him tied. You know where to take him. Make sure no one sees you."

"Will you be coming soon?" one of the hooded figures asked.

"A few more days and I'll have Lord Drian convinced of our cause. I'm going to stay here until I'm sure of him."

"What about Prince Ard?"

"With the weirling out of the way, he should come around. If he doesn't, we'll have to do this without him. Lord Drian is the important one anyway. We'll concentrate on him."

"Will Lord Tennebar be—"

"Enough! The weirling is listening to everything we say." Alfar pinched Kalna's arm. "Aren't you, Kalna? You've disrupted my plans long enough, weirling. Your friendship with Prince Ard is at an end, and with luck, Ard will follow his father into war against your people."

Alfar stepped back. "Better wrap him in a blanket. No sense in going through all this only to have him die of the cold."

Kalna regained consciousness several times in the next hour; each time he was more alert and more aware of the discomfort of riding stomach down across someone's lap.

The lopers stopped. He could hear the Yorrga whispering among themselves. The one who held Kalna remained silent. The lopers stomped restlessly and made soft noises of displeasure, as if anxious to be on their way.

Kalna thought about escape, but knew he had little chance of success while wrapped tightly in a blanket with his head covered and his arms lashed to his sides. Should he even try to call up fire, he would end up burning himself worse than his enemies. He would have to bide his time and wait for an opening. Meanwhile, he could try to improve his position, which might help the dull ache in his head.

"May I sit up?" he asked.

"You're fine right where you are," the Yorrga growled.

"I promise I won't try anything."

The Yorrga snorted. "And I'm to believe that?"

"Please, I—"

"Another word and you'll be gagged as well as tied!"

Kalna subsided, not willing to challenge the Yorrga's mood. Minutes later the Yorrga continued on their way. Time quickly lost all meaning for Kalna as discomfort and a growing pain in his head filled his every thought. When the riders finally halted several hours later, he was pulled from the saddle unconscious.

Night gave way to morning and eventually Kalna roused to the sound of low voices. He didn't remember where he was for a moment or two, for he had been dreaming about Ard and the dream had been so real that it was a jolt to waken and be reminded of his status as prisoner.

He rolled to one side and the blanket corner covering his head fell back. He saw four weirmen seated around a small campfire sharing breakfast; all were typical weir with prominent cheekbones, narrow slanted eyebrows, and red-brown hair. They were dressed in loose-fitting tunics, leather pants, and leather coats, all of which had seen better days. Two wore ankle-length moccasins; two wore calf-length boots more typical of the Bree. Cloaks and hoods lay in a pile nearby, along with the Yorrga masks. Kalna studied each face but failed to recognize anyone. Who were these weir who followed Lord Alfar's orders? And why did they hide behind Yorrga masks?

One of the weirmen turned and saw Kalna was awake. He stood and walked over to where Kalna lay. "Hungry, weirling?"

Kalna nodded.

The weirman squatted down and untied the ropes around the blanket and pushed it aside, then hauled Kalna up and toward the fire.

Kalna was conscious of the contemptuous glances cast in his direction as he hobbled forward and sat down.

The one who had released him handed him a fire-warmed roll, a chunk of cheese, and a cup of hot broka, a strong, tangy drink made from beans grown on the edge of the Morican Plains. The hot drink was a welcome relief from the chill and stiffness caused by his inadequate clothing.

Kalna assessed his chances for escape while he ate, but it was quickly apparent that a jolt or two of fire would avail him nothing and leave him too weakened for flight.

The weirmen lingered around the fire after they were finished eating, their silent glances leaving no doubt in Kalna's mind that they saw him as the enemy even though he shared their weir blood. Why would weir turn against weir? He kept asking himself that question over and over again. What could these weirmen hope to gain by siding with Lord Alfar? And what in the name of all that was sacred was Alfar doing parading as a Yorrga?

One of the weirmen stood up. "Time to get started. Kill the fire and get ready to move."

Kalna was allowed a minute for personal needs, then retied, blanket and all, and pushed back up into the saddle. He was allowed to sit upright this time.

The weirman who mounted behind Kalna had a strange cast to one eye. Kalna thought he might be blind in that eye for he held his head sideways while he rode.

Kalna decided to chance a question. "Where are you taking me?"

"A place where you'll be out of the way for a little while, where no one will ever think to look for you."

"Why are you doing all this? Why are the Yorrga killing people?"

A rough hand slapped over Kalna's mouth. "Enough talk! Keep quiet and behave yourself and you may yet come out of this alive, weirling! Clear?"

Kalna nodded and slowly the hand dropped away.

The riders avoided the main road north and chose smaller, less-traveled pathways. The pace was steady, the stops to rest were brief. The end of the day found Kalna half dozing in the saddle. He was aware of his surroundings, yet strangely removed, as if a part of him were somewhere else. In his mind's eye he saw Ard and Raney standing on a small outthrusting rock overlooking Lake Mataral. The House of Char rose behind them, its gray stone lighted by the westering sun. Ard looked grim; Raney worried.

Ard glanced down at something he held. Kalna saw that it was one of his crutches. Ard's lips moved but Kalna couldn't hear what he was saying.

Raney nodded and together the two of them turned and started back toward the palace.

*Ard! Raney!*

Kalna's silent call went unanswered. Neither man stopped or turned.

Kalna was startled from his dreamlike state by a hand clamping over his mouth again. His eyes flew open and he saw a band of six riders headed down the road toward them. The weir who held Kalna pulled back on the reins and quickly guided his mount into cover beside the trail. The other riders quickly followed.

"One sound and you're dead," the weirman hissed in Kalna's ear. Those words were accompanied by the prick of a knife in his side.

The six riders coming from the north passed their position a short time later. The weirmen waited until the riders were out of sight, then turned their mounts out onto the road again.

"Who are they?" one of the weirmen asked.

"Men from the House of Char. The same ones who came with Alfar earlier. After seeing what remains of

Kirlyle, I'm sure they're convinced that the Yorrga are on the move, which means that the treaties will soon be broken."

"And that means war!" another of the weir cried. "War with the Bree and victory for Lord Tennebar!"

# CHAPTER 10

Kalna looked around the stone cell where he'd spent the night. It had been dark when he was thrown inside, but with the coming of morning, a shaft of light had appeared from a narrow slot overhead. The opening was out of reach and far too small to offer any chance of escape; still, it was better than darkness.

The cell was large. A raised platform stretched along one wall. It was damp and moldy, proof that the cell hadn't been used in a long time.

Kalna had no idea where this place was; he knew only that it was some kind of old ruin, because the night before he'd seen a tower and some crumbled walls silhouetted against the nighttime sky.

Two weirmen came with food and water. They were in and out of the cell so quickly that Kalna hadn't a chance to even contemplate attacking them with fire. He eyed the food with misgiving, but finally ate what was brought, reasoning that the weir masquerading as Yorrga wouldn't go to all the trouble of kidnapping him if they only meant to kill him later.

While he ate he thought about Alfar, who had spoken as if there was another in command, someone who saw him as being useful in the future. Useful how? he wondered. He also remembered that his abductors had twice used the name of Lord Tennebar. He had always believed the name was only used to frighten children into obedience; perhaps he'd been wrong. If Lord Tennebar was a real person, it meant that evil incarnate now walked the mountain pathways, and if he was all the legends said he was, both Bree and weir were in great trouble. He shuddered at the thought even though it led to a possible explanation of the emergence of the killer Yorrga.

It was impossible to measure the passage of time. He dozed fitfully and woke to noises he heard but could not identify. The last time he woke, it was dark in the cell. He lay awake for a while, then grew restless, and stood up and limped around the confines of the cell, groping along the wall with his hands. Twice he heard something scurry out of his path. When he reached the cell door, he put his face to the grating and called out, asking for water. No one answered.

He stood at the grate for a long time listening, wondering if he had been left alone to die. He finally retreated to the moldy platform and curled up in the blanket they'd left him. He had never been afraid of the dark before; but then, until the coming of the Yorrga, the darkness had held nothing to be afraid of. At that moment he was as much in need of light as warmth. He thought about calling up his inner fire, but after a minute of consideration, he rejected the idea. Not only would it drain him of energy, but there was nothing to burn in the damp cell but his blanket or his sleeping tunic, and neither would provide light or heat very long.

Time passed and his thoughts drifted. He thought about all that had happened to him since the day he'd delivered Rops's medicine, all the pain and grief, all the fear and uncertainty. His thoughts finally centered upon Ard and what he would think of his abrupt departure, and whether or not he would even think to blame Lord Alfar.

No, he thought, Ard will think I left on my own; Alfar will make sure of that, which means that I'm on my own and that I cannot sit here waiting for someone to rescue me. When they open the door the next time, I must be ready.

The shaft of light returned and began its slow trek across the floor. Kalna slept on, lost in dreams and unaware of the three weirmen who entered his cell quietly. One carried a crude wooden bowl and a large cup filled with water; the second acted as guard and remained near the door; the third walked over to the sleeping platform and peered down at Kalna, as if making sure he still lived. Satisfied, he signaled the other two out and closed the door carefully behind him.

Kalna woke to the sharp squeaks and chittering noises of several small rodents fighting over the contents of his food bowl. He threw back his blanket and made a dive for the bowl, knocking one of the rodents away; the other nipped him on the finger before scuttling off under the platform. He limped back to the platform with what was left of his food and water and divided the remnants, eating half and saving the remainder for later.

He was left undisturbed the rest of the day. With nothing but his own thoughts for company, he eventually fell asleep again, his last conscious thoughts of Ard and Raney.

*Kalna's spirit lightened even though the day was overcast. He was seated behind Ard riding down a long, winding dirt road protected by overhanging bigleaf trees, their fall colors muted by the darkening sky. He turned and saw Raney riding beside them. He smiled, but Raney didn't respond in kind.*

*They rode on a little farther and the road divided. Ard turned to look at Raney. "Left fork or right?"*

*Raney stopped his mount, stepped down, and inspected the ground. "The left fork," he said, remounting.*

*"Are you sure?" Ard asked.*

*"It shows the most recent travel."*

*Ard shook his head. "It seems wrong to me. Check again."*

*Kalna felt Ard's frustration as if it was his own; it was a feeling of wanting to hurry without knowing where you're going. Where were they going? he wondered.*

*Raney studied the two roads carefully and pointed left. "I'm sure," he said, remounting. "They went this way, and from the looks of it, we're a good day behind them."*

*"Who are we following, Ard?" Kalna asked.*

*Ard raised a hand. "Someone's coming! Let's get out of the way."*

*They left the road and waited, shielded by the trees, until a small group of riders passed by. "Alfar," Raney growled softly.*

*"Let's find out what he's up to," Ard responded.*

*"No, Ard! He's with the Yorrga! He's the one who . . ."*

Kalna wakened to a threatening crack of lightning followed by a deep roll of thunder. He sat up, dazed for a moment. Where was he? He'd been riding with Ard and Raney.

Another bolt of lightning hit somewhere nearby and in the second the cell was lighted, he remembered where he was. Despair washed through him as he gathered his blanket more closely around himself. All a dream. All just a dream. But it had been so real!

He woke the next morning with a terrible headache. Part of his blanket was wet where rain had dripped on him from above, and he was cold.

He felt worse as the day passed; his chest and shoulders ached and his head grew warm. Large red blotches began to appear on his arms and chest and soon he was itching all over.

He lost track of time as his fever rose, not caring if it was day or night. All he wanted was an end to the terrible itching.

When his daily meal was brought, he tried to summon the will to sit up and lash out at those who kept him a prisoner, but he had no energy; it was all he could do just to raise the water cup to his lips and drink. One glance at the stew he'd been given and he turned away, swallowing quickly. If he ate anything, he knew it would just come up again.

Exhausted and feeling so ill that he hardly cared whether he lived or died, he finally fell into a fitful sleep where he dreamed about a strange, golden Yorrga whose face glowed in the dark; he cringed away from its burning eyes and cruel laughter and he flailed at its hands as it grabbed at his arms and pulled him close.

*You will be mine!* it cried triumphantly. *Open to me and you will understand what it is to be a god!*

"No!" Kalna screamed.

The Yorrga cursed and twisted Kalna's arm, forcing him to his knees. Kalna heard the beat of wings; then a fist smashed into his mouth and dream became reality. He opened his eyes and saw a Yorrga leaning over him, shaking him by the arms.

"Up, weirling! Now! You're wanted!"

Fear etched through the fuzziness in his mind and brought the Yorrga face into focus. It was a twisted-nose and he wasn't alone. There was another Yorrga with him, a long-tongue, who stepped close and grabbed his other arm. Both wore gold-colored wrist bands with the image of a crowned serpent coiled for attack.

They pulled him off the platform and propelled him toward the cell doorway. There was a short, dark corridor beyond the doorway, then steps leading up and outside.

Kalna squinted into the bright glare of daylight and took stock of the great stone walls that surrounded them.

Some were still intact; others lay crumbled and broken. Old timbers slanted down from the vine-covered walls, the last remnants of floors and ceilings, and scattered here and there lay broken furniture green with moss and lichen. Encha vines and fern overran what was left of the stone floors on level ground.

The ruins were extensive, at least as large as the Palace of Char. When Kalna turned and saw the single great tower that stood to the north wall and the ornately carved stone gate that had once guarded the main courtyard, he knew where he was. He had heard of the ruins of Rithe's Keep and knew the story behind its fall, for it had once belonged to the weirfolk, who upon being driven out of their last foothold in the Lakeland Forests had chosen to destroy their home rather than leave it for men to claim.

They passed a place where the Yorrga had built shelters for themselves and their mounts using freshly cut logs and several of the more substantial walls. He began to count the people he saw as he was pushed along. Only a few more Yorrga masks; the rest were weir, though some could have easily passed as true men.

Questions filled Kalna's mind. Who were these weir? Where had they all come from and what were they doing here? And most important of all, who was leading them? Alfar was a part of it all, he knew that, but there was someone else involved, someone who called himself Lord Tennebar.

The Yorrga who escorted Kalna became impatient with his limping stride; as he stumbled, they literally dragged him off his feet and splashed through several puddles, heedless of his attempts to regain his footing.

Cold, wet, and shivering, he was brought to stand under an improvised shelter next to the tower wall. The roof of the shelter was little more than wooden poles overlaid with bow greens. There was a small fire just at the edge of the shelter and a haunch of taural cooking on a spit. The smell of meat made Kalna nauseous. He turned away, trying to ignore the odor as well as the achy pain in the back of his head and neck.

A voice came out of the shadow at the rear of the shelter. "Bring him closer."

Kalna was filled with a sudden foreboding as Twisted-nose pulled him farther under the shelter, for of all those seated within the shelter, only two were not masked. He sensed antagonism and loathing from several of the closest Yorrga, but overriding that was a feeling of maliciousness that made the hairs on the back of his neck rise.

As his eyes adjusted to the half-light, he saw one of the Yorrga stand up. He was tall and strong looking and, like the others, he wore a gold-colored armband. His heavy cloak was slit at the sides, allowing him to move his arms freely. As the Yorrga moved closer, Kalna's attention went to his mask, which was different from the others. But for eye, nose, and mouth holes, it was featureless, and it looked to be overlaid with the same gold-colored material that made up the wrist bands.

His dream! He had dreamed of fighting this Yorrga— and in his dream he had lost! He shrank back as the Yorrga reached toward his face.

Twisted-nose caught Kalna's arm and bent it up behind his back, holding him still.

Gold-mask reached out again and touched the blood on Kalna's lip, then put the finger into the mouth hole of his mask. The gesture was obscene and it made Kalna feel sick to his stomach.

Gold-mask reached out again, caught Kalna by the chin, and lifted his head to stare into his eyes. "You don't look well, weirling, not well at all. But it's no wonder, dressed as you are. We shall have to do something about that."

The aura of wrongness emanating from Gold-mask surrounded Kalna with an icy cold. For a moment or two he had thought it might be Alfar behind the gold mask, but it wasn't Alfar's voice he heard. This voice was deep and hollow sounding and totally unlike any he'd ever heard before. He sensed evil in the weir behind Gold-mask, and more than that, he sensed madness that was strong enough to sway anyone who came within his sphere of influence. Was this then Lord Tennebar?

"He's trembling!" Twisted-nose crowed delightedly.

Gold-mask moved a half step closer and looked down at Kalna. "Is it illness, Kalna? Or do you fear me?"

Kalna didn't respond; his thoughts were centered on his inner fire, but try as he might he couldn't make it obey his command. It was there, he could feel it, but each time he gathered it to himself, it slipped and squirmed away. He realized that his illness was to blame.

"I've learned much about you these past few weeks, Kalna," Gold-mask continued, unperturbed by his silence, "but I need to know more. I know that you're responsible for killing one of my followers—perhaps more than one—and I know that you have shown certain talents with fire, talents that would some day make you a formidable enemy. A small amount of fengla in your food took care of that problem. Have you never heard of it? Your mother would have recognized its scent, I'm sure. Her death wasn't planned, by the way, but I think it was for the best, because she would have caused us great difficulties had she learned what we were about."

Anger and frustration overrode fear as Kalna twisted free and launched himself at Gold-mask, his one thought to kill the weir responsible for his parents' deaths. His inarticulate cry of rage tore the air like the howl of a crazed velhund.

Gold-mask failed to counter the attack, but stood calmly waiting as Kalna's weight carried him back a step or two. He even allowed Kalna to grab him around the neck in a choking hold. Then he moved; he brought his hands up and caught Kalna's head, his fingers splayed and cupping at the temples and around the back of the head.

Kalna dug into the Yorrga's neck with his fingers, squeezing with all his strength. Suddenly sharp needles of pain lanced through his head wherever the Yorrga's fingers touched. He arched back, teeth bared in a grimace of agony—but he didn't give up his hold.

Gold-mask tried to push Kalna to arm's length but failed. He went down on one knee, pulling Kalna down with him. Twisted-nose saw he was in trouble and moved in, a stout branch in one hand. He raised it and brought it down on the side of Kalna's head.

Kalna woke to find himself bound hand and foot, lying near a firepit. His enemies were seated around him, talking. He rolled his head to one side and instantly regretted it as pain lanced upward from his neck to the top of his head. He groaned softly and settled back, his eyes closed.

His movement, though slight, caught the eye of one of the Yorrga. "He's stirring, Lord Tennebar."

"Sit him up!"

Two of the Yorrga eagerly obeyed, jerking Kalna roughly to a sitting position. Though his head felt as if it was about to fall off, Kalna glared at Gold-mask, sorry that he had failed to kill but more than willing to try again.

"See the hate in his eyes," Gold-mask said to his followers. "He would gladly kill us all—and in doing so become one of us. Is that what you want, Kalna? To be one of us?"

The tall Yorrga knelt beside Kalna and reached out to touch the swollen lump at the side of his head. Kalna leaned away from the touch and the pain it caused. Gold-mask's hand dropped down to Kalna's neck.

"You don't answer," he purred, his fingers massaging Kalna's throat. "I can feel the hate in your blood, weirling. It will choke you to death if you don't get rid of it. Feel it pump through your veins?" The fingers closed tighter around his throat.

Kalna was past all fear at that moment. He knew they were going to kill him. He looked into Gold-mask's eyes and spat.

Gold-mask's hand was a blur as he backhanded Kalna

across the face, knocking him backward. Kalna again tasted blood in his mouth.

Gold-mask reached down and pulled Kalna back to a sitting position. "You want death that badly, do you? Then death it will be! But not the kind you hope for. There is another kind of death, weirling. A living death that only I can give and then only to those who have earned it. It is a type of joining, but not the kind you are accustomed to."

Gold-mask snapped his fingers. Twisted-nose handed him a Yorrga mask with a downturned mouth and a long nose; it was painted black except for the large white eyes; there were no eye holes.

"I have many names," Gold-mask said menacingly. "The one I prefer is Lord Tennebar. It means darkness, and that is what I am to my enemies. I had thought to use you for another purpose, but I see now that this will be a better way." He held up the mask.

"I have learned some of the secrets of the Ancients and I know what must be done to twist souls to my bidding. This mask will make you mine, as those around you are mine. You will struggle a little, I think, but you won't win because I have fashioned this mask myself and the spirit trapped within it is strong and it hungers for a body that will make it fully alive! There is but one drawback for the wearer, however. You see, this mask causes blindness that will remain even if the mask is removed. Shall we try it on?"

Kalna shrank back from the mask as Lord Tennebar pushed it at his face.

"Hold him still!" Lord Tennebar growled.

Twisted-nose and another Yorrga threw themselves on top of Kalna while a third clamped his hands to either side of Kalna's head.

As Kalna saw the inside of the mask drop toward his face, the anger that had sustained him began to drain away, fear taking its place. He didn't like the *feel* of the mask; he sensed perverted power and auras of lust, envy, and hunger layered one over the other.

Suddenly a voice broke into the proceedings. "What goes on here?"

Gold-mask stopped what he was doing and looked up. Lord Alfar stood there, hands on hips, his glance disapproving. Four men stood behind him, their hands close to their weapons.

"I said, what are you doing?" Lord Alfar repeated.

"Nothing that concerns you, Alfar!" Lord Tennebar replied.

Alfar glanced at the eyeless mask. "You plan to make him one of your special Yorrga?"

"Why not?"

Alfar shook his head. "You could never trust him."

"I won't have to. A few days with this mask on and he'll be mine forever. There'll be no Kalna; there'll only be a Yorrga pleased to do my bidding."

"I thought you were going to use him as a hostage."

Lord Tennebar looked down at Kalna. "I've changed my mind. I think it will be wiser to keep him near me, and there's only one way to do that. Now, if you have no more objections..."

Alfar looked at Kalna a moment, then shrugged. "He's yours. Do with him what you will."

Lord Tennebar brought the mask back in front of Kalna's face. "It's time for you to feel a little taste of living death, weirling."

Kalna squirmed under the hands that held him as the mask was brought down upon his face. Fingers fumbled with the leather strap that passed around his head and fastened in back. They drew the mask so tight, he gasped in pain.

His next awareness was of something cold against his forehead. He opened his eyes to darkness and moments later felt the presence of the Yorrga's spirit like a cloying syrupy wetness; it entered through his nostrils and swirled down into his mouth. He choked and gagged, trying to spit it out, but it only moved faster. He tried to call up his inner fire, preferring to burn himself to death rather than allow this nightmare to take him over, but even that was denied him. There was nothing to do but retreat before its snakelike coils, flinching as its slimy tendrils caught hold of him.

*No!*

His silent scream shattered its hold momentarily. Kalna turned and ran and finally came to a dark cave where he'd never been before. He quickly moved inside and walled the entrance behind him. Moments later he felt the Yorrga push at his newly made wall. He leaned against it, holding it with all his being. Here he was safe! Lord Tennebar had not won!

# CHAPTER 11

Kalna heard someone call his name. The voice sounded familiar. He concentrated on the voice, trying to remember whom it belonged to. It was dark where he was, and warm and safe, and somewhere in the back of his mind that safety was overshadowed with a feeling of danger should he leave his hiding place.

The voice was insistent; it wouldn't let him slip back into that quiet waiting place that knew neither time nor pain. He listened and this time he knew the voice. It belonged to Ard—or someone who sounded like Ard.

He tried to answer but words wouldn't come. He tried to move and found himself imprisoned behind a strange wall. He looked for another exit but found none.

"Ka, it's Ard and Raney! Come on, wake up!"

The urgency in Ard's voice stirred memories, and suddenly Kalna knew where he was and why. Fear gripped him and he stopped pushing against the wall. Suppose it was a trick? Suppose it wasn't Ard who called him, but the Yorrga named Lord Tennebar disguising his voice so it sounded like Ard? He would not put it past the one he thought of as Gold-mask.

Ard called him again.

He tried to quell the flutter under his rib cage. There was only one way to find the truth. The wall would have to come down.

It took moments of concentration but slowly the wall dissolved. When it was gone, he stood within the cave-like opening staring out into the darkness, a new fear tickling his backbone. He was lost because he didn't remember how he'd gotten there or how he could get back.

Then Ard called his name again and he latched onto the sound of his voice and followed it up, up and out!

". . . isn't going to work, Ard," Raney hissed softly. "We'll have to carry him. If it comes to a fight, we'll just have to put him down and do the best we can."

Kalna couldn't see. He reached up to feel for the mask but found it gone.

"Ka? Are you awake?" Ard said, excitement in his voice.

"The mask. Where is it?" he asked, his voice trembling.

Ard caught his arm and pulled him up. "We smashed it! Come on, stand up. I'll help you walk."

"Is it night?"

"Yes. Keep your voice down. We killed two guards already but there are others all around the ruins. We'll have to move quickly and quietly."

Kalna reached out and caught at Ard's arm. "I can't see! I can't see anything. Is it that dark outside?"

Ard and Raney exchanged glances. "There's a moon out, Ka," Ard said, as he pulled Kalna's blanket around his shoulder. "Can't you see anything?"

"Noooo!" Kalna wailed. "I'm blind, Ard! The mask . . . it did something to my eyes!"

Ard's hand crushed against Kalna's mouth. "Shssh. We'll talk later, Ka. Right now we have to get out of here!" He pulled Kalna to his feet, grabbed his arm, and

started him toward the cell doorway. Raney followed
close behind.

They walked down the short damp corridor and
passed up the shallow flight of steps to the outside.
Kalna followed the pull on his arm, but without his sight,
he stumbled and fell on the uneven ground. Escape
should have been uppermost in his mind, but at that moment, all he could think of was Lord Tennebar's threat:
"This mask will make you mine forever!"

Ard helped Kalna up and hurried him on, retracing
the route they'd followed coming in. Suddenly a shout
rose behind them.

"They've found the guards!" Raney cried, moving up
beside Ard. "We'll have to run for it!"

"You go ahead," Ard said. "I'll carry Ka."

Kalna felt himself being hoisted up over Ard's
shoulder, then Ard was running. Kalna held on as best
he could, his blindness forgotten in the threat of falling
into Lord Tennebar's hands again.

Ard saw Raney ahead of him, then someone jumped
out of the bushes right in front of him, cutting him off
from the lopers. He stopped, bent low, dropped Kalna
off his right shoulder, and in a continuing movement
spun around, drawing his sword just in time to meet the
attack of the weir hurtling toward him.

Shaken but unharmed, Kalna sat up, knocking a
branch out of his face. He heard the clang of striking
swords and flinched; there followed the grunt of pain and
someone fell into the bushes nearby. They thrashed
around a moment, then stilled.

"Ard?" There was fear in Kalna's voice.

"Right here, Ka," came the quick reply. "Are you all
right?"

"Yes."

"Good! Here we go again. Hang on!" Again Ard
hoisted Kalna over his shoulder, and moments later they
had reached the place where Raney awaited them. Ard
flung Kalna into the saddle and mounted behind him.

Raney was already mounted. "Which way?"

"North!" Ard snapped.

"But there's nothing to the north!" Raney countered.

"They know that as well as we do, so they'll figure we'll head south and try for safety in one of the small towns between here and the House of Granfiel. I think we'll have a better chance to outrun them if we go north, then swing east, then south."

"We can try," Raney said, leading out. They kept their lopers to a walk, moving as quietly as possible until they were some distance from the ruins, then they pushed their mounts to a faster pace.

Kalna listened for the sounds of pursuit, but heard nothing but the soft thud of loper hooves on pine-needle–covered ground. He looked up, straining to pierce the darkness surrounding him. Giving up, he swallowed and tried to keep the tremor from his voice. "Ard, I can't see. It was the mask. Lord Tennebar said it would cause blindness."

Ard was silent a moment before speaking. "You couldn't have had it on very long, Ka, an hour or two at the most. We got to you as quickly as we could. We saw them bring you from the center of the ruins back to the place we found you. We didn't dare move until it was dark."

"I don't fault you or Raney, Ard. I'm just glad you came."

"It could be the blindness is only temporary, Ka," Ard said gently. "Warmth, food, and a good night's sleep and perhaps your sight will return."

*And perhaps it won't.* Silent tears fell from sightless eyes.

"Ka? Who is this Lord Tennebar you speak of?" Ard asked.

Kalna cleared his throat. "He's the head Yorrga. He wears a gold-colored mask."

"I saw that one, but only briefly. Did you recognize any of the weir back there?"

"No. The only one I knew was Alfar. Did you see him?"

"We saw. That's how we found you. When you disappeared from the palace, Alfar kept saying that you'd probably just decided to go home. But Raney found your crutches on the ground outside your room hidden in some bushes, so we figured that if you left, you had some help. We searched the ground and sent out riders but no one saw you. Two days later Lord Alfar said he had to return to the House of Dar-rel.

"To this day I'm not sure what made me decide to follow him, but I'm glad we did. Raney and I were out trying to find your trail one morning when Alfar and several of his men passed us by. They were headed east instead of north, which was the wrong direction if they were making for the House of Dar-rel. We decided to follow them and ended up at the ruins of Rithe's Keep."

"I saw you on the trail," Ka said softly.

"What?"

"Nothing, just something I dreamed. Ard," he said, changing the subject, "how did you know I was there?"

"We didn't until we saw them lead you from those underground cells up through the ruins. By the time we had worked our way closer, they were carrying you back to the cells. We were worried about you but there wasn't anything we could do until darkness. There were just too many of them to tackle by ourselves."

"Were you surprised to find Alfar meeting with the Yorrga?"

"Not really. I guess that in the back of my mind there was something about Alfar's surviving the Yorrga attack near Black Lake that never set well, some feeling that he was lying about something, and the more I think about it, the more I begin to see the layers of intrigue surrounding that first Yorrga attack. Can you guess what Alfar was aiming for all along?"

Kalna turned his thoughts from darkness, thankful for the distraction Ard offered him. It didn't take long to piece the story together. "Prince Jurandyr was heir to the House of Dar-rel. He dies and it all belongs to Alfar. And your death?"

"My death was arranged in order to bring my father into the war Alfar had planned. The House of Char is a leader among the Sister Houses. Alfar couldn't win a war without us siding him. And the reason for a war? The House of Dar-rel is small by most standards. What better way to increase his territory than to start a war and get others to fight his battle for him? With the weirfolk driven farther back into the Black Forest, he could claim a vast amount of territory to the north and east of Black Lake, and as the one who championed the war, who would deny him his choice of lands won?"

"What about the Yorrga? What are they after? And why deal with Alfar if he only means to rob them of lands belonging to their own people?"

"That I haven't figured out yet."

Kalna sat quietly on a blanket on the ground, the sun warm on his back. He heard the lopers slurping water nearby and Raney speaking to them softly. Ard was going through a pack beside him and cursing under his breath when he didn't find what he wanted.

It had been two days since Kalna's rescue, days of riding and hiding as the Yorrga harried them farther and farther north. Twice they had come close to being recaptured, so close in fact that Ard was sure that the Yorrga knew who he was. That meant that they wouldn't allow him to slip past them, for if he carried the truth back to his father, the war against the weirfolk might be called off, and Lord Alfar's plans would be nothing but smoke in the wind.

Kalna felt a cloth brush against his arm, then a hand was laid against his forehead. Ard's voice came out of the darkness. "You're still running a fever, Ka, and I haven't anything more to help. Are you thirsty—or hungry at all?"

Kalna shook his head. He'd tried to eat that morning but had lost everything a short time later.

"Are you warm enough?"

He nodded. They'd given him some of their own

clothing, which in both cases was too large but better than the sleeping tunic he'd been captured in.

Ard settled down beside him. "Things don't look good, Ka. There's nothing but wildlands north of us now and we're cut off to the west and south. It leaves us no choice but to head east, straight into weir territory, and considering that most of those who are chasing us are weir, it isn't much of a choice."

"We have to go east, Ard. If we can find Thekis, he'll protect us!"

"You sound sure of that. What happens if he's in league with the Yorrga who are after us?"

"Thekis would never betray me!"

"He might not betray you, but what about us?" It was Raney speaking. Kalna hadn't heard him approach.

"You'll be safe with me! You don't understand anything about weirfolk if you think—"

"Easy, Ka," Ard said, interrupting. "Raney wasn't insulting your people. He's just being cautious. Tell me, how are we to find this uncle of yours?"

How indeed, thought Kalna, with me blind and unable to guide you? He cursed silently and clenched his fists, his fingernails biting into the palms of his hands. He would *not* succumb to the self-pity that had ridden with him the past two days. He would *not*!

"I can't show you the way," he said finally, "but I can tell you what to look for. I'm not sure how far north we've come, but if we turn east, it couldn't be more than a two-day ride to the Black Forest."

Ard turned to his friend. "What do you think, Raney?"

"I think that we don't have much choice unless you want to turn around and try to break through their net again. We've failed twice. Maybe a third time will be the charm."

"There's one more alternative," Ard said. "We could go to ground and hope they pass us by."

Suddenly Kalna rolled over onto his left knee, used his casted leg as a brace, pushed up with his arms, and brought his good leg under him and stood up. "I can feel them, Ard," he cried. "They've found us again. We've got to move quickly!"

Ard stood and caught him by an arm. "Are you sure?"

"Yes! They're coming this way!" He pointed south. "I swear, Ard! I can feel them! They're in that direction."

Raney looked at Ard and shrugged. Ard shook his head but started moving. He was more willing to believe, yet still not sure how Kalna knew the enemy was close. Once before he had warned them, and they had run—just in time.

It took only moments to gather their things and mount. Raney shared a saddle with Kalna this time, and Ard took a defensive position in the rear. They avoided open ground and kept to cover wherever possible; their course was east toward the Black Forest.

Something whipped past Kalna's head and *thunked* into a nearby tree. Raney pressed Kalna forward and down over the pommel of the saddle, shielding him with his own body.

"What was that?" Kalna demanded, as Raney urged his mount to a run.

"Arrow! Keep low and hang on!" Raney yelled.

"Where's Ard?"

Raney looked back. "He's coming! There are two right behind him. We'll have to try to outrun them. Their lopers must be as tired as ours!"

It was a terrifying thing to ride blind; all Kalna could do was hold tight to the saddle flaps and keep his head down to avoid whipping branches. Twice the loper rose in the air to clear a fallen log or low bush. If not for Raney's riding skills, they both would have fallen from the saddle on the last jump, for the loper landed wrong and stumbled before recovering his balance.

They rode on. Kalna heard the splash of water as their mount crossed a shallow stream, then they were riding uphill. The loper's hooves began to slip and churn on the moss-covered slope. Raney cursed and jumped off to lighten the load. Still holding the reins, he scaled the steep grade beside his mount and called encouragement to keep it going.

"Do you want me down?" Kalna cried, feeling the loper heave beneath him.

"Stay put! We're almost to the top!"

Moments later the loper scrambled onto level ground. Raney paused to look behind him and saw Ard below crossing the stream. There was no sign of the Yorrga. Had they lost them?

Ard motioned for them to go on. Raney swung back up behind Kalna and kicked his mount to a run again. It was breathing heavily but still had some speed left. Kalna stayed low at Raney's command and prayed to Yaril to lend their mount strength.

Several minutes passed. Raney let their loper slow to a canter and turned to look behind. Ard was nowhere in sight. He finally pulled his mount to a halt.

Kalna sat up. "What's wrong?"

Raney peered through the bare branches behind them. "I'm not sure."

Kalna listened. The forest was quiet. "Do you see Ard yet?"

"No. But he should be right along."

When Ard failed to appear, it left Raney two choices: either ride on without him, believing him dead or captured, or go back and see what had happened to him.

Kalna, though ill, was sensitive to the emotions surging through Raney at that moment, and it didn't take much guessing to know that the man feared for his friend. Kalna brought his right leg up and over the neck of the loper and slid from the saddle before Raney realized his intentions. Raney caught at the back of his tunic.

"What are you doing?" he demanded angrily.

Kalna twisted around and caught Raney's arm. "You must go back and find Ard! I'll stay here!"

"No!"

"I'd only be in your way, Raney. Leave me here. I'll be all right until you come back."

"But what if I don't—"

"There's no time for argument!" Kalna pulled away and took several lurching steps backward. "Ard has to be in trouble or he'd be here by now! Go back and find him!"

Raney sat there a moment, undecided, then he leaped to the ground and pushed Kalna back against a nearby tree. "You stay here and don't move! I'll be back as quickly as I can!"

Kalna touched the tree behind him, suddenly terrified. Raney squeezed his shoulder, then ran to his loper and flung himself into the saddle. He nudged the loper close to Kalna and made two wide gashes in the tree high above Kalna's head. "I've marked the tree, Kalna. Now don't move away from it! Promise?"

Kalna felt Raney's indecision as he sat there; he knew the man was torn between going and staying. Trying to quell his own fear of being left, he put on a show of false courage. "I promise. Go!"

The loper's bushy tail flicked against his face as Raney swung the animal around. He listened as the loper pounded back down the trail, the hoofbeats quickly fading.

It was terrifying to be blind and alone in a forest where there were more enemies than friends looking for you. As Kalna waited for Raney's return, his mind whirled with imaginary scenes of Ard and Raney fighting Yorrga, or the two of them riding the forest paths bent over their mounts, the Yorrga in hot pursuit. What if the Yorrga had captured Ard? Or worse, killed him? What if Raney was captured? Would anyone come looking for him?

Yes, he thought. Gold-mask would come if no one else did. He knew that as surely as he knew he was blind. I should hide, Kalna thought. Move some distance away from the marked tree. No. I promised Raney I'd stay here.

The minutes crawled by, every one twice as long as the one before. He jumped at each sound, his mind filled with visions of Yorrga sneaking up on him. Twice he called out, sure that someone was standing nearby watching him. He wanted to run but had the presence of mind to realize that his only chance of survival lay in staying where Raney could find him ... if he made it back.

There was no way for Kalna to tell the passage of time, but gradually he felt a shift in the breeze and the small patch of sunlight that had warmed the side of his face departed. The cooler air meant that night was approaching.

*Raney, where are you? Please come back. Don't leave me here alone.*

Kalna sat at the base of the tree, his arms wrapped around his good leg, his head cradled on his knee. He heard a noise and woke from a light sleep. His mouth was dry, his head was hot, and his back and shoulders ached so terribly that he couldn't keep from moaning softly to himself as he shifted positions.

He knew that Ard and Raney weren't coming back; he knew that somehow the Yorrga had claimed them both. He also knew that if he didn't move soon, the Yorrga would find him by retracing Raney's trail.

He uncurled and stood up using the tree for support. The trees around him moaned softly in the wind, as if they saw what he was doing and disapproved. He ignored their warning and started out feeling his way as best he could. It was in his mind to try to find shelter under the low, sweeping branches of a pine tree, to sleep until he felt better, then to sit calmly and think over his next move.

The ground was uneven and his casted leg made his movements awkward. He lost his footing twice and fell, and each time he got up a little slower, his determination to go on fading as his strength seeped away.

He stumbled and fell again but managed to protect his bad leg by falling to his left side. He tried to push himself up, but his arms seemed to have lost all their strength.

*Lie down. Sleep here. No one will bother you.*

*No*, he argued with himself. *The Yorrga will come and find me!*

*They have Ard and Raney. Why should they want you now?*

*Gold-mask wants me to serve him!*

*No. You are nothing to him—nothing to anyone. That's why Ard and Raney didn't come back for you. They've gone on without you. You were a burden they didn't need.*

"No!" Kalna cried aloud.

*Yes. You know it's true.*

Kalna's head dropped onto the ground. "Raney promised. He said he'd come back for me."

*He lied, and you were a fool to have believed him.*

"He'll come! I know he will!"

*How can he come if he's dead?*

"Raney's dead?"

Kalna finally managed to sit up. He was confused. It was so hard to think. Whom had he been talking to?

He heard the sound of running water somewhere off to his right and licked at dry lips. He was so hot and thirsty. If only he could get a little drink of water and some sleep, maybe he could think things through.

He used his last reserves of energy and struggled to his feet. He stood swaying a moment, then turned and hobbled toward the sound of water. Hands out, he felt for branches and trees. They tore at his arms and face but he was no longer mindful of such minor irritations. He continued on, his sole purpose now was to find water to quench the raging fire within his body.

He misstepped and fell one last time. His right shoulder slammed into a tree trunk, throwing him sideways. There was one brief moment of gut-wrenching agony as his bad leg twisted, then mercifully he passed out.

# CHAPTER 12

Kalna woke to pain and cried out as hands slipped under his back and legs. "Easy, Kalna. It's Raney. We've been looking for you since first light. You should have stayed where I left you."

"Put me down!" Kalna cried. "It hurts!"

"I'm trying not to hurt you. Hold on just a minute and I'll have you into the saddle. Ard, take his arm."

"I've got him."

Kalna recognized Ard's voice, and for a few seconds the haze of pain receded. "Ard? Raney?"

"We're both here, Ka," Ard answered. "You're going to be all right. Here, lift your leg so you can sit astride. That's it."

Kalna pushed at the black curtain threatening to enclose him. "What happened to you? I thought—you were both dead. When Raney didn't come back—"

Ard cut him off. "It was a close thing, Ka. If Raney hadn't returned, I probably would be dead. My loper fell and broke a leg. I was pinned and couldn't move. Raney found me, but before he could do anything to help get me free, he saw two Yorrga coming down our trail."

Raney took up the story. "Ard was in no position to fight, so I did the only thing I could think of and led them away from the stream. It took me an hour to lose them and longer to find my way back to Ard. It was growing dark by then. By the time I got him free and we'd followed the trail back to where I'd left you, it was dark. When we found you gone, we feared the Yorrga had captured you again. We stayed there the night and in the morning found your trail." Raney dropped a hand to Kalna's leg.

"It must have been terrible waiting there not knowing if we were coming back."

Ard interrupted. "We'd better get moving, Raney. There's no telling how soon the Yorrga will pick up our trail."

Raney nodded. "I'll lead out."

"When you tire of walking, let me know and we'll switch places," Ard offered.

"Your leg's too swollen to do much walking. I think it best if we find a place to go to ground for a day or so. You both need tending."

"Look for a place, then," Ard agreed, "but make sure it's a defensible one. Here, Ka, lean back against me and try to rest."

"No," Kalna cried softly, pulling away from Ard's hands. "Let me sit up. It hurts to be touching anything." Kalna's mouth was so dry he could barely swallow. "Do you have water?"

Ard lifted a hide flagon from the saddle horn and put the spout to Kalna's lips. Kalna grabbed the flagon and drank deeply, trying to quench the fire burning him up inside.

Ard pulled the flagon away before Kalna could drink himself sick. "You can have more in a little while. Take hold of the saddle horn and hang on. If you feel yourself falling, yell out. All right?"

Head down, breathing deeply, Kalna nodded.

Raney read the worried look on Ard's face and agreed. Kalna was very ill. If they didn't find him help soon, it was possible that they'd lose him.

Ard looked up as Raney parted the bushes screening them from the narrow trail they'd been following the past hour. He'd tried to make Kalna as comfortable as possible while Raney went to refill the water flagon from a nearby stream. The small thicket they'd found provided them with little more than a hiding place for a few hours; it was too small for a lengthy stay and it was not defensible, but both men had decided that Kalna could not go on.

"How is he, Ard?" Raney said, kneeling.

"He's burning with fever. We've got to get him cooled down. If we bathe him, it might help. I'll get his clothes off, you find something to use as a cloth."

Ard was gentle, but Kalna's skin was so sensitive to touch that he couldn't keep from moaning as Ard freed him from his too-large pants. Raney began to lave him with cold water as Ard pulled his tunic up and over his head.

When Ard saw Kalna's back, he cursed softly under his breath.

"What's wrong?" Raney asked.

"Look at his back, Raney! No wonder he's got a fever. It looks all infected. It's even warm to the touch. There's two bad spots here and here. What in the name of Gander's Hell did they do to him?"

Kalna flinched as Ard's fingers brushed several tender places high on his back.

"There are no lacerations or puncture wounds anywhere that I can see," Raney said. "I wonder what caused it?"

"I'd say that there's some kind of poison in his system."

"You think the Yorrga poisoned him?"

"It doesn't matter right now. All that matters is killing his fever. I'll hold him up, you keep bathing him."

Kalna felt some relief as the water touching his skin evaporated in the air, but it still hurt to be touched anywhere on his back, chest, or arms. Raney used up all the water and went for more.

By the time he returned, Kalna was in a stupor, all coherent thought twisted into fragmented reality. He didn't know where he was nor did he care who held him. All he knew was the throbbing beat of pain.

Ard looked up as Raney dropped the flagon and knelt to begin the bathing process again. "He's hurting so bad I can feel it. We've got to do something more. He's slipping away from us."

Raney heard the desperation in Ard's voice and thought quickly, reviewing all he knew of medicines and home remedies, anything that might help. He glanced at Kalna's back and the two egglike protrusions over the shoulder blades. The skin was so swollen there that it was discolored a blotchy red and brown.

Raney licked at dry lips and turned to face Ard. "If it's poison it has to be let out. I remember my grandmother once lancing a boil on my sister's arm. She was running a fever, too. We had to keep the cut clean and drained but we finally got rid of the infection and she was all right."

Ard considered a moment, then nodded. "It's worth a try. Build a fire to sterilize your blade. I'll hold him while you cut."

"A fire may be dangerous. If the Yorrga see smoke, they'll come running."

"We'll have to risk it. We'll douse it as soon as we can."

It didn't take long to build a fire to heat the blade. Raney signaled to Ard he was ready. Ard changed his position slightly, pulling Kalna up against his chest and holding him tightly, one hand at the back of his neck, the other around his waist.

Raney lifted the blade and took a deep breath. "This is going to hurt," he warned Ard. "Be ready to shut him up if he yells."

Ard nodded, his jaw clenched.

Raney said a quick prayer, placed the knifepoint against the swollen skin, jabbed it in and drew it down in a quick but shallow cut. Kalna arched in Ard's arms; his scream was cut off by Ard's hand across his mouth. A moment later he slumped unconscious.

Raney watched the blood flow down Kalna's back along with a light-yellow liquid, then something else slithered out; it looked like a piece of light-brown rope.

"What in the name of..." Raney muttered, as he wiped carefully at the skin around the cut. He caught the ropey piece of dead skin and brought his knife up. "I'm not sure what this is, but it doesn't look healthy."

"What what is?" Ard demanded, glancing down. Kalna's forehead was beaded with sweat and his face was white. Suddenly Ard's hand shot out, catching Raney's wrist.

"Wait! Don't!"

"Best to do this while the boy is out, Ard."

Ard shook his head. "No, Raney. Don't cut it."

"Why not? It's just a piece of dead skin."

"Raney! Think!" Ard snapped. "What did I tell you about Ka's mother?"

Raney frowned, not understanding. "You said she'd saved your life... that she was beautiful..."

"And?" Excitement lit Ard's face.

"And—that she was a darkling."

"A darkling! Yes! If what I think is true, that *thing* you're holding is a wing!"

Raney released the stringy flap of skin as if he'd been burned. Ard reached out and took it gently in his hand and saw that under the smear of blood there were traces of a ruffled edge, as if something was rolled up. "Look, Raney. Look close."

Raney looked and shook his head slowly. "But I thought they were born winged."

"So did I," Ard said, a strange, mystified smile on his face, "but apparently we've been misinformed."

"Why didn't Kalna tell us? Gods, I might have cut it

off!" He rubbed his bloodstained hand against his pants leg as he looked at the other lump on Kalna's back. "Shall I cut the other one free? I mean, maybe we should've let them sprout on their own."

"I think it's too late for that now. Better cut it free while he's still unconscious and hope that we're doing the right thing."

When Kalna woke his fever was gone and the pain in his back and shoulders was little more than a dull ache. He lay on his side, breathing deeply of the crisp cool air, and was suddenly filled with a strange sense of euphoria. He remembered running from the Yorrga and being left alone in the forest; and he remembered Ard and Raney finding him again, but after that, nothing.

"Ard?"

"Here, Ka," Ard answered from nearby.

"Is it night?"

"No. Morning. How are you feeling?"

"I feel better, a lot better."

"Your fever broke last night. Would you like to sit up?"

"Yes."

Ard took Kalna by the arms and pulled him to a sitting position and steadied him until he was sure he had his balance.

"Are you hungry, Kalna?" Raney asked.

"Starved. Have we anything to eat?"

"A little. I'll get you something," Raney said, as he reached for a pack.

"Ka, what do you remember of last night?" Ard asked.

"Nothing. Why? Did the Yorrga come again?"

"No, Ka, this has nothing to do with the Yorrga." Ard glanced at Raney, who nodded. "Ka, do you feel anything when I do this?"

A strange crawling sensation ran across the back of Kalna's shoulders. He couldn't suppress a shiver and with that slight motion, something thumped softly against his back. He sat a bit straighter. "What was that?"

"A part of you—darkling," Ard said gently. "You sprouted wings last night . . . with our help."

*Wings!* Kalna moved his shoulders slightly and again felt the strange sensation of muscles coming to life. He reached back with his left hand and felt one of the leathery ropelike things dangling down his back.

"They're beginning to unfurl," Ard said, touching one wing carefully. "Is there anything we should be doing to help, or will it happen by itself?"

Kalna's spirit soared. "Wings! I've grown wings!" Oh, Mother, Father, if only you could've seen! Tears of joy trickled down his cheeks. He felt like crying and laughing at the same time.

"Kalna, did we do wrong in cutting them free?" Raney asked, worried by the tears he saw. "We didn't know they were wings when we cut you. We thought it was some kind of infection. If we've harmed them, I'll not forgive myself."

"Harm?" Kalna laughed. "No, you did no harm. You did exactly what you should've done. The fever—the pain—I should've guessed, but the probability that I would be darkling was so remote that it didn't even enter my thinking. I had always dreamed of having wings, but . . ." Kalna swallowed the lump in his throat unable to go on.

Ard stood up suddenly and looked off through the trees. Kalna's joy was creating an echolike effect that resounded in his own body. The throb of excitement and the surge of emotions were akin to sexual arousal but on such a level that he feared he could not contain such feverish ecstasy in silence. He strode away from their small camp quickly, disappearing into the shadowed pines nearby.

Raney was surprised by Ard's abrupt departure, but stayed with Kalna, saw that he calmed down and ate something, then went in search of Ard when he failed to return. He found him watering their single mount in the nearby stream.

"Sir, is something wrong?"

"Raney, please call me Ard. We've been through too much together for formalities."

Raney nodded, his glance touching Ard's face, then moving to his hand, which twisted a lock of the loper's mane. "Are you all right?"

Ard's blue eyes were clouded with worry. "I don't know." He took a deep breath and released it slowly. "It's Ka, Raney. I felt what he was feeling and—I've never felt such joy before. This isn't the first time it's happened, but this time his emotions were so strong they nearly overwhelmed me. It's the *joining*. It has to be! It's done something to both of us. He tried to warn me once, but I didn't believe such linking was possible. I laughed at him and told him not to worry. What did it matter if some of my memories were his now and some of his, mine? But this—this side of the *joining* scares me because I'm not in control and I can't shut his feelings off."

"Like just a little while ago?" Raney guessed.

"Yes! When it happens, I feel like I'm not me anymore, but rather an extended part of him and that if I don't get away, I'll cease to be me!" Ard snorted. "It sounds crazy, doesn't it?"

Raney looked away. "No, not crazy. You've got to remember that you're dealing with one of the weirfolk, and what sounds crazy to us is not crazy to them. I don't completely understand this *joining* but I do know that it saved your life, and we are all grateful for that."

Ard looked at his friend and tried to smile. "So you're telling me to live with it." He shook his head. "I guess I'm just tired."

"We're all tired. It's this damn hide-and-seek with Lord Alfar's masked friends that's crazy! We have got to get back south somehow and tell Lord Drian what's going on!"

"I know, but now that we're down to one mount, it's going to make it even harder to elude the Yorrga. If only

Ka could see, then I wouldn't feel bad about leaving him in weir territory to go his way alone. To be truthful, I am not happy with the thought of looking up Ka's relatives."

"Neither am I, especially considering the possibility that some of them may be Yorrga. But what choice do we have? We can't just leave him here to fend for himself."

When Ard didn't respond, Raney's heartbeat quickened. "Ard? Is that what you were thinking about? Leaving him here?"

Ard hesitated, then nodded. "It crossed my mind."

"But we can't. He's too weak yet to—"

Ard interrupted. "We won't leave him, Raney. It was just something I had to think out. Come on, let's get back to camp. He'll be worried with both of us gone, and we shouldn't be lingering around here much longer anyway."

"Agreed," Raney said. "Let's go."

# CHHAPTER 13

Kalna heard running hoofbeats. He reached to his right and found Raney's shoulder. "Raney, someone's coming."

Raney rolled over and sat up, rubbing his eyes. He'd been the last on watch and hadn't slept very long.

"It shouldn't be Ard already," Kalna said. "He hasn't been gone that long."

"If it's not him, we're in trouble." Raney pushed Kalna down flat. They were partially hidden between two large pine trees, their low branches forming somewhat of a shelter against the wind. "Stay here and be quiet."

With his sight gone, Kalna's other senses seemed to have come to life. The scent of pine was pungent in his nostrils; he could also smell the earth, fallen leaves, the dried sweat of his own body. He listened as Raney moved away and heard the soft crush of leaves beneath his feet, the sound of cloth brushing against a tree branch, and over that, the solid thump of hoofbeats fast approaching.

His senses of taste, touch, smell, and hearing had become so acute in the past few days that he marveled at his new awareness, realizing how much he had over-

146

looked before. He reached out mentally for the identity of the rider. He had no name for the inner awareness that had sprung to life within him, but it enabled him to tell Ard and Raney apart without touch or voice reference. It was a knowing that came from inside, an ability to sense each man's special aura and recognize differences. He had said nothing to either man about it, fearing to waken the doubt he sensed growing in both men as they neared the Black Forest. He thought about the wings beneath his loose-fitting tunic and wondered for a moment if it was him they were uncertain about, if his becoming a darkling had changed the way in which they viewed him. Then again, it might not be him, he reasoned, but rather their destination. All their lives they had been told not to trust weirfolk, to avoid all contact with them, and now that their lives were threatened by weir-masked Yorrga, it was easy to understand why they were reluctant to enter forbidden territory.

They had a right to be wary, he thought, knowing in his heart that the safe conduct he had promised them would be worthless until they found Thekis or another who might know him. Could he protect them long enough? he wondered.

He finally caught the aura of the rider. It was Ard and he was so charged with tension that Kalna withdrew contact immediately, knowing only one thing that would stir Ard to such an agitated state—the Yorrga had found them again!

He ignored Raney's order and got up and began rolling the blanket he and Raney had been sharing. He did it clumsily but was almost finished when Raney returned on a run.

Raney passed Kalna and began gathering the rest of their belongings. "They've found our trail again!" He quickly tied a rope around the small bundle and stood and handed it to Ard, who rode up and halted his mount between the trees.

Ard took the rolled bundle and settled it across his knees. "Your hand, Ka."

Kalna reached up and Ard swung him up behind him. Raney had already started off through the trees.

"Are they close?" Kalna asked, as they started after Raney.

"Close enough. I was checking our backtrail and saw them down in the valley near the river we forded last night. It won't take them long to find out where we left the river."

"How many?"

"I counted nine."

"All Yorrga?"

"Too far to tell, but I wouldn't be surprised if some of Alfar's men are on the trail, too. They know that if we carry the truth back to my father, Alfar's plans for enlarging the House of Dar-rel will be worthless. He has to kill us all and he knows it."

"How close are we to the Black Forest?"

"If I'm not mistaken, the river we crossed last night should empty into Black Lake, which means that we're on the edge of the Black Forest right now."

"Home," Kalna said softly.

"For you, Ka, but not for us. If we had any other choice right now, we'd be—" Ard reined the loper in sharply.

"What's wrong?" Kalna asked, sensing trouble.

"Shssh," Ard whispered. "Raney's signaling that there's something ahead." He brought his right leg up and over and slid to the ground, favoring his bad leg. He tied the reins to a branch and started away. "Stay in the saddle, Ka. I'll be right back."

Moments passed. The loper stomped restlessly. Kalna reached down and patted it, for his own comfort as well as the loper's. He hated being left alone because his blindness made him feel vulnerable. He stretched out his awareness, seeking for life signs. He located Ard and Raney ahead, then a short distance beyond them there were others. They were mere flickers of warmth to him. They moved south past Ard and Raney. He counted seven.

Some minutes later Ard returned and took up the

reins and led the loper forward. "It was just a small group of riders heading south," Ard said, keeping his voice low. "We're going to mix our trail with theirs and hope that we lose those who follow us."

"Who were they?"

"Bree this time. Alfar's men, I think, trying to cut us off from reaching your people now. If you're right and the Yorrga Alfar has with him are not Black Forest weir, there's a chance we can stop this war by exposing all parties to the truth. If the Black Forest weir don't back Alfar's Yorrga and the Sister Houses don't back Alfar, there simply won't be any war."

It sounded logical, but Kalna had doubts about it working just the way Ard laid it out. What troubled him was Lord Tennebar and what he hoped to gain by such a war. Until they understood that, they were like children floundering in the dark after a candle is blown out. Lord Tennebar is the key, he thought. Now all we have to do is find the locked door and what he hides.

They reached the trail left by Alfar's men and followed it for a short distance, then carefully exited the trail near some overhanging pine trees. Raney took a branch and brushed gently at the pine needles covering the forest floor, moving backward as he did so to help obliterate their trail. Moments later they were moving east once more, safe for a little while longer.

Raney stood on a fallen tree, the shadows of late afternoon turning the bright carpet of red and yellow odd-bark leaves to rust and gold. They had been climbing steadily all afternoon. The higher they climbed into the mountain forest, the closer winter seemed, for there most of the trees were bare and the wind moved easily through the open spaces between the trees and bushes.

"Have you any idea of where we are?" Ard asked Raney.

Raney shook his head. "No. I'm lost."

"My turn to walk for a while," Ard said. He and Raney had changed positions off and on all day.

Raney looked at Kalna, who dozed in the saddle, his cheek against Ard's back, his arms around his waist. "You'll wake Kalna if you move. Let him sleep a little longer. He's been irritable all day. He needs more rest."

"We all need rest," Ard growled. "It will be dark in another two hours. We'd best find a place to stop the night, preferably out of the wind. Do we have anything left to eat?"

"A piece of hard bread and a handful of dried fruit. I'll set some snares again tonight. Perhaps we'll be lucky and catch something for breakfast."

They entered a section of the forest where pine trees outnumbered the larger oddbark, bigleaf, and dewberry trees. The tangle of briar bushes in and around the trees seemed to form an almost impenetrable barrier. Raney skirted the pines heading south and finally came to an open place that looked like some kind of path.

"More than an animal trail," Ard said. "Let's follow it a ways. If nothing else, the pines will offer us some shelter from the winds."

Raney nodded agreement and led the way in. After a few twists and turns, the narrow pathway opened outward and passed freely under the branches of the pine trees.

Ard halted the loper and studied the blue-green depths that stretched before them. "Someone's done a lot of work here. Look at the way the lower branches have all been trimmed, then stacked off to each side."

"Weirfolk?" Raney said softly.

"Who else?"

Raney walked close to one of the trees. "The cuts are old, Ard. It could mean no one's passed this way recently. Think it's safe to go on?"

"No, not really, but I don't see that we have much choice. We certainly can't go back the way we came. Let's just hope that when we find Ka's people, they give us a welcome."

Twice the trail branched off, once to the south, once to

the north. They stayed on the trail headed east until it became so dark under the trees that it was difficult to see.

Raney finally spotted a place off the trail that would afford them some security. It was a small hollow that was partially surrounded by pine trees whose branches brushed the ground. The remains of several old fires told them that they were not the first to use the place as a campsite. When Raney saw the fire pits, he suggested they keep moving. Ard said no, that they would take a chance and camp there the night.

"It's too dark to go on," Ard said, lifting his leg over the saddle horn. Kalna stirred at his movement. "And this place is low and out of the wind. I think we can even have a fire if we're careful it's not too large. I could use some hot broka if we have any left."

"We have a little. Enough for tonight, though it'll be weak."

Kalna sat up, fully awake. "Where are we, Ard? Is it time to stop?"

"It's night, Ka, and I don't know where we are. We've been following a pathway cut for passage for the last few hours. Piles of branches line the path both sides and we've found a place where we can stop the night and be out of the wind a little."

Kalna made a face. There were hundreds of forest paths cut and maintained by the weirfolk throughout the forest. Ard's description told him nothing about where they were or how far they had yet to go to reach one of the small weir settlements west of Pavion.

Ard slid out of the saddle and helped Kalna down. Raney peered around the hollow feeling very ill at ease. "What if some of the weirfolk find us here?"

"If we're found by weir, we'll ask them to take us to Thekis," Kalna replied. "It's what we want, Raney."

"Maybe it is, and maybe it isn't," Raney said. There was a hard edge to his voice as he continued. "I still think our best bet would be to swing south and try for one of the Sister Houses. Alfar's people can't be everywhere! There's got to be a way to slip past."

"We've tried it, Raney," Ard said, "and it hasn't worked. We've no choice now but to trust in Ka and his people. I know it's hard to walk into what we've always thought of as enemy territory, but if we're to stop Alfar from starting a war, we're going to need the weirfolk on our side."

Raney glanced at Kalna. "And what if they aren't on our side, Ard? What if Ka is wrong? After all, the Yorrga are—"

"I'm not wrong!" Kalna was hard pressed to keep the anger out of his voice. "The Yorrga who killed my mother and father are not—could *not* be any of the weir from my section of the Black Forest! You don't know my people! You don't understand what Graya was to them. She was darkling! She was..." Kalna choked back a sob, turned and faced away from the two men, hands clenched at his sides.

Ard scowled at Raney. Raney flinched from the look. "I'll see to the loper," he muttered, and moved off.

Ard came up behind Kalna and put hands to his shoulders. Kalna jerked away, took several steps, and stumbled over an upraised tree root.

Ard hesitated, then bent down to help Kalna up. "Raney said what he did because he's worried and he's tired. We're all tired, Ka. Why don't you move over here and lay down and rest awhile. I'll fix you a place and—"

"I'm not a child!" Kalna yelled, pulling away again. "Nor am I helpless! Leave me alone! I can take care of myself!"

Ard's fists clenched in anger. "What I ought to do is turn you over my knee, but that I fear would serve little purpose. Be alone, then! And welcome to it!"

Kalna heard Ard stalk off and instantly regretted his remarks. Ard was right, they all were tired, hungry, and scared, and fighting among themselves wasn't the answer to their problems.

He took several deep breaths, trying to quell the emotional storm threatening him from within; but the well of sadness that was a mixture of grief and self-pity had reached a level that could not be dammed up any longer.

Raney heard Kalna's muffled sobbing when he returned from caring for their mount. Struck with remorse, he turned from the camp and busied himself with gathering firewood from down along the pathway. Ard was nowhere in sight. By the time he returned with his first armload of wood, Kalna had quieted. He lay curled on one side, his face hidden by an arm. Raney dropped the wood in a pile and left for more, deciding it would be better to let Ard comfort Kalna when he returned.

Kalna was aware of Raney's comings and goings but he didn't move. Never had he felt so alone and so emotionally unstable. One moment he was angry, the next moment he was in tears, and try as he might, he couldn't seem to control feelings of anger toward the two men though he knew they were his friends. He finally drifted off to sleep wondering what was wrong with him.

*The smell of putrefied flesh was strong in his nostrils. The gagging stench came from ahead. He turned to go back, feeling his way along the labyrinth of passages that seemed to go on forever. He couldn't remember where he was or how he'd come there. All he knew was that he wanted out!*

*He slipped and lost his balance; the floor was slimy with mud and moss, and the darkness made it all the more gruesome. His right arm slammed against a wall as he fell; the pain was nauseating. He pushed to his feet, his hand touching something wet. He hoped it was water but he feared it was blood. Visions of bloody corpses strewn about a hall made him break out in a chilling sweat. So much blood. It was everywhere. It seeped from the walls like tears from the eyes and it clung to whatever it touched.*

*A flicker of warmth touched him and suddenly he remembered something—Ard in trouble. He had to find him. That's what he was doing in the dark maze—he was looking for Ard!*

*Something moved in the tunnel ahead of him, something that came out of the loathsome smell below. His special awareness touched a twisted soul, mad with revenge and the thirst for power. He knew it from before, and it frightened him for he knew it meant to kill him. He could feel its hate and its malicious thrill in the hunt. He backed away as quickly as he could but it kept pace with him; he could hear its heavy breathing. An inhuman laugh reverberated down the tunnel, echoing back and forth along the walls.*

*He turned and ran and moments later fell again, splashing into knee-deep water. He struggled out, pulling himself up by using the wall for support. Something splashed into the water behind him as he darted forward; taloned fingers caught at one wing. He moaned in panic, fear constricting his throat muscles. He turned and struck out; his fists hit something soft and he was wrenched around with a jerk. He screamed in pain as the grip tightened on his wing.*

A hand struck his face sharply once, then again. He fought the hands that shook him.

"Ka, wake up! You're dreaming!" Ard's voice came out of the darkness. He recognized it and stopped struggling. Then there was another voice filled with worry.

"Is he all right?"

"I think so, Raney. Put more tinder on the fire, will you?"

Kalna's hands moved up sinewy arms. "Ard?"

"Yes, Ka. I'm right here."

"I thought—I felt someone grab at my wings." He shivered. "I didn't know where I was. I was looking for you, but the tunnel kept going on and on and I couldn't find you. Then *it* came and it smelled terrible. I ran but I couldn't get away. It caught at my wings."

"It's all right. You were just dreaming. There's nothing here to hurt you."

"It was real, Ard! I could smell it! I could feel its hate! It meant to kill me!"

"Ka, it was all just a dream. You're right here with us,

and there are no tunnels anywhere—no one is going to harm you."

Kalna licked at dry lips, his heartbeat slowly dropping back to normal. "Could I have some water?"

While Raney went to fetch the water flagon, Ard helped Kalna sit up. Kalna flinched as a muscle spasm caught him high in the back. "My wings hurt."

Ard lifted Kalna's tunic up and gently pulled his wings out, first one then the other. Kalna moaned softly as the wing muscles were stretched.

"You must have rolled over and caught them under you, Ka," Ard said. "It also looks like the outer layer of skin is starting to peel off. Is that supposed to happen?"

"I think so." Kalna drank deeply while Raney held the flagon to his lips. As the dream began to fade, Kalna remembered his behavior before falling asleep. He also remembered his fear that Ard would decide to leave and not come back. Embarrassed at having to be wakened from his dreams like a child, he pushed the flagon away. "Enough."

Ard watched Kalna and sensed that something was still amiss. "Ka, are you all right?"

Kalna nodded. "I want to apologize to both of you," he said softly. "I said things I shouldn't have, not after all you've done for me. I know that without you, I'd still be—"

Ard interrupted. "There's no need to say it, Ka. We understand. Why don't you lie down again, on your side this time, and try to sleep a little longer."

"No. Let me take watch. I don't want to sleep again right now. If I hear anything, I'll wake you, I promise."

Ard hesitated, then patted Kalna's shoulder. "All right. It's your watch. Wake one of us if you start feeling sleepy."

# CHAPTER 14

Kalna was cold, wet, hungry, and totally miserable but he didn't complain because Ard and Raney both shared his discomfort. It had begun raining not long after they'd started out that morning, and the rain had turned to wet snow by midafternoon. They needed a place to stop and shelter, somewhere where they could build a fire and get warm and try to dry their clothes.

Raney came to another fork in the forest pathway. He looked back at Ard, who shared the saddle with Kalna again. "Which way?"

Ard studied both paths. Without the sun as a guide, it wasn't easy to tell what direction they were going, especially since they had entered a section of the tall timber where the pine trees blocked out the sky most of the time.

"Let's try the left-hand fork," Ard said. "It looks a bit lighter that way. We have to find some open ground or a river, something that will give us a hint as to where we are. I don't see how your people use these trails without having them marked, Ka."

"The trails are known to those who patrol them," Kalna replied. "Since we haven't encountered any of my people thus far, I'm guessing that we're a lot farther north than I thought. It might be a good idea to turn south the first chance we get."

"Kalna thinks we should take the right-hand fork, Raney."

"All right. You ride on ahead and I'll cover our tracks for a short distance, just in case the Yorrga are still behind us."

An hour later Ard stopped the loper, dismounted, and had Raney take his place.

"I'd just as soon walk a little longer, Ard," Raney offered.

"No. It's my turn. Anyway, my leg feels stiff. It needs exercising."

"Have we anything left to eat, Raney?" Kalna asked, as they started out again.

"Nothing, Kalna, I'm sorry. I'll set snares again tonight and try once more. If we were out from under these pine woods, we'd have a better chance of catching a yrax or two. Meat again, now doesn't that sound good!"

"It sure does," Kalna agreed. Yrax were long-furred, burrowing mammals; their vegetarian diet made them extremely tasty and their prolific nature provided a constant staple for weir and man alike. "It seems forever since I've had a good hot meal. When we find Thekis, the first thing I'm going to—"

"Quiet!" Raney said, interrupting

The loper stopped. "What's wrong?" Kalna asked softly.

"Ard's signaling us to stay where we are."

Several minutes passed. Kalna grew impatient. "What's he doing?" he whispered. "Can you see him?"

"He's standing by a tree, no—he's starting to move down the trail. We've reached the end of the woods, I think. I see sky beyond the edge of the trees."

Kalna was suddenly struck by lahal and the premonition of danger ahead. "Raney! Don't let him out of your sight!"

"But he signaled us to wait."

"Raney, we're not alone anymore! Someone's watching us! Come on, let's go. We've got to warn Ard!"

This time Raney didn't question Kalna's special knowing. "Hang on, Kalna!" he cried, and kicked his heels into the loper's sides.

The mad dash down the pathway ended as something darted out from behind a tree and launched itself at Raney and Kalna as they rode past. Raney had one brief glimpse of a face and horns before he was knocked from the saddle. Kalna somehow managed to catch the back of the saddle and hang on though he was dangerously close to falling. The loper managed only another ten strides before it was caught by its bridle and drawn mercilessly to a halt, its cry of pain sounding loud in Kalna's ears.

Suddenly hands were dragging Kalna from the saddle. He fought but to no avail, for his attacker was far stronger. He heard the sounds of fists striking flesh somewhere to his left and the crackle of bushes as someone either fell or was thrown off the trail.

"Ard!" he yelled. "Raney? Answer!"

His head was jerked back; something cold was laid against his throat. "Silence," a deep voice growled.

"Please, who are you? What . . ."

A blade pressed against his throat; it was followed by a sharp pain and a warm trickle of wetness. Sudden anger consumed Kalna, and without thinking of the consequences, he called up his inner fire. He thrilled as it built within him, but when he tried to direct it, it slipped away from him like water through a holed dam. His failure brought shock and also brought him back to his senses. Breathing deeply to try to clear his mind, he listened and realized that the sounds of battle had ceased. All was still but for the heavy breathing of several people nearby.

He became aware of the musky odor of beran; he

moved his right hand and felt the furred leg of the one holding him. Weir! They'd found weirfolk. He sent a silent prayer to Yaril that they did not wear Yorrga masks.

His heartbeat slowed as he rehearsed what he would say when given a chance to speak. Until then he sent his awareness outward, searching for the two auras he had come to know so well. Ard was to his right standing between two people; Raney was lying on the ground to his left, another person standing over him. Though he couldn't see either man, he felt Ard's anger and Raney's fear. He wanted to speak to them, to reassure them that the weirfolk wouldn't harm them, but the knife pressed at his throat kept him still.

"We are within our rights to kill you all," the weir holding Kalna snapped. "Who are you? What do you do in weir territory?"

"My name is—" Kalna began.

His head was jerked backward, the knifeblade pressed down again. "The white-hair will answer first!" the beran said.

Ard glared at the man-beast holding Kalna. "I'm Ard, of the House of Char. My friend on the ground is Raney, and the one you threaten with your knife is weir, one of your own. We've come to help him find his uncle, a dweorg named Thekis."

The beran was brown furred, his horns were black, and his amber eyes glinted with suspicion. He was dressed in nothing but a heavy overvest and taural-hide boots. He turned Kalna around to face him. "You claim weir blood?" he demanded.

"Yes," Kalna said firmly.

The beran's glance took in bone structure, features, eye and hair color. "It's possible," he murmured.

A weir man with prematurely white hair and dark-amber eyes spoke up. "If he's weir, what is he doing traveling with two Bree?"

"A good question," the beran said. "Answer!"

Kalna hesitated. If these weir knew of the Yorrga depredations against the Bree and approved, it would mean that they were a part of whatever was going on. If not, they might be convinced to allow them free passage, perhaps even an escort to Pavion.

The beran became impatient for an answer and squeezed Kalna's arm painfully. "Why do you ride with Bree? Why do you bring them to our sacred meeting ground?"

Kalna's mind caught on the last phrase—the sacred meeting ground. *Ilyaset!* That meant they were two days north of Pavion near a sacred valley dedicated to Yaril. A small community of weir lived there, following Yaril's teachings and practicing the special techniques of healing with a knife.

"Answer!" the beran growled, angry with Kalna's silence.

Kalna cleared his throat. "These men are my friends. I would be dead now but for their help. We've come to warn the weirfolk of a conspiracy against them. I must reach my uncle in Pavion. His name is Thekis."

"Thekis-ar-Kenyon?"

"Yes. Do you know him?"

"I know him and his children," the beran said. "Whose son do you claim to be?" There was a definite challenge in the beran's voice.

"My father was Dari, my mother Graya. Dari was Thekis's youngest brother."

"And your name?"

"Kalna."

"I think that you are a liar," the beran growled. "The one whose name you use is dead! He was burned to death months ago, along with his parents."

"Not true! I escaped the fire!" Kalna caught his breath and tried to calm the flutter under his rib cage. "Listen to me, please. I *am* Kalna, and if the news I carry doesn't reach the weir High Council, there will soon be war between the Bree and the weirfolk."

"If war comes, it comes," one of the weir said. "We've fought the Bree before."

"You don't understand," Kalna cried. "There must

*not* be war between our two people! It's the Yorrga who must be fought! They are the ones who killed my parents. And they've killed people in the Breedors. There's a man named Alfar—somehow he has rallied a group of Yorrga to help him start a war in order to gain more land. They—"

"You will not speak of the Yorrga before these men!" the beran rumbled. "They are Yaril's own and not to be discussed before such filth!" he caught Kalna by one shoulder, then signaled to his comrades. "We'll keep this one for the moment, until we learn the truth. Kill the Bree."

"No!" Kalna screamed. He tore from his captor's hold and hobbled toward the place he felt Ard standing. "Ard! Raney! Fight them!"

The beran was caught off guard, but he recovered quickly and lunged after Kalna. Kalna reacted instinctively as the beran grabbed his tunic; he spun around and jabbed his elbow into a furry stomach. Cloth tore and again he was free. He headed straight for Ard, feeling him rather than seeing, and slammed into one of the two weir grappling with his friend. He was knocked off balance and fell; he rolled over and came to his hands and knees, senses alert. He searched frantically for the two auras he knew and found both men fighting for their lives.

"Stop!" the beran bellowed. "Omecon! Lachen! Enar! Jylak! Hold!"

The fighting didn't stop instantly, but tapered off as Ard and Raney finally realized that the weir were trying to disengage from combat.

Kalna pushed to his feet, wings vibrating with tension. He didn't know what had stopped the fighting but was aware of the sudden shift in emotions around him. He sensed surprise and shock coming from the weir. He turned as the beran approached him slowly. What remained of his tunic lay dangling off one shoulder.

Silence descended on the crude roadway. Kalna heard the men and weir breathing heavily; sweat trickled down his sides, and he smelled the musky odor of beran as the weir stopped before him.

"Ard? Raney? Are you all right?" he demanded.

"Yes, Ka," Ard answered.

The beran looked from the men back to Kalna, who stood waiting, still unsure what had put an end to the fighting. The beran moved a step closer. Kalna felt his nearness but didn't flinch away. He sensed confusion in the beran as he reached out and gently caressed one of Kalna's wings.

"How long since you've winged, darkling?" he asked softly, all hint of anger gone from his voice.

In that moment Kalna understood what had put an end to the fighting, and he began to breathe easier, aware that his becoming a darkling had drastically changed the way in which other weir would perceive him.

"Why didn't you tell us you were darkling?" the beran asked. "We might have hurt you."

"We'd not heard that there was a new darkling in the forest," another of the weirfolk said, as if defending himself.

The beran's glance went to Ard and Raney, who had moved closer together; their defensive posture was unmistakable. "Who helped with the cutting?" he asked, turning back to Kalna.

"My friends. There was no one else," Kalna answered.

Another of the weirfolk came up on Kalna's other side. "Who are you? What was all that about . . ." The weir's voice trailed off as Kalna's ragged tunic slipped off his shoulder, baring his chest.

"A male darkling!" There was disbelief in the tone of voice. "Laric, look! She's a he!"

The beran Laric pulled the scrap of tunic away, his eyes wide in wonder. "Who are you? You're not Ek-nar. I've seen him and he's much older and the hair color is wrong. Is it true—you've just winged—and no one knows about you?"

"I told you, my name is Kalna. I *am* Dari's son. As

for anyone knowing about me, you are the first other than my friends."

The beran hesitated, as if unsure what to do next. A red-haired weir with a broken nose and large ears moved around behind Laric and pushed in front of Kalna. "My name is Enar," he began. "We made a mistake, all of us. Please, Kalna, accept our apology and tell us what we may do for you."

"Apology accepted," Kalna said. He turned, sensed Ard's aura, and beckoned him forward. "All I ask that you do for me now is greet these two men as my friends and help us get our message to my uncle Thekis."

Laric eyed the two men warily as they approached. "We'll help you with your message," he promised, "even though we don't understand what you were talking about."

"And my friends?" Kalna pressed.

"They are safe with us."

Kalna sensed the beran's inner struggle to accept the men and knew he couldn't push the matter any further, at least at the moment. Ard and Raney would be safe but unwelcome. It was a beginning.

"My name is Laric," the beran said. "These are Omecon, Lachen, and Jylak." He pointed the others out.

"He can't see, Laric," Ard said, carefully keeping a neutral tone to his voice. "He's blind. The Yorrga did it to him."

The weirfolk exchanged glances, several shaking their heads as if they couldn't believe such a thing possible.

Kalna reached out toward the beran. Laric caught his hand and held it firmly.

"I can't see your face, Laric, but I can feel your heart and I know we are in good hands. Please, all I ask is for you to listen to our story and see us safely to Thekis in Pavion. We've not come here to cause trouble, but to stop it."

Laric hesitated, his glance falling on the one introduced as Jylak, who stood only waist high to him. Jylak looked up and nodded. Laric glanced at Ard and Raney.

"You two will have to give us your weapons if you want to travel any further into weir territory."

"Do it, Ard," Kalna said. "They won't harm you now."

Reluctantly the two men handed the weir their swords and knives.

"Lachen, Enar, you two stay and watch the trail. Jylak, Omecon, come with me." Laric gently took Kalna by the elbow and led him down the trail. Ard and Raney fell in behind, followed closely by Omecon and Jylak.

Some time later Ard, Raney, and Kalna sat at the supper fire with Laric, Jylak, and Omecon. The other two weir had come in, eaten, and returned to the road to watch for any other uninvited guests.

Ard and Raney let Kalna do most of the talking, for it was obvious from the beginning that the weir didn't trust them. It was also obvious that Kalna's growth of wings had greatly improved his status among the weirfolk.

Ard watched the weir watching Kalna and as their glances darted from his face to his wings, then back again, he felt a small pang of jealousy, for in those glances he read the gleam of possession. He isn't yours, he wanted to say, he's mine! I'm the one who saved his life! If not for Raney and me, he'd probably be dead by now!

"Is something wrong?" Raney whispered, touching Ard's arm. "You look as if you don't feel well."

Ard shook his head. "No. I'm fine," he said grimly.

Laric heard their murmurs and glared at the two men, his eyes telling them to be silent while Kalna was speaking. Ard met his look defiantly. Laric glowered at the Bree a moment longer, then turned back to Kalna, who had almost reached the end of his story.

"...and the last time we saw the Yorrga was about four days ago. We lost them by mixing our trail with some of Lord Alfar's men who passed us headed south. Since then we've been following the trail we were on hoping to reach Pavion."

Jylak was the first to speak. "I don't doubt anything

you say, Kalna, but the true Yorrga are not as you describe. They don't kill, they heal—at least, that's what they're supposed to do."

"So I was taught," Kalna agreed, "but the Yorrga who are running wild through the Breedors and the ones who killed my parents have no compunction about killing, and they must be stopped. I beg you to help us reach Pavion."

Laric looked at the two Bree. "We'll help, Kalna. You and I will leave for Pavion tomorrow. Your friends will remain here."

"No!" Ard and Kalna spoke as one.

"We go together," Kalna said. "Ard and Raney have a message to carry also, to Lord Drian and the House of Char. The weirfolk will deal with the Yorrga, and Ard and his people will deal with Lord Alfar. I want them to ride with me as far as Pavion where I'll ask my uncle to give them an escort back to the House of Char. They have earned it."

"It's forbidden to bring men to Pavion."

"Who forbids it?"

"Our laws," Laric said firmly. "It is stated that no outling shall ever enter Pavion alive."

"That law was made to protect us from our enemies, not our friends," Kalna said. "Ard and Raney must come with me. I want them to talk to my uncle."

Laric looked as if he wanted to argue, but Jylak forestalled him with a shake of the head. While Laric glared at the two men as if they were somehow responsible for Kalna's obstinacy, Jylak took Kalna's hand. "I'm not sure it's wise to bring men into Pavion,—but if it's what you want, you'll have our aid."

# CHAPTER 15

It was painfully evident from the beginning that the weir were trying to make up for their earlier actions. That first night in camp, Jylak mended Kalna's tunic and thoughtfully cut out a section in the back to allow him free wing movement. Laric provided a heavy blanket to keep the night chill away; and in the morning, before they started out, Omecon gave Kalna his own knife and sheath.

Ard and Raney watched it all in silence, ignored for the most part by the weir. As for Kalna, he was so happy to be back among his own people and out from under the immediate threat of the Yorrga that he didn't feel his friends' displeasure until late the following morning when they were out on the trail.

Kalna had been given a mount of his own to ride; it was led by Jylak. Ard rode to Kalna's right. Laric took the lead, leaving Raney, Omecon, Lacher, and Enar to follow.

"Ard, you've been quiet all morning," Kalna said. "Is something wrong?"

Ard glanced at Jylak, who would hear anything that was said. "No. There's nothing wrong."

Kalna sensed the lie. Instincts alerted, he reached out with his special awareness and probed at his friend, seeking the truth. Ard's emotions were churning with uncertainty and suspicion and deeper yet, at the core of his feelings, there burned a small flame of jealousy. Startled, Kalna withdrew.

It was his turn for silence now, as he tried to sort it out. He could understand Ard's misgivings about riding into Pavion, of walking among people he had been taught to fear, but surely that could not be grounds for jealousy. He thought back over the past few days, wondering what had sparked such an emotion. He had felt nothing but Ard's pride in helping him become a darkling. It could not be that.

Jylak leaned over and caught Kalna's arm. "We'll be coming to the small village of Ryton in a few minutes. We'll stop there and get some food for the next day, and something else for you to wear."

Kalna nodded in response, but his mind was elsewhere, for Ard's emotional turmoil had suddenly flared to life. In that instant he centered on Ard's jealousy and was amazed by what he found, for the simple truth was that his friend was afraid of losing him to the weirfolk. Was the joining responsible for Ard's feelings toward him? he wondered. Or was it something that had been growing between them since their first meeting—a friendship at first based on mutual need but slowly changing to something much deeper?

He reached out with his hand. "Ard?"

"What?"

"Take my hand, please."

Ard frowned but did as Kalna asked, jealousy submerged in a burst of concern. "Is something wrong, Ka?"

Kalna searched for the right words. "I just wanted you to know how much I value our friendship—and that I'm glad you're here." It wasn't as much as he wanted to say, but the words for stronger emotions caught in his throat.

Ard saw Jylak watching and turned away, embarrassed by Kalna's avowal of friendship yet strangely pleased at the same time. He squeezed Kalna's hand, then released it and returned to the ride with a lighter heart.

It was midday when Laric signaled that they were approaching another village. They had passed through several small villages the day before and one that morning, and the news that a young male darkling had winged spread quickly. Before the small party was able to leave the last village, food and gifts appeared as weirfolk eagerly pushed love tokens at Kalna and those who rode with him. In the excitement, many overlooked the fact that two of those attending Kalna were Bree. Those who did notice viewed the men with either curiosity or silent contempt.

Kalna was somewhat overwhelmed by all the attention he was getting and began to understand why his mother and many of her sisters chose to live away from populated areas. Thinking back, he remembered how often he'd thought about becoming a darkling, dreaming about what it would be like to be special among so varied a race, to be listened to and asked his opinion. As the crowd pressed around him, he realized that wanting something and receiving it were not always one and the same thing.

Ard and Raney, having seen more weir in the last two days than most Bree saw in a lifetime, still could not suppress their wonder at the differences in size, shape, and coloring of the El-ar-kil. It was exciting and frightening at the same time. Ard saw a good number of the horned weir known as beran, and around them stood child-sized, furred beings who emitted a strange keening sound.

Kalna sensed Ard's curiosity and explained that the sound was an expression of greeting among the rella.

"They are kin to the beran and are excellent builders despite their small stature."

"Do they speak?"

"Yes, but you have to listen close to understand them."

Ard saw a tall manlike being whose crest of tawny hair ran down its neck and over its shoulders like a cape. Large, sharply pointed upper teeth were visible and its widely spaced eyes stared boldly at the riders, especially the men. It was dressed in a short kilt and soft leather boots that laced up the sides. A hand ax rode in a sheath at its belt.

"How are the fanged ones named?" Ard asked, keeping his voice low.

"They are leondar, our fiercest warriors. They are loners usually and prefer the high mountains for their homes. I was told that a few live in and around Pavion."

"Are there female leondar?"

"Yes, and they are equal to their male counterparts in temperament, I'm told. To be truthful I've never met one, but my father had."

Ard's glance continued to rove the crowd that followed them into the center of the small town. Not all among the weirfolk were beastlike; there were many who could've passed for true men; some were most handsome, especially the women who mingled freely among the menfolk, unlike the women in his own society.

Jylak drew his mount to a halt in front of a store. The porch was lined with open shelves, most of them bare. A few hardy vegetables and fruits were displayed near the main door.

Someone touched Kalna's arm, another hand touched his leg. Voices rose around him as one weir after another greeted him and wished him long life. Someone pushed a bundle of cloth into his lap, congratulating him on his winging. Others from the crowd pushed forward, anxious to see and speak to the new darkling.

Laric saw what was happening and signaled Jylak.

Jylak had promised Kalna something special to eat for lunch, but one look at the growing confusion around Kalna's mount and he agreed with Laric's decision. He quickly turned his mount around and pulled on the lead to Kalna's. Someone yelled as the loper stepped on a foot. Startled, the loper jumped to one side, nearly unseating Kalna and scattering the crowd.

Ard kicked his loper in the sides and moved close to Kalna; he caught him by an arm and helped him regain his seat, then Laric was there, guiding his mount through the crowd and waving them off. Between the two of them, one riding to either side of Kalna, with Jylak in the lead, they finally managed to bring Kalna out of the crowd and away to the edge of the village. Raney, Omecon, Lachen, and Enar followed.

"Ka, are you all right?" Ard asked, noticing how tightly Kalna gripped the saddle horn.

Kalna laughed shakily. "I thought I was going to be trampled there for a minute."

"It'll be worse when we reach Pavion," Laric said. "The news is running ahead of us and there's no stopping it now. I should have thought of that sooner and taken back roads into the city." The beran looked straight at Ard. "You moved quickly back there. Our thanks to you for that."

Ard was startled but managed to hide his surprise behind a show of concern for Kalna's welfare. "You spoke of other roads into Pavion. If it would be safer to go another way, I think we should take it."

"Jylak?" Laric asked.

"It would take a bit longer but it might be easier on Kalna and us."

Kalna spoke up, embarrassed to be the center of attention. "I'm all right. It was my mount that was afraid of the crowd, not me."

"I still think it would be best if we try one of the back roads, Kalna," Laric said. "Thekis would never forgive any of us if something happened to you. We'll go by way of Isen's Dam and down through the quarry. No one will be working there by the time we ride through. We'll have to pass through the village of Ingline, but if we move quickly, we can be in and out without any problems. From there to the Cotril Gate is only a five-minute ride. Galen Keep lies just beyond. When we reach the keep, we'll enter through one of the lower doors and try to find Thekis before those looking for you realize you've already arrived."

Jylak eyed Ard and Raney. "What about the men?"

"I believe we can trust them to behave," Laric said. "Let's go."

"What do we do?" Raney asked softly as he rode up alongside Ard.

"We stay with them—for now."

Kalna heard, but said nothing.

The roar of water over Isen's Dam was like the growling of a huge, angry beast chained forever in one place. The mist rising above the waterfall became more noticeable as they approached the ribbon of land that led out to the bridge rising up over the main spillway. Both men marveled at the construction of the dam, for there was nothing like it in all the Breedors. Ard and Raney were beginning to realize that the weirfolk were not the primitives they were said to be. They would have much to tell Duval when they returned to the House of Char.

It was dark by the time they reached the salt quarry that provided the weirfolk with a tradable commodity. Kalna was acquainted with the movement of the salt caravans that four times a year made their way down out of the mountains to the Moricanian capital of Bragadar, because his father had once been an active member of the Weir Traders and, like any father, had told his son of his finer days before settling down.

As Laric promised, the quarry was empty. Kalna tried to get a *feel* of the place, but without his sight it was impossible.

"Ard? What do you see? Describe it for me please."

Ard looked around as they rode down a long narrow

trail that wound in and out among great boulders. "It's getting dark, Ka. All I can see are huge rocks, and off to my left there are shelflike formations and what looks like giant caves."

For the hundredth time in the past few days, Kalna mourned the loss of his sight; he feared that he would walk in darkness for the rest of his life, even though Jylak held out the hope that healers in Pavion might be able to help him.

They reached Ingline a little while later and rode straight through. Laric stopped to greet one or two people who came out to see who was passing while the others went on ahead.

"Any trouble?" Jylak asked, as Laric caught up with them.

"No. I guess the news hasn't reached here yet. Let's keep riding."

"Ard, can you see Pavion yet?" Kalna asked a short time later.

"I see lights in the valley ahead," Ard answered. "There are hundreds of them. There's a large place in the middle of the valley that's all dark."

"Shadow Lake," Jylak provided. "It's in the center of the valley. It gets its name from the morning shadows of Galen Keep. It's very beautiful there in the morning with the sun just rising and the moon slipping down out of sight. Galen Keep is to the east side of the lake."

"Tell me what else you see, Ard," Kalna asked again.

Ard sensed Kalna's loss as an emptiness that brought tears to his eyes. If only I had been able to get to Kalna quicker, he thought, I might have prevented his going blind. Regret consumed him for he knew it was too late to change anything now.

"Ard?" Kalna probed his friend's silence and was bombarded by sorrow, grief, regret, and anger. "Ard, what's wrong?"

Ard angrily wiped at the tears streaming from his eyes. "It's my fault that you're blind! I should have known Alfar was planning something against you! If I had put an extra guard at your window or come back to check on you that night . . ."

"No, Ard, don't!" Kalna cried softly. "It's not your fault!"

"It is!"

"No!"

"Damn it! I can't stop crying. I don't know what's wrong with me."

Kalna picked up on Ard's emotional surges and suddenly realized what was happening. "It's not you, Ard—it's me, and the joining!" He hadn't known Ard was picking up on his emotions because Ard hadn't said a word. But perhaps he didn't understand how deep the joining had been.

Kalna took a deep breath and tried to calm down. "Ard, listen to me! You are feeling what I'm feeling. It's the joining! It's linked us too closely together. I can feel the echo of my emotions running through you right now."

"What's wrong back there?" Laric growled, halting his mount.

Jylak pulled Kalna's loper to a halt and the others followed suit. "There's something wrong with the white hair," he said, answering Laric's question.

Kalna ignored everyone but Ard, who was fighting hard for self-control. "Ard, take a deep breath and hold it and think of something else, something good, something that makes you happy." As he spoke to Ard, Kalna tried to empty his own mind of sadness and loss, for only in doing so could he help Ard regain his own emotional balance. "You have to separate yourself from me—from what I'm feeling. Think about your home, a friend's smile. Think of happy days spent riding or hunting."

"I hear you," Ard managed. He closed his eyes and tried to follow Kalna's suggestions. Slowly the emotional turmoil within began to subside and he felt his sense of self return. When he opened his eyes, he found himself the center of attention.

Raney was the first to speak. "Are you all right, Ard?"

Ard nodded, not quite ready to test his voice.

Jylak looked from Ard to Kalna, who sat quietly braced in the saddle, as if he feared any movement from his direction might set Ard off again. "Did I hear Kalna speak of a joining?" he asked.

"It was necessary," Kalna said, carefully keeping his tone of voice neutral. "I will explain later. I think it best if we all go on now. Ard, it might be better if we didn't ride so close together."

"I agree," Ard responded, pulling his loper back and away from Kalna's. "We'll talk about this later."

Laric caught Jylak's silent signal to proceed and turned his loper around. "Let's move. It's getting dark."

As they neared the entrance to the valley and the Cotril Gate, Laric halted the small band. "Getting into Galen Keep will mean getting past the guard. Raney can easily pass for one of us, I think, but not you, Ard. Jylak, see if you can't rig some kind of a hood for him to wear."

It took Jylak only a few minutes to fashion a blanket into a hooded cloak, which Ard donned without comment. A short time later they were moving up on the Cotril Gate. When Ard saw the torchlight flooding the roadway and the two guards standing at the gate, he pulled the makeshift hooded cloak more tightly around his face.

"Hunch over," Laric said to Ard, "and don't speak, either of you. Your accents would give you away."

"Perhaps it would be better if we just went back and tried to find our own way back into the Breedors," Raney suggested softly.

"You're too deep into our territory," Jylak said. "You'd only be picked up by someone else, and without Kalna to vouch for you, you'd be in serious trouble."

"As far as I can see, we can't be in much more trouble than we are right now!" Raney snapped. "Ard?"

Ard looked from Raney to Kalna. He hesitated, then

committed himself. "If we're to find out who's behind the Yorrga attacks, Raney, one of us has to stay with Ka. Laric, would you or one of your people be willing to guide Raney back to Black Lake to see that he—"

"I won't leave you here by yourself, Ard," Raney began, only to be interrupted by Laric.

"You both have to come with us now. It's too late for other choices. Wiser heads than mine will have to decide if you're what you say you are."

"What happens to Ard and Raney if we're caught before we reach Thekis?" Kalna asked, anxious now for his friends. He had thought that as long as they were with him, they would be safe. If not, it might be better for them both to leave, with or without Laric's permission. It would mean a fight, but if that was the only way to ensure their safety, he would back them.

"They won't be caught if we're careful," Jylak answered. "The number of winter guests has dwindled every year for the past ten years so there are hundreds of unused rooms in the lower keep. We'll find a place for all of you to hide, then one of us will go and locate Thekis and bring him to you. After that, whatever happens will be up to him."

"That didn't answer my question," Kalna said.

"Enough!" Laric growled low. "We look suspicious sitting here arguing. The gate guards are looking at us right now. Let's go!"

Laric did all of the talking when they reached the gate, but while he spoke to the one guard, the other moved around to one side to inspect the riders. The weir was one of those called a faun. He was short and compact and clumped toward them on hooved feet, his only garment a heavy belted tunic with long sleeves.

Raney suppressed a shiver as the faun paused near him and looked up into his face. A tilt of the faun's head exposed a pair of menacing horns and the most beautiful face Raney had ever seen. Amber eyes glinted in the torchlight as the weir stared at him. The faun's hand dropped to his knife sheath.

"Who are you?" he said darkly.

Kalna felt Raney's fear and turned in his saddle. "His name is Raney and he can't speak."

The faun glided up alongside Kalna. "You have a quick tongue, weirling. Too quick, I'm thinking." There was a threatening tone in the faun's voice though the words were spoken softly enough.

Jylak saw the knife in the faun's hand and glanced at Laric, who was still talking to the other guard. Fearing the faun might do something foolish, Jylak leaned across Kalna's lap.

"Only a fool would draw a blade on a darkling!" he hissed at the guard. "Put your knife away. Now!"

The faun raised his knife. "I see no darkling! What are you trying to—"

"Show him!" Jalak ordered.

Kalna protested. "But Laric said to hide . . ."

"Show him, Kalna," Ard whispered carefully keeping his face lowered and covered by the hood. He, too, saw the knife and was worried.

Kalna shrugged and untied the lacing at his throat and let the makeshift cloak drop back. The guard's eyes grew large when he saw the flutter of wings. He backed away, then turned and dashed for the gate, skidding to a halt beside Laric and the other guard. He spoke fast and low.

Laric turned and glared at those behind him, but seconds later he signaled them to pass through the gate. Omecon led Laric's mount and stopped so the beran could remount.

"What happened?" Laric demanded. "How did the guard find out about Kalna?"

"The guard drew his knife on Kalna. It was the only way to stop him without beginning a fight."

"Well, it stopped him, all right, but it won't be long before everyone knows he's in the city, and that means that we'll have to move quickly. We'll ride to Brandon's Market and leave our mounts at the stables, then enter the main keep through the nearest door. I know a place where Kalna and his two friends will be safe for a little while. You and Jylak will stay with them, while I go to find Thekis."

"You trust the men to stay with us?"

Laric glanced at the riders ahead. "You're armed, they aren't. Just stay with them and keep them all quiet. I'll get back to you as soon as I can."

Ard paced restlessly around the room Laric had chosen as their hiding place. He was growing more and more nervous as the minutes passed, and he couldn't even tell if it was his own nervousness or Kalna's.

He glanced at the two exits to the room, thoughts of entrapment uppermost in his mind. Surely by now Laric had had time enough to find Thekis and return.

The room they were in was large; it was furnished with three beds, a trestle table and benches, several chests, and four chairs, all handmade by weirfolk. Jylak had said that most of the rooms in the keep were furnished though in recent years many went unoccupied during the cold winter months.

Jylak sat with Kalna at the table. "Each year we are fewer," he said. "Our birthrate has dropped the past three generations and each year we lose some of our people to the outside."

Ard settled down on one of the straw-covered beds. "What do you mean by 'outside'?"

"He means that some of our people become traders," Kalna answered. "We have people among the Morican and Urst and even a few among the Bree. Most live as traders, though a few do settle down in one place."

"Not all weir are born talented," Jylak continued, "or with that special stamp upon body or face. Many of us can easily pass for true men and often do so. I have a brother who travels now with the Urst. It's been seven years since I've seen him. He married an Urst woman and has three children now. Two he has with him, the third child was dweorg like me. He brought her back to us to raise. She lives with my wife and me. We have no children of our own."

Omecon, who stood near the door, turned at the sound of footsteps in the stone hallway outside. "Someone's coming."

"About time," Raney muttered, getting up from one of the chairs.

Kalna swung his legs over the bench, excitement stirring. It would be wonderful to see Thekis again. Thoughts of Thekis brought thoughts of his parents to mind. A knot of grief suddenly rose to his throat. He swallowed and blinked back tears, determined not to embarrass himself in front of everyone.

Ard heard the hollow clump of hooved feet in the hallway and unconsciously brushed his hand against his empty knife sheath. Omecon, who stood in the open doorway, turned suddenly, frowning.

"It's the keep guards," he hissed. "I don't see Thekis!"

Jylak moved with the quickness of a bird, signaling Ard and Raney to the back exit while he grabbed Kalna by the arm. "That way, quickly!"

Kalna followed the pull on his arm, his mind spinning with throughts of betrayal. If Thekis wasn't with those coming down the hall, it meant that Laric had summoned the guard. They had been fools to trust Laric!

Jylak halted abruptly, his hand tightening on Kalna's arm.

"What's wrong?" Kalna demanded, his special awareness blocking by his own anger.

There wasn't time for an answer for keep guards appeared at both doors and poured into the room. Several were beran, three were faun, and the rest were weirmen.

"Take the Bree!" someone ordered.

"No!" Kalna cried.

Omecon caught Laric's arm as he came through the front hall doorway. "What happened? Where's Thekis? Why the guards?"

Laric ignored the questions as he plunged into the mass of bodies surging around Kalna and the Bree. "Be

careful, you fools!" he bellowed. "Don't hurt the darkling! Jylak, where are you?"

"Here!" Jylak cried, trying to pull Kalna away from
the weir surrounding Ard and Raney, who were fighting
back.

Kalna managed to break free of the dweorg's grasp.
"Don't hurt them!" he yelled, hitting whoever was before him. "They're under my protection!"

One of the berans turned, his elbow catching Kalna a
glancing blow to the side of the head. Kalna fell backward but strong hands grabbed him before he hit the
floor. His rage over Laric's betrayal overshadowed any
fear of fighting blind and he struck out, trying to reach
his friends.

Ard saw Kalna pulled down a second time and feared
that he'd be trampled. "Get up, Ka!" he yelled, as he
struggled against the hands that held him. Using his enemies for support, he brought both feet up and kicked out,
knocking two of the weirmen down. A beran swung
around and punched Ard in the stomach; as he doubled
over in pain, the beran slammed a huge fist down on the
back of Ard's neck, driving him to the floor.

Raney had lost his fight and stood backed against the
wall pinned by the arms, a knife pricking his side. He
saw Ard crumble, then heard a cry that twisted his in-
sides. One of the weirmen had caught Kalna by an arm
and a wing while trying to subdue him.

The excruciating pain in his back and shoulder smothered Kalna's rage and left him semiconscious and dangling from the weir's hands.

Laric finally reached him and struck the weir's arm,
numbing it from the elbow down. "Fool!" he bellowed,
catching Kalna's limp form. "He wasn't to be harmed! If
you've injured him, I swear, I'll chew you into little
pieces!"

Laric readjusted Kalna's weight in his arms and
looked at the nearest guard. "Take the men to the upper
cells and see that they're kept well away from everyone.
Barack will see them later."

Omecon and Jylak hurried after Laric and his burden, catching up with him outside the doorway. "What happened?" Jylak demanded. "Where's Thekis?"

"He wasn't in the keep," Laric answered. "I was told he'd be back some time late tomorrow night. He's somewhere on Council business. I thought about waiting but decided that someone should know about Kalna and the Bree before the entire city was out looking for them. I found Barack and told him what was going on. I thought he'd just assign a few guards to go with me to watch the Bree, but instead he gave orders that they were to be taken to the cells and that Kalna was to be brought to his quarters as soon as possible."

Kalna stirred, spoke Ard's name, then slipped back into unconsciousness as Laric climbed the first flight of stairs leading up to the level where Barack lived.

Jylak glanced at Kalna. "He isn't going to forgive you for this, Laric."

The beran frowned. "It's not as I wanted it, but who am I to argue with one on the High Council? Personally I hope that Thekis returns soon because I think we're going to have our hands full handling Kalna when he wakes up."

# CHAPTER 16

Kalna heard the door open and close. He remained still, feigning sleep. His empty stomach told him that another mealtime had slipped by. He mentally counted the number of missed meals and reckoned that he'd been in Galen Keep two days not counting the night he'd arrived. Where was Thekis? Why hadn't he come?

"Shall I wake him?" It was a woman's voice.

"You can, but I doubt you'll get him to eat." The second voice was also female. "He's being obdurate. He won't eat, won't speak, won't change his clothes, won't allow anyone to touch him. If Glanna were here, she'd set him to rights quickly enough!"

"She's been sent for, hasn't she?"

"Yes. She and Jarad usually winter in Endwall, but when they hear about Kalna, I'm sure they'll come running. He was given up for dead, you know."

"Yes, I know. It's a miracle that he survived the fire."

"And another miracle that he winged. Those who brought him in claim that the two captured Bree had a hand in the cutting, that without them he might have died."

"It's a wonder they knew what to do."

"Men can surprise you sometimes."

"I've heard that they're planning a Naming celebration for Kalna even though he's a year young for it."

"I think it would be wiser if they'd wait on the Naming until they're sure his mind is balanced. The way he's acting now has led some to say he won't make the change successfully."

Kalna rolled over, stretched, and sat up, letting his audience know he was awake. He'd heard all he wanted to hear. He knew he was being stubborn, and that his actions were causing people to doubt his sanity, but until Ard and Raney were released, he would not cooperate with anyone!

"Good, you're awake, Kalna," one of the women said. "We've brought you some delicious wildbird stew and some fresh bread still warm from the oven."

Kalna pushed his awareness out until it caught the two women approaching. One was nervous; the other, determined. The determined one set his food tray on a nearby table, wafting the bread under his nose as she did so. A fragrant aroma brought saliva to his mouth and a clawing sensation to his stomach.

The determined one caught his right hand at the wrist and placed a slice of bread in his hand. "Eat now while it's still warm. It tastes best that way," she said.

He let the bread drop to the floor. He felt the weirwomen's anger as he hitched himself backward until his back rested against the headboard.

The determined one caught at his shoulder. "Please, Kalna, you must eat!" It was a command, not a request.

He shrugged out from under her touch and turned his face away. The two weirwomen looked at each other, the younger one with a worried frown, the older one with an expression of frustration. The older woman moved toward the door. The younger woman started to pick up the tray, but the other one shook her head, telling her silently to leave it.

Kalna listened to their footsteps go to the door, then the door closed behind them. He turned, felt around on the tabletop, and found the tray. It was tempting, but he was as determined as they were and withdrew his hand.

Time passed slowly in the continual darkness. Kalna had never thought much about what it would be like to be blind; now he realized that no one really appreciated life's gifts until they were forced to do without them. A lump of self-pity rose to his throat for he was sure now that he'd never see again.

His thoughts drifted to his home and to the day the Yorrga had come. He saw his father lying dead on the floor and his mother lashing out with her inner fire in his defense. Grief mixed with anger as he relived his own feelings during those brief moments of terror. If only he'd left Ard lying in the woods... if only he'd fought back somehow before the Yorrga pushed into his home.

Kalna pushed off the bed and stood up wanting to strike out at something, anything, anyone; then slowly he sank back onto the bed, remembering that they'd taken his newly acquired crutches the day before, after finding him wandering along one of the inner hallways. He had sensed Ard in a room somewhere below and had set out to find him, but when he had made a fuss about being allowed to visit the Bree, whoever was in charge had dismissed his rantings as a bout of fever and had ordered him taken back to his room. After that, he had stopped speaking again.

His thoughts on the subject were interrupted as the door swung wide, banging against the inner wall. He ignored the footsteps that approached the bed, thinking it was one of the weirwomen returning to see if he'd touched his food.

"Ka?"

Kalna's head snapped up. Only five people had ever called him Ka: his mother and father, Rops, Ard, and ... "Thekis?"

There was a bounce on the bed, then strong arms went around him, pulling him close. Lips brushed his cheeks and forehead in the ritual kiss of kinship; then he was being rocked back and forth as if he were still a child. He returned the embrace, knowing no other but Thekis would treat him so.

Thekis was a dweorg, small in stature but strong and quick for his size. He had wiry gray hair, snapping green eyes, and a dour expression that belied his true happy nature.

Thekis finally released Kalna and pushed him to arm's length. He wiped at the tears on his face and cleared his throat, his eyes eagerly drinking in the face before him.

"And so the dead return to life," he said softly, squeezing Kalna's arms. "In the name of Yaril's Folly, Ka, what happened to you? We were sure you'd died in the fire!"

Kalna swallowed, fighting his own emotions plus the surge of relief and joy Thekis was giving off at that moment. "It's a long story, Thekis, but before I tell you what happened, you must promise to help me free my friends. I'm afraid for them! They won't let me talk to them; they won't listen when I tell them that they've come here to help us discover the truth about the Yorrga."

"You're talking about the Bree."

"Yes! You know about them?"

"I've heard a little bit. It was wrong to bring them here, Ka, no matter the reason."

"So I've been told over and over!" Kalna said loudly. "But they're my friends, Thekis! I would be dead twice over but for their help!"

Thekis moved his hand in front of Kalna's eyes, testing. There was no response. It was as he'd been told. His nephew was blind. He drew his short legs up onto the bed and crossed them comfortably and patted Ka on the arm.

"Let's hear your story, Ka. I want to know everything that's happened to you—from the beginning."

"All right," Kalna agreed, "but before I begin, I want your promise that Ard and Raney will be freed."

"Ka," Thekis said reprovingly.

"No, Thekis. What I have to tell you is very important to our people, but the Bree are a part of it, too, and I won't speak unless you promise that my friends will be released unharmed."

Thekis looked at Kalna in silence, then his look softened. "Right now you remind me very much of your father, Ka. Stubborn was his middle name when he was growing up, and I can see now that you've inherited a good portion of that trait."

Kalna sensed that Thekis wasn't really angry with him. "Sometimes being stubborn is the only way to survive, Thekis."

"So it is," Thekis agreed. "Come now, tell me your story. You have my word that the Bree will be released."

Kalna had been braced for more of a battle; winning so easily made him suddenly wary. Would Thekis lie to him? He didn't want to believe it, but . . .

"Ka, what's wrong now? Don't you trust me?"

"I trust you. It's only that—in the past months everything and everyone I knew has either changed or died. It's left me doubting a lot of things."

"I'm sorry, Ka. I know that seeing your parents die must have been horrible. I can't even imagine it." Thekis squeezed Kalna's arm gently. "Talking it out might help."

Kalna hesitated, then pushed his fears aside and began his story, starting with the day he'd found Ard wounded in the forest. It was difficult to tell about the Yorrga battle in his own home, and when he reached the moment his mother died, his voice was whisper soft. Thekis understood something of what he was going through and didn't interrupt.

As Kalna continued with his story, Thekis watched him closely, noting changes in the weirling he'd known just a half year ago. Other than the obvious—the dirty, ill-fitting clothing, his thinness, the hint of facial hair on his cheeks and upper lip, the casted leg that stuck out stiff before him, and the pair of wings that had begun to shed their leathery outer skin—there was a difference in the way Kalna held himself, in the line of his jaw and the way he spoke; and more than that, there was a feeling about him, a sense of strength and determination that far outmatched his age. Adult in mind, not in body, he thought, not yet darkling but beginning to grow aware. Tears stung his eyes as he thought of Dari and Graya and how proud they would have been to see him changing.

Thekis meant to wait for Kalna to finish his story before asking any questions, but when Kalna spoke about the Yorrga he called Gold-mask and the Lord of the House of Dar-rel and their plans for igniting the mountain people in war, he couldn't keep quiet any longer.

"Ka, are you sure those you saw were Yorrga? Not just men parading in masks that looked something like Yorrga masks?"

Kalna shook his head. "I don't know about all of them, Thekis. The Yorrga spirit that almost claimed Ard was real. I know because I fought it; and the Yorrga within the mask they forced upon me was real or it could not have taken my sight! The other masks might not be true Yorrga masks. I've no proof one way or the other. But Gold-mask, or Lord Tennebar, as he calls himself, spoke as if they all were real masks, their spirits his for the taking. He frightened me, Thekis. I sensed a madness in him. He won't care how many die in this war. We've got to stop him!"

"How many others know about all this, Ka?" Thekis asked. "Who have you spoken to?"

"Only you. I told Laric and Jylak a little of what had happened to me, but they didn't want me speaking ill of the Yorrga, so I didn't. I just kept telling them to take me to you."

Kalna licked at dry lips. "Thekis, Jylak said that one of the healing Yorrga might be able to give me back my sight. Is that true?"

"What they took away they should be able to return.

And they will, if I have anything to say about it!" Thekis hesitated, his mind whirling with questions. "What I can't understand is how anyone could so pervert the Yorrga's natural gift for healing that it could cause pain and suffering rather than alleviate it, unless..."

"Unless what?"

"Unless someone has discovered the rest of Yaril's children."

"I don't understand. Aren't we Yaril's children?"

"We are, but so are the Yorrga." Thekis slid off the bed, his feet thumping to the floor. "I'm sorry, Ka, I can't stay any longer and I can't say anything more about the Yorrga right now. It's imperative that I speak with the High Council as soon as possible." His glance fell on the tray of untouched food.

"I see you haven't eaten yet," he said, changing the subject abruptly.

"Never mind about the food," Kalna said. "What is this about the Yorrga and Yaril's children?"

Thekis looked at Kalna and argued silently with himself. If anyone had earned the right to know the secret of the Yorrga, it was Kalna; but he had taken an oath in Yaril's name and he couldn't divulge even part of the truth without going against that oath.

"Ka, you must trust me for a short time. I want to answer your questions but I can't, not unless I get permission from the Council. Please, stay here, eat, rest, and be good and I'll return as soon as I can with the answers you want. I hope."

Kalna sensed that Thekis could not be pushed or wheedled into speaking further on the subject of the Yorrga. "What about my friends?"

"When the Council hears your story, I'm sure they'll reconsider the status of the two Bree," Thekis promised.

"And if they won't?"

Thekis heard the challenge in Kalna's voice. He smiled to himself, admiring the youth's unflinching loyalty to his new friends. "I promised you that they'll be freed, Ka, and they will, one way or another."

Fresh food was brought soon after Thekis left the room. Kalna was sure it was at Thekis's orders. He excused the two weirwomen, preferring to feed himself without the embarrassment of an audience. They said they'd be back later to see to his bath and fresh clothes.

While he ate, he thought over Thekis's enigmatic comment about Yaril's children. It was obvious that his uncle knew something special about the Yorrga, something that wasn't common knowledge among the weirfolk. What secret did the dweorg hold so carefully? he wondered. And how would it affect himself and his friends?

After he had finished eating, he stretched his arms and legs and flexed his wings, then reached up behind him as far as he could and rubbed at the thick membrane that was beginning to peel from his wings. An older darkling had come into his room the day before to speak to him. Though he didn't speak back, she warned him that his wings would be extremely sensitive for a few weeks, but that once the outer membrane wore off, they would grow in length and would be less fragile.

Kalna didn't hear the door open, but suddenly he was aware of another presence in the room. "Thekis?"

There was no answer.

He thought it might be one of the weirwomen returning for the tray. He'd forgotten their names. He heard the sound of leather rubbing against leather as his mysterious visitor moved around to his right. He followed the movement with his head. The invisible tendrils of his new awareness stretched outward; he touched hate and envy and flinched away, suddenly frightened.

"I know someone is in the room," he said, trying to keep the quaver from his voice. "I can feel you. What do you want? Who are you?"

Mouth-drying fear enveloped him as the visitor approached the bed. Kalna could feel him strongly now; it was a he, and he meant him harm! Kalna had no weapons with which to fight off an attack, and without his crutches, he couldn't flee. There was but one thing to do. He dipped down within himself and gathered his inner fire; it coursed down his arms and tingled in his fingertips; never had it answered him so quickly. A single thought and it would be released. He raised his hands toward his visitor, palms out, threatening.

"Leave my room," he snapped. "Now!"

Darkling fire was not a thing to ignore. One moment the visitor was there, the next he was gone, gliding out of Kalna's field of perception as silently as he had come.

Kalna lowered his hands as he quelled the fire from within. Beads of sweat covered his forehead and upper lip and he shook visibly. The knowledge that he had an enemy within the keep left him cold and frightened.

# CHAPTER 17

Ard and Raney left their room and walked down the stone corridor, both conscious of the guards stationed at either end of the hall. They had been free for two days but still felt like prisoners. They reached Kalna's room a short time later and barely avoided a collision with a striking, but grim-faced, female darkling as she stalked out through Kalna's doorway. She gave them an angry look and kept going, her wings folded primly against her back. Her open-backed tunic was belted at the waist and fell full length to the floor. It was blue in color with an intricate white thread webbing pattern sewn on the bottom half of the skirt.

Ard watched appreciatively as she moved away from them. "Beautiful," he murmured.

"But definitely not happy," Raney added. "I wonder what's wrong now."

"Only one way to find out." Ard knocked on the open door. "It's Ard and Raney, Ka. May we come in?"

"Come in. I've been wondering where you two were."

"We were talking to Jylak and a beran named Runner

about the Yorrga we saw in the ruins at Rithe's Keep. They're about the tenth delegation we've spoken to in the last two days, all asking the same questions. I'm beginning to think they don't believe us."

"There are factions among the weirfolk, Ard, just as there are among your own people. Runner even knows me from before, yet I've been going through the same thing. It's almost as if they don't want to know the truth!"

"Did Thekis find out anything about the intruder in your room yet?" Raney asked.

"Not yet, but they haven't given up. It's why there are guards stationed at both ends of the hall."

Raney cocked an eyebrow. "I thought they were for our benefit."

"In a way they are," Kalna conceded. "They keep you safe at the same time they guard my door."

Ard sat in one of the chairs near the bed. Raney took another across the room. Both men regarded Kalna silently a few seconds. Bathed, his hair combed, his clothes properly fitted, Kalna looked like a different person, more mature, less vulnerable.

"Who was the female darkling who stormed out of here a few moments ago?" Ard asked.

Kalna grimaced. "Glanna, my mother's true sister. She and her husband, Jarad, have come to protect me from the rowdy elements inhabiting Galen Keep during the cold season. They want to take me with them back to Endwall."

"And you don't want to go," Raney guessed.

"I'm not going anywhere until I learn the truth behind my parents' deaths. My aunt thinks I'm being foolish and stubborn. Perhaps I am, but I won't leave until this business with the Yorrga is taken care of, even if—"

"Glanna only wants what's best for you, Ka," Thekis said from the doorway. "Although there may be a bit of selfishness involved, too. It would bring a lot of prestige to Endwall if she could persuade you to make your home there. But not to worry, no one here will force you to do anything you don't want to do."

Kalna hadn't spoken to Thekis since the day before when he'd brought Ard and Raney up from their cells. His visit had been brief but he had promised to return and talk about the Yorrga as soon as he could.

"Have you any new information on the Yorrga, Thekis?" Kalna asked.

Thekis eyed the two Bree as he came into the room, his hands behind his back. "Nothing new on the Yorrga you three speak about, but I do want to talk to you about the Yorrga masks, Ka. It might be better if we speak alone."

Raney started to rise.

"No, Thekis," Kalna said. "Ard and Raney are a part of this now, and I want them to hear what you have to say."

Thekis saw how it was to be and let his hands drop to his sides as he walked toward the bed. "So be it, Ka."

When the two men saw what he held in one hand, they both stood up quickly, their chairs making noises on the floor as they were pushed back. Thekis set the Yorrga mask on the bed and motioned the two men to return to their seats. When Ard started to speak, Thekis put a hand to his lips and shook his head.

There was something in the dweorg's eyes that warned Ard to obey, but his own experience with a Yorrga mask was still alive in his mind and he was afraid, for himself as well as for Kalna. He had never had cause to question his own courage until his contact with the Yorrga mask. Memories of fear, of trying to run and hide from the mad spirit who had threatened his sanity, left a metallic blood taste in his mouth.

"Ard? What's wrong?" Kalna demanded, sensing his distress.

Thekis was aware of Kalna's sensitivity to the emotions of those around him. He looked at the men and tried to think of a way to reassure them that there was no danger in the Yorrga mask they eyed with such alarm.

But before he could speak, Ard moved to the side of Kalna's bed.

"Thekis has brought a mask into the room, Ka," Ard said. "It's on the bed to your left."

"Mask? A Yorrga mask?"

"Yes!"

Though Kalna couldn't see the dweorg, he knew where he stood. "Why did you bring it here?" he demanded.

"Easy, Ka. You know me too well to ever think I'd do you any harm," Thekis said placatingly. He glanced at Ard, wishing the big man had had sense enough to follow his lead. He had wanted to approach Kalna unaware, to use the Yorrga mask without upsetting him. Now he would have to do it the hard way.

"I brought the mask here to see if I can do something about your blindness; but now, before I can do that, you must be made to understand fully what a Yorrga mask is."

"I know what they are! They're evil and they're deadly, and I want nothing to do with it!"

"Nothing? You want to remain blind and crippled the rest of your life?" Thekis snapped angrily.

Kalna swallowed nervously. "No, but I don't trust the Yorrga!"

"Ka, you can't have it both ways. Now listen to me. The mind is a strange and powerful thing, and belief is essential in coping with life, belief in parents, in friends, in oneself, and in this case, belief in the Yorrga. A Yorrga mask can't heal by itself; it needs acceptance and free access to the mind because that is where most healing takes place—within yourself. At the moment your fear and hatred of the Yorrga is too strong for me to fight against. We'll have to break down the barrier you've built up or we'll get nowhere with the healing."

Thekis glanced at Ard and Raney. "All of us will have to work together because you, Ard, have become linked to Kalna in a special way. If you want him to see again and walk again, you'll have to put aside prejudice and old ways of thinking. Most of all, you'll have to put your fear aside and promise to trust me. Are you willing to try?"

"I want what's best for Ka," Ard said. "We'll do as you ask."

"Thekis," Kalna said, "I want to see again and I want to walk without crutches, but I'm not sure I can trust myself to a Yorrga."

"You aren't trusting yourself to anyone but me," Thekis said firmly.

Kalna was still afraid but was anxious not to offend Thekis or lose a chance for the return of his sight. His leg he thought he could live with, but his sight—that was something else again. "What do we do?" he asked softly.

Thekis jumped up onto Kalna's bed and made himself comfortable. "We begin at the beginning," he said. "I'll start by asking what you men know of Yaril."

"Ka has told us her story," Ard answered.

"And did you believe it?" Thekis pressed, eyes intent upon the handsome, scar-faced man.

"I believe Ka told us what he *thought* was the truth. Duval, a historian among my people, thought Kalna's facts might be somewhat skewed, but he had no proof one way or the other. He was most interested in reading some of the books Ka told him about. No one, it seems, realized that your people took such pride in keeping records."

"Truth has a way of blurring if it isn't written down somewhere," Thekis said. "Yaril began the *Book of the El-ar-kil* and gave it to us to continue, which we have done to this day. It holds our past and is the truth as we see it."

"And the Yorrga," Raney challenged, "are they in this book?"

Thekis's chin raised proudly. "They are, but the full truth behind their origin rests in the minds of only a few who can be trusted."

"Perhaps that is where you've gone wrong," Ard said calmly.

"What do you mean by that?" Thekis snapped.

Ard studied the dweorg. "I mean that it is possible you've trusted the wrong people. Who better to change the Yorrga from their intended purpose than someone who really understands what they are?"

Thekis nodded at Ard. "That is very perceptive, but the truth we are speaking about would not be enough to enable anyone to pervert the Yorrga masks into something they aren't. Yorrga do not kill. They may numb the mind of the weak-willed to a point where the mask wearer kills himself accidentally, but they do not kill wantonly, as you all say they have done."

"We say it because it's the truth," Raney said loudly.

Thekis took a deep breath and released it slowly as he fastened his gaze on Raney. "I don't doubt what you've told us, I'm only saying that the Yorrga, as we in the Black Forest know them, are not killers."

He turned and picked up the Yorrga mask he'd brought with him. It was a long-tongue with a comical, silly expression on its face. It was painted red and had white hair dangling down both sides of its face.

"Yaril was a great healer among the Ancients," Thekis began, "and the Yorrga mask was one of her tools. As she grew old, she realized that she had to teach the weirfolk how to use the mask and, because we were growing in numbers, how to reproduce it. When she brought us out of Sandu-valgara, she also brought certain equipment with her, equipment she secreted away in a place she called the Grotto. Then she showed the Grotto to one of her most trusted followers and taught him how to use the equipment found there; thereafter he or she was known as the Guardian. Knowledge of the Yorrga masks was passed down this way for generations—until some forty years ago, when the Guardian disappeared."

Thekis held the mask toward Ard. "Take it and look inside."

Embarrassed to show fear before the dweorg, Ard accepted the mask gingerly, holding it well away from himself.

"See the metal band inside the forehead?" Thekis said. "There lies the healing power. When you place the mask on your face, the metal band is in contact with your forehead and you instantly become a Yorrga, a strange mixture of being and nonbeing with an awareness capable of diagnosing and treating most illnesses."

"You speak as if the mask is some kind of machine," Ard said, eyes narrowed in speculation.

"It is and it isn't. On Yaril's home world, which she called Terra, the Yorrga was a machine, but on this world it has become something more. Yaril discovered that the metal band of information, when linked to a certain kind of tree, produces a resonance, a charge of energy that in turn creates a symbiotic relationship among weir, tree spirit, and Yorrga knowledge; in other words, the masks become alive."

Kalna was struggling with concepts and words that produced more questions than answers. Ard and Raney were in a similar state.

"I don't understand some of what you're saying, Thekis," Kalna said. "What is a symbiotic relationship?"

"Those are Yaril's words, not mine, but what they mean is a type of joining between two very different life forms, a joining that is beneficial to both and makes them more together than they are alone. Think of the cuplike fungus that grows on the oddbark tree. The fungus needs the tree for nourishment and the tree uses the catchbasins of rainwater formed by the fungus. Two separate life forms together creating a working unit."

Ard eyed the mask in his hands. "You said that the information for healing comes form the metal bands inside the mask. How are they made?"

"I can't tell you that for the knowledge died with our last Guardian, if dead she is."

"How long do the masks live?" Ard asked.

"A long time if properly cared for. The outer mask must be rubbed with the oil of the numbberry root twice each year and the interior must be kept clean and dry. It's not unusual for a mask to live for fifty years."

Ard looked down at the mask. "You said that the Guardian disappeared forty years ago, so that means no new masks have been made since then?"

Kalna was surprised at how quickly Ard had accepted the concept of the living masks and wondered if it had something to do with their own joining.

Thekis took the mask back. "Yorrga masks are made every year," he said, "but the *special* Yorrga masks that carry the metal band haven't been made in forty years, and no more will be made until we find Yaril's Grotto or the Guardian."

Kalna interrupted. "Thekis, you're telling us that there are two kinds of masks, then. One for healing, and the other?"

"The others are symbolic only, hung in individual homes for good luck, a living reminder that Yaril's spirit watches over us still. The symbolic masks are alive just as the Yorrga masks are, the only difference being that they don't possess the healing knowledge that was Yaril's legacy to us."

"My mother once said that he who wears a Yorrga mask wears death while he dances," Kalna said. "Which kind of mask was she talking about?"

"Both. There are many stories told about the Yorrga masks. Some are true, some not. But there is one truth that is a constant, and that is that the masks are cut from living trees. I'm not free to tell you what kind of tree, but these trees are very special. They are aware, not perhaps as you and I are aware, but there is a sense of being in them, and how that being is manifested often depends upon the person who cuts and carves the mask; it's almost as if the masks take on an inner image of the mask maker. Those who wear the masks for healing or only ritualistic dances can easily lose their own identity if they aren't strong enough to resist the lure of joining the masks offer."

"How many of the real Yorrga masks are there?" Kalna asked, his fear slowly being submerged by curiosity.

"There are twelve now functioning. Half will probably cease to live within the next two years. The others might live another ten years, no more."

"My mother knew about the masks, didn't she?"

"Yes. Your father also."

"How many others know?"

"Not more than twenty in any one generation."

"What about the Yorrga who have ravaged the Breedors recently?" Ard wanted to know. "And those who killed Ka's parents? Where are they coming from?"

Thekis gnawed his lip, unsure how much more he could tell the two men, for already he had overstepped the bounds of his promise to the High Council. "We don't know," he said, "but we're trying to find out. When Runner came and told us of Rops's death and the burning of Kalna's home, we were stunned. Just the day before, I'd spoken with Dari about the mask he'd found and I had not yet presented it to the High Council."

Thekis shook his head. "I took news of the deaths of Dari, Graya, and Kalna very hard, and it was several days before I had the presence of mind to do any investigating. At first I thought it was a local matter, someone angry or jealous of Dari or Graya, but that didn't explain Rops's death at the hands of five Yorrga. Runner was out of the cabin when they struck and walked into their trap unknowing. He saw that Rops was dead and somehow broke free. He went to your cabin, Ka, and found it in flames; then he came here.

"We've been questioning people ever since. Runner and I have tracked down hundreds of masks trying to find one or two that he might recognize, but so far we've had little luck. Some of the masks are so similar that it's virtually impossible to tell them apart at a quick glance, and that's all Runner had before he bolted.

"Now you three come to us with your story about Yorrga invading the Breedors, and things have taken on a new light. The High Council has two theories at the moment. The first theory is that some among our people have taken it upon themselves to start a war with the Bree in order to regain lands once ours."

"And somehow they've convinced Lord Alfar to aid their cause," Ard finished for him. "What have they offered him, I wonder?"

"Land," Raney offered. "And he wins out no matter who loses the war. If we win, he'll enlarge his holding northward and eastward into the Black Forest. And if the weirfolk win, they give him whatever he's asked for, repaying him for stirring up trouble between us. If not land, then something else of value is at stake here."

"Thekis," Kalna asked, "What is the Council's second theory?"

"That someone has found the rest of Yaril's children and has brought forth a new kind of Yorrga, one that kills instead of heals."

"What do you mean by 'the rest of Yaril's children'?" Ard asked.

"I'm sorry, but I can't tell you that right now. Later perhaps, with the Council's approval." He looked at Kalna. "So, Ka, you now understand what a Yorrga mask is—at least, this one. Will you allow me to show you how the mask works?"

Kalna's stomach knotted and his heartbeat quickened. "Are you sure it will be all right? After what happened the last time, I'm frightened."

"Everything will be fine, Ka, I promise. Both Ard and Raney are here and they won't let anything happen to you." He took Kalna's hand. "Here, touch the metal band behind the mask's forehead."

Kalna felt the tingle of power he'd experienced before and quickly withdrew his hand. Suddenly his mouth was dry and he couldn't swallow.

Thekis slipped the wooden mask over his face and tightened the leather straps at the back of the head. Ard and Raney watched, both intent upon the dweorg's every move.

Thekis sat quietly for a few seconds; his silence was frightening, ominous. Kalna reached out with his inner awareness. Ard and Raney were both tense and Thekis was—for a moment it was as if Thekis wasn't there, as if he was hidden behind a filmy curtain. "Thekis? I can't feel you!"

Thekis opened his eyes and peered out of the mask. "I'm here," he said softly. "It takes a few moments to adjust. Be patient."

The dweorg's emotional emanations blossomed to life so suddenly that Kalna was caught off guard. He felt concern and a wraparound warmth that pushed fear aside gently but firmly.

"I'm ready to begin," Thekis said, his voice made slightly hollow sounding by the mask. "Give me your hand and relax."

Ard's hands clenched into fists as Kalna gave his right hand to Thekis. He had all he could do not to jump up and physically prevent the Yorrga-who-was-Thekis from touching Kalna.

Kalna felt the tingle of power as it fed upward from his hand to his arm and chest; then suddenly there was nothing but a feeling of floating with no anxiety or pain or fear.

Kalna sensed another presence; it was wrapped in layers of strength and was old beyond measuring; it mourned its separation from the whole, yet rejoiced in its new freedom and the subtleties of life found within the ephemeral being who called itself Thekis. So this is a Yorrga, he thought. Why was I so afraid?

"Thekis? Is Ka all right?" Ard asked, worried.

The Yorrga turned. "He suffers from a type of hysterical blindness. Fear has blinded him. Fear is ignorance. Erase the fear and ignorance and he will see again."

Ard glanced at Kalna. "Ka? Do you hear what he says?"

"He hears but cannot answer," the Yorrga said. "He must learn himself and seek within for that which frightened him. We shall assist."

The Yorrga pulled Kalna from the peaceful floating void toward a pulsating light. He entered a place that

he'd never been before; here all was color but in sub-
dued tones that let the eyes absorb the images that appeared fleetingly then disappeared. Time lost all meaning
as he relived his past: joys and sorrows, loves and hates,
excitement, despair, hopes and dreams. The twin spirits
of the Yorrga mask showed him how to see and feel yet
not lose his way. At last they came to the image of Gold-
mask and the moment when an eyeless Yorrga mask was
forced upon him.

Sudden terror rose in his throat as something cold
touched his eyes. He fought . . . or tried to. A voice came
to him.

*Open your eyes. It can't take if you won't give! It's
strong only if you are weak. Fear is its mightiest
weapon. Don't let it wield it against you! Open your eyes
and see!*

*I can't. The dark . . . it clings to me!* Kalna wailed.

*It's their dark . . . not yours! Open your eyes!*

*I'm afraid!*

*Only a fool is unafraid. Is it the dark that frightens
you?*

*Not the dark . . .*

*What then?* the Yorrga demanded.

*Something in the dark. I can feel it!*

*What is it?*

*I don't know, but it hates! Can't you feel it?*

*Yes, we feel it, but its madness can't hurt you unless
you let it! Let your fear go. Open your eyes and see that
which your fear would deny you!*

The voice was impossible to resist. Kalna blinked
several times, and gradually the darkness faded and light
and blurred images became solid. There was a brief
glimpse of a silly-looking mask, then it was pushed up
and Kalna saw Thekis grinning at him.

"Ka?" Ard asked, hardly daring to hope.

Kalna's eyes blurred with tears. "I can see, Ard! I can
see!"

Ard never remembered getting up or moving to the
bed, all he remembered was an infusion of joy that drew

him irresistibly to its source. He sat down on the edge of Kalna's bed and embraced the one he had come to look upon as a younger brother. Tears wet his face as he shared Kalna's happiness.

Thekis looked on, his smile fading to a frown of uneasiness. He glanced over at Raney and saw that he, too, looked worried.

Raney caught his look and shook his head slightly. "It's been like that ever since Kalna freed Ard from that Yorrga mask," he said softly. "Look at them. They're in a world of their own right now, not even hearing what I say."

"It bothers you?" Thekis asked, carefully keeping his own voice low.

"Because Kalna's weir? No, it's not that. It's Ard. He once told me that he was afraid of losing himself to Kalna. I'm not exactly sure what he meant, but—this joining Kalna spoke about, is it dangerous? I mean, is there harm for either of them in this closeness?"

No dull wit this one, Thekis thought silently. He has a gift for seeing the truth. How do I answer to his satisfaction?

"A joining is not lightly done, Raney, but don't fear for your friend. Kalna would never do anything to harm him, nor he Kalna."

A few moments later Kalna stirred and pushed Ard back. His eyes sparkled with life as he grinned. "It worked, Ard! The Yorrga showed me how to fight the darkness!"

"I know," Ard said. "I know." He turned and looked at Thekis. "Thank you, for whatever it was that you did."

Thekis acknowledged Ard's gratitude with a nod, then he looked at Kalna. "Well, that is one thing taken care of, now comes a different matter, your leg."

Kalna glanced down at the dirty, battered cast that enclosed his leg from midthigh to calf. "Can the Yorrga do anything about it?" he asked, sobering.

"Yes. It will require surgery and someone with a steadier hand than mine, but we have several good physicians who've worked under a Yorrga's guidance many times. According to the Yorrga, you have a partially ruptured meniscus, that is, the cartilage at the knee. The damaged cartilage will have to be cut out, which will mean that you'll have to wear a hard cast similar to the one you have on for at least a month, then a lighter one for another month. By the end of that time, you should be walking without any pain."

"When can you do this?" Ard asked.

"I think I'll send for Vidler. He's one of our best physicians. If he's keeping to his schedule, he's four days east of here in the village of Adria's Gap. He should be back by the end of next week. We'll plan the surgery for then."

# CHAPTER 18

The Council chamber was a good-sized room lighted by lanterns on the side walls. There was a large table and a dozen chairs in the center of the room and a scattering of couches and padded chairs at the far end, away from the main door. There were two doors to the room but no windows, for the room was located deep inside Galen Keep, literally under the mountain.

It was here that Kalna was introduced to the High Council. Following the introductions, Thekis spoke about Kalna's healing and his request for a Naming. As the weir elders talked, Kalna glanced around the room. It had been barely twenty-four hours since his healing and he still couldn't get over the feeling of wonder he felt at the return of his sight. Wherever his glance rested, he was struck by beauty: a lantern, the carved leg of a table, a hand, a face, a shadow, a cup. Each was exquisite in its own right and not to be overlooked. How much he had missed before! Never again, he thought, would he take his sight for granted.

"Ka?" Thekis's voice brought him back from his musings.

He turned and looked at the elders. They were six: two were beran, three were weirmen, and one was darkling. The darkling's name was Alvenna; she was very old but one could still see the beauty in her features, the delicate bone structure of wrists and hands, her bird-bright eyes glowing amber and her gold-tinted wings.

"Could you tell us again how you felt when the healing Yorrga touched you?" she asked, her well-modulated voice reminding him of his mother.

"Warm. Safe," he answered truthfully.

"It was not the same then as when the false Yorrga touched you?" This question came from the oldest weirman, a seer by the name of Larch.

"No, not the same," Kalna agreed. "Instead of warmth there was cold, and instead of safety there was fear and darkness." It was strange, he thought, even his aversion to thinking about that day was gone. Thekis had said he'd never heard of hysterical blindness, but the Yorrga's knowledge was not to be refuted. The eyes see, but the mind will not accept.

"What else do you remember about the false Yorrga?" Larch asked.

"All I remember is feeling enclosed, as if I couldn't breathe. I must have passed out a short time after they put the mask on me because I don't remember anything else until Ard and Raney woke me up."

"According to all that Thekis has told us," Alvenna said, "the two Bree went through a great deal to rescue you. Can you tell us why?"

Kalna sensed no challenge in the question so answered truthfully. "I believe the joining between Ard and me was partially responsible for his going out to search for me, and Raney goes where Ard goes. We have become good friends, all of us."

"You sensed no ulterior motive for their entry into weir territory?" This question came from the large, barrel-chested beran with silver fur. His human face was heavy with wrinkles and the horn at his right temple was broken off at the tip. Djan would have been considered ugly by men's standards, but among the weir he was accepted without comment, for the mind that dwelt within the beran body was quick and efficient and was balanced by a gentle heart.

"Ard and Raney entered weir territory at my invitation," Kalna answered, being careful not to show anger, for these few weir held the lives of his friends in their hands. "They came with me to see me safely home and to warn you about the killer Yorrga. Their people are being ravaged by these false Yorrga, as you call them, and I think it's only right that they be allowed to help us find out who is behind them."

The weirman named Barack turned to Thekis, an angry glint in his eyes. "It sounds to me as if you've been talking more than you should have. The boy has just recently winged and is too young to be meddling in Council affairs!"

"This is more than a Council affair!" Thekis snapped, barely holding onto his own temper. "These false Yorrga killed Ka's parents and almost succeeded in killing him! Who better has a right to know what's going on?"

"You've told him *everything* about the Yorrga?" Barack sputtered. "You took an oath to keep that information to yourself! You jeopardize all we have—"

"I jeopardize nothing!" Thekis cried. "Nothing but a false security that is tied to the Yorrga masks! I begin to think that it's time for us to try to heal the rift between weir and men, or at least try to get along a little better, and that will mean a sharing of our knowledge that should extend to the Yorrga masks! We have much to offer each other if both sides can only be brought to remember that once we were brothers and sisters!"

"You speak suicide!" Barack shouted. "Men don't share, they take! It's how we lost Rithe's Keep and all of the Lakeland Forests!"

"Please! Please, this gets us nowhere." Zehav was a female beran, youngest on the High Council. She was slightly smaller in stature then Djan, and more slender, but when she spoke her voice was crisp and clear and it brought instant silence.

"What has been done is done and there's no going back. I for one am inclined to agree with Thekis. We've had little luck searching out these false Yorrga. Perhaps the men can succeed where we have failed. It sounds to me as if they may be based in Bree territory."

"Are you suggesting that we should open the search for Yaril's Grotto?" The last elder to speak was Jandro, a weirman, a delver who was renowned for his success in searching out minerals and subterranean water. His summer home was on the Nikon Plains where his talent was much in demand.

"That would not be wise!"

All heads turned at the sound of a new voice. Kalna barely stifled a gasp when he saw the male darkling approach.

Ek-nar was in full prime and made as striking a figure as any female darkling. His hair was a burnished red and framed a face as beautiful as any Kalna had ever seen. He was of average height but thin when compared to most weirman; yet he moved with a wiry strength and easy grace that belied any weakness. Most striking of all were his wings, which he carried partially open, for they were tinged with a red-gold color that seemed to glow in the lantern light.

Barack hurried toward the darkling. "Ek-nar, we didn't know that you'd arrived! How long have you been here? Please, come and join us. We have much to tell you."

The rest of the Council rose as Ek-nar approached. Kalna followed their example, bracing himself with his crutches. He had heard of Ek-nar but had never thought to meet him, for it was said that the darkling lord seldom left the Nikon Plains.

Jandro greeted Ek-nar warmly, kissing him on either cheek, then he stepped back. "We hadn't thought to see you for another week or more, but we're glad you came so quickly. Things have gone from bad to worse since our last message to you."

Ek-nar nodded, acknowledging Jandro as his glance swept the others on the Council. He nodded to each and accepted their kisses. Finally he came to Thekis and Kalna. He accepted Thekis's murmured greeting, then let his glance rest on Kalna.

"Upon entering the city, I was told that a weirling had winged recently. You must be Graya's son, Kalna."

Kalna nodded, unable to find his voice. He wondered if Ek-nar had come about the false Yorrga, or was it something else that had drawn him from his home; the winging of another male darkling perhaps?

Djan took his seat again, offering the place beside him to Ek-nar. "Please join us, and we'll bring you up-to-date on the false Yorrga."

Ek-nar ignored Djan's invitation and continued to look at Kalna, who grew nervous under the close scrutiny and glanced at Thekis for guidance. Thekis shook his head ever so slightly, signaling Kalna to stand quietly. Kalna met Ek-nar's gaze once more and tried to calm the sudden flutter in his stomach.

"Turn," Ek-nar said briskly. "Let me see your wings."

Several of the elders stiffened at the tone of Ek-nar's voice. A tinge of red touched Alvenna's cheeks as Kalna hesitated, then did as Ek-nar commanded.

Eyes downcast, Kalna turned around, awkward with his crutches. Conflicting emotions chased through his mind as he came back around: hurt, anger, and confusion.

"Ek-nar, what was the meaning of that?" Alvenna demanded, her face mirroring disapproval.

Ek-nar turned to his sister darkling and spoke calmly, as if he'd done nothing wrong. "I was told that there was to be a Naming. I was also told that the one to be named was a cripple, and possibly insane. Our laws state that for the betterment of our race, those who are less than whole either mentally or physically are not to be given adult status."

Kalna lifted his head in anger, his shame forgotten, but before he could speak out Thekis angrily jumped to his defense.

"We know the laws," he snapped, "but the one you refer to does not apply to Kalna. His leg was crippled in an accident. It is not a birth deformity! Vidler will operate on it as soon as he arrives. As for Kalna's mind, it is as sound as your own!"

Ek-nar's chin lifted. "I was told otherwise."

"Well, you were told wrong! Kalna will be named, as is his right!"

"Thekis," Djan reproved, "Ek-nar is our guest."

Thekis started to say something in response, but Alvenna interrupted. "Thekis, the Council has much to discuss in the next few hours. We appreciate you and Kalna coming to answer our questions. Why don't the two of you go get something to eat. If we need you again, we'll call for you."

Kalna knew a dismissal when he heard one, but his anger made him feel defiant. He glared at Ek-nar and felt a surge of raw energy course up his spine and down to his fingertips.

Thekis saw one of Kalna's hands twitch and realized what was happening. He had been too long around darklings not to read the danger signs of a darkling during change. His own anger forgotten, he caught at Kalna's belt.

"Come, Ka," he growled loudly, hoping to break through Kalna's growing rage. "I've something I want to show you."

Kalna heard Thekis as if from a long distance off. The haze of anger slowly subsided and he glanced down and saw Thekis watching him, a worried frown on his face.

"Coming, Ka?" Thekis asked.

"Where?"

"To talk to Ard."

Kalna thought about it moment, then nodded and swung along behind Thekis as the dweorg started for the door. He glanced back once as they passed the large table in the center of the room. Ek-nar was watching him, a smug look on his face. A flush of renewed anger burned Kalna's cheeks.

"Easy, Ka," Thekis warned, as they passed through the doorway leading out of the room. "A display of anger won't help your cause right now."

"What cause?" Kalna demanded. "Ek-nar can't stop me from being named! Who does he think he is?"

"He's a male darkling with power aplenty if he wants to use it!"

"Let him try!"

"Kalna, stop it! Listen to me."

"I'd like to singe his wings a bit and burn that self-satisfied look right off his face! Just one chance is all I ask. Who is he to tell me that I can't be named!"

Thekis swung around on Ka and grabbed at his crutches, physically stopping him. The dweorg was small in stature, but he was strong and he caught Kalna unaware.

"Stop it, Ka! Right now! Now you listen to me! You aren't going to do anything to Ek-nar. You're going to return to your room and you're going to stay there until you calm down. Ek-nar is no fool. He was baiting you on purpose. He knows you winged recently and he knows how unstable that can make a darkling. It's almost as if he was trying to push you into a fight, one you couldn't win. He's powerful, Ka, both physically and influentially, and you are no match for him right now. In time perhaps, but not now."

Kalna saw Thekis through a red haze of anger. A part of him wanted to strike out at the small intense being who prevented him from moving, to shut off the voice that demanded things of him; but another part of him recognized that voice and knew he should obey it.

"Now behave yourself and do as I tell you." Thekis softened his voice. "Ka? Do you hear what I'm saying?"

The anger slowly slipped away. Kalna nodded as he tried to focus on Thekis's face. Suddenly he felt hurt and confused. "I feel so strange," he said softly. "What's wrong with me, Thekis?"

Thekis caught Kalna's right hand and gave it a squeeze. "Nothing is wrong, Ka. It's just something that darklings go through at change. It's a kind of chemical imbalance in the body as you change from weir to darkling. Emotions play an intricate part in the change, and you haven't had an easy time of it these past few weeks. Had you winged with other darklings in attendance and been able to rest properly afterward, the change would have been easier, though for some it is never easy; and not every darkling makes the change successfully. Some die; some go insane."

"How long will it last?"

Thekis smiled at the worried look on Kalna's face. "Not long, fourteen to eighteen days is usual. Now don't worry, all you need is rest and quiet."

"Mother never said anything to me about this."

"She wouldn't have. The chances of your becoming a darkling were not high, though it's something every darkling mother hopes for. The darklings don't talk much about the change because to them it's like a madness they have to go through but don't want anyone to know about. It was your bad luck not to wing with any darklings in attendance, and when you arrived here things were in such turmoil with this Yorrga business that everyone either forgot about the change or thought you'd already gone through it. That's our fault, not yours. Come, let's go back to your room and get something to eat, then you are going to lie down and take a nap. It will be the best thing for you."

"Thekis, why would Ek-nar try to stop me from being named?"

They started down the corridor. "I don't know, Ka. It doesn't make any sense. I would have thought he'd be overjoyed to know another male darkling had winged."

They reached the end of the short corridor and turned and walked right into someone. Kalna's wings spread

open as he was knocked off balance; they buffeted
Thekis in the face.

A hand shot out, caught Kalna by an arm, and drew
him back to his feet. Kalna looked up into a pair of
amber-flecked brown eyes that seemed to swallow him
whole. A high arched nose divided the weirman's face,
giving him a somewhat predatory look. The hand on his
arm dropped away as the eyes narrowed in recognition.

"Best watch where you're going, darkling!" The voice
was soft yet somehow menacing. Without another word
the weirman stepped around Kalna and continued on his
way up the corridor they'd just left.

A roiling mass of fear churned in Kalna's stomach as
he watched the weirman step through the doorway
where the elder's were meeting. "Who was that?"

"His name is Jagivan. He's Ek-nar's brother."

"Talents?"

"Foresight and telekenisis, both very limited. He's
made a place for himself as a loo woods wachter; he's
one of the best. He isn't the friendliest of weir, but he's
accepted by most."

"Because of Ek-nar?"

Thekis frowned, then nodded. "Yes, I guess so."

Kalna shivered. "I know him, Thekis. We met once
before."

"Where?"

"In my room a few days ago. I told you about it, remember? Someone came into my room but wouldn't
speak. I became frightened and threatened him with fire.
The person I *touched* felt just like Jagivan did a moment
ago."

"I know you have a talent for empathy, Ka, but you
were blind that day and with the darkling change coming
over you, it's possible that what you 'felt' wasn't even
real. No one saw anyone come into or go out of your
room."

Irrational anger surged upward. "You don't believe
me!"

"I believe you," Thekis said placatingly, "that's why

I've been asking around for witnesses. I've just not come up with anyone yet, but I'm not giving up. As for Jagivan coming to your room, it's possible, I suppose. It may be he was just curious."

Kalna shook his head. "It was more than curiosity; it was hate like I've never felt before. I don't understand why though! What have I done to either of them to make them hate me so?"

Thekis thought back on Ek-nar's performance just a short time ago, a new idea forming. "It may not be what you've done, Ka. It may be what you are. There's been some talk of making you the official Ra-ling of the Black Forest, just as Ek-nar is Ra-ling of the Nikon Plains."

"Ra-ling?"

"The term is old; it means Sun-child. A Ra-ling is always a male darkling, one filled with a talent for darkling fire. It's been over a hundred years since we've had a Ra-ling in the Black Forest."

"You're talking about Mirab?"

"Yes, he was our leader for sixty of his eighty-one years. He was a great tactician. Without him we might well have lost the war against the Bree a hundred and fifty years ago. We did lose Rithe's Keep, but we survived as a people."

"Is a Ra-ling always a war leader?"

Thekis gave him a smile. "A Ra-ling is whatever he wants to be."

# CHAPTER 19

Runner touched Kalna's shoulder. "Come, you must bathe and be in the Naming Circle before the sun crests the mountains. Jylak said he'd meet us by the Morning Pool with your clothes."

Kalna turned from looking out over the terrace wall that stood twelve stories above the valley floor. He'd been watching the flickering lights on the roadway that led to the Naming Circle. It was still too dark to see the people, but they were there, moving west toward the far side of the valley. Had this been a simple Naming, not more than a hundred would've turned out, those either related to or close to the family of the one to be named. Today was different. Today a Ra-ling was to be named, which meant that the Naming Circle would be filled to capacity. He shivered at that thought and suddenly wished himself wingless and safely back in his own home.

He pressed a hand to his eyes and rubbed them, knowing there was no going back. He cared nothing about being named Ra-ling, not after all the arguments it

had caused the past three days, especially among Ek-
nar, the Council, and the other darklings; but he did want
to be named officially as was the right of every weir who
was competent to stand before his peers. Without the
Naming one could not marry, father children, or ever be
considered an adult in weir society.

Gradually the sky grew light to the east and there was
a warmth in the air that was unusual for that time of
year. Runner said it was going to be a mild winter. If
true, it would mean a continuation of the Yorrga raids
into the Breedors. It was an unpleasant thought and not
one he wanted to dwell on.

He turned and looked at Runner, who had become his
constant companion in the past few days. The young
beran looked almost as nervous as he felt. He thought
back, remembering the first time he'd seen Runner. Rops
had been alive then, and so had his mother and father.
Another thought to avoid.

"How are you feeling?" Runner asked, as they left the
room and started down the outside steps leading to the
next level.

"Like I'd like all this to be over with," he answered.

"It will be soon, just remember to stay calm. Ek-nar
would like nothing better than to have you prove yourself emotionally unstable today."

"You don't like Ek-nar, do you?"

"I wouldn't chose him for a close friend, no," Runner
answered bluntly. "He thinks too much of himself and
too little of others."

"What do you think of Jagivan?"

Runner eyed Kalna closely. "I think you'd best put
both of them out of your mind right now for your own
good."

Kalna nodded, accepting Runner's rebuke. The beran
had been good for him; his easy ways, his humor, his
calming words when Kalna so easily flared to anger.
Thekis had been wise in his choice, he thought.

The Morning Pool was small and was only used for
special occasions. It was lined with rainbow-colored

stones and was springfed, which made the water extremely cold even during the summer. Kalna bathed quickly at the side of the pool and turned gratefully to the blanket Jylak held out to him. While he was rubbing down, Runner went to a nearby altar and unfolded a long tunic, all gold and gossamer.

"Hold up your arms," he said, lifting the tunic over Ka's head. The silken garment slipped down, covering Kalna from wrists to ankles. A deep yoke in back allowed his wings to be free outside the tunic.

Kalna looked down at Jylak as the dweorg handed him a comb. "Is this all I'm to wear? I can see right through it."

"The material is called linthav. It creates the illusion of clothing the body yet discloses the truth. It symbolizes that you come before the weirfolk hiding nothing from anyone."

Kalna nodded, accepting the explanation, his mind already darting to something else. "Where's Thekis?"

"He's already in the Naming Circle."

Kalna shivered suddenly. Thekis had gone over the day's events with him, but still he was unsure of his role. "Are you sure I'm not to say anything during the ceremony?"

"No. Your darkling sisters are the speakers this morning. It's your duty just to stand and listen and hear the words of power spoken. When the ceremony is over, there'll be a feast to which all are invited."

As they started down the winding trail that would bring them to the veld and the Naming Circle, Jylak paused and turned to Kalna. "There is one more thing— your crutches. You must set them aside before you step up on the Naming Rock."

"Thekis said nothing about that."

"He probably forgot. With all that's been going on, it's no wonder. The Naming Rock is sacred to us, Kalna. Nothing may touch it but the flesh of the body. The stone is flat. Only three steps and you'll be at its center. Once there you face east and wait for the sun to crest the

mountains. As the sun's rays touch the valley, the darklings will come forward. When they reach the stone,
they'll form a circle around it and then they'll sing the
three songs of power. Listen to the words, let them enter
your mind freely. You may not understand all you hear,
but time and growth will change that. When the ceremony is ended, you'll be escorted to the Garden of Eos.
There you'll meet those who came to witness your Naming. The rest of the day will be spent feasting, providing
the weather holds."

They stopped at the edge of the veld. The sky was
growing lighter by the minute, but Runner assured Kalna
there was no need to hurry.

"Take your time, Kalna. Jylak and I will follow behind you."

Kalna looked around the veld. There was a huge
round depression in the center and tier upon tier of log
seats around the Naming Rock. Many people were already seated; more were still coming. A few torches
burned here and there about the veld but most of them
had been extinguished.

Kalna readjusted the crutches under his arms and
took his first steps out from the pine trees lining the
pathway from the Morning Pool. He heard several of the
weirfolk whisper as he started down the gradual slope to
the center of the veld. Heat rose to his cheeks as he
thought of all the eyes following his progress. He tried to
take his mind off the skimpiness of his attire by looking
for familiar faces.

He saw Thekis smile at him. Glanna stood beside him
with Jarad next to her. Thekis nodded to his right. Kalna
saw Ard and Raney in the row behind him. He'd not
seen either man since the day he'd spoken with the
elders. Thekis had thought it would be less stressful for
him if he had no visitors. Both men nodded to him as he
passed by. What had Thekis told them about darkling
madness? he wondered.

He saw several others he knew: Laric, Omecon,
Zehav, and Barack, and beyond Jarad sat the elder Djan,

his massive, silver-furred body taking up two sitting places.

He reached the Naming Rock and carefully lowered his crutches to the ground. The step up onto the rock was no more than a foot or two, but as he stood looking down, it seemed twice that height. He stepped up with his good leg and brought his casted leg up, then hobbled the few feet to the center of the rock. His wings opened wide as a pain darted up his knee to his hip and for a moment he thought he would lose his balance.

He regained his footing and stood flushed with embarrassment as he realized the sight he must have presented. He lowered his head, unable to look out at the faces around him. A well of sadness opened up within and tears began to trickle down his face. He realized that the darkling change was still affecting him, but knowing that didn't stop the tears.

Runner somehow sensed his distress and came to stand in front of him, being careful not to touch the Naming Rock.

"Kalna," he said softly, "you have many friends here and soon you'll have many more, and no one laughs at a friend. Look to the east and watch for the sun. Keep your mind on that alone and you'll be fine. Soon you'll be named and given the title of Ra-ling, Sun-child, friend to all weirfolk. So lift your head proudly and remember that you are darkling, and very special to the hearts of our people."

Kalna silently called upon Yaril's name and stood a little straighter. His head rose a moment later and he looked to the east. There were some clouds in the sky but they were gathered far to the north. A sign of winter's return, he thought absently. He looked to the east again and saw the sun's rays shooting upward outlining the mountains in gold.

Runner smiled at Kalna and returned to his place by Jylak. If he noticed the wetness that glistened on Kalna's face, he never after spoke of it.

Others filed in and soon the veld around the Naming

Rock was filled. A pathway was left open for the darkling's approach. The moment finally came. Kalna saw
the first rays of the sun break over the mountains and
touch the upper edge of the veld with the illusion of
warmth. His stomach muscles tightened. The waiting
was at an end. Soon he would be named and as an adult
he would be free to take on whatever responsibilities he
chose, which for him meant the killer Yorrga, and finding
out who was behind them.

He drew three deep breaths to calm the thunder in his
chest, and carefully positioned his bad leg, letting his
good foot carry most of his weight.

The seconds slipped by as he stood facing the sun. A
minute passed, then two and three. There was no sign of
the darklings. Kalna looked to Thekis and saw that he
was frowning. Jylak and Runner were craning their
necks to look up to the top of the veld where the darklings were to appear.

Another minute passed and as Thekis stood and
started up toward the top of the veld, Kalna could hear
the whispered questions floating about the crowd.
"Where are the darklings? The sun is up, someone must
go and tell them it's time. Thekis is going to find out
what's wrong. I'd heard there was an argument between
the darklings and the Council; I wonder if . . ."

Thekis was halfway to the edge of the veld when Ek-
nar stepped into view and stood looking down at the
gathering. Thekis stopped. A hush swept across the veld
as the other weirfolk became aware of the darkling lord.

Ek-nar started down the open aisle toward Thekis.
Ten or twelve female darklings stayed behind at the edge
of the veld.

Ek-nar carried himself proudly and moved with an
easy, graceful stride. He was dressed in light-brown
pants and a green, open-backed tunic. Calf-length boots
and a belt of gold-colored disks completed his attire.

Thekis passed Ek-nar without a glance and continued
on up the pathway toward the darkling women; he knew

something was wrong and meant to find out what was going on.

Kalna noticed movement at Ek-nar's shoulders, then suddenly a pair of red-gold wings unfolded. He gasped at their size, for they were five times the length of his own. As Ek-nar came to a halt before the Naming Rock, he opened his wings wider, as if stretching them for battle.

Kalna shrank back a step as Ek-nar's winged shadow blocked off the sun. One quick glance beyond the darkling lord and he realized that the rest of the darklings were not coming down to sing to him. His heartbeat quickened with uneasiness. What was Ek-nar doing there?

The darkling lord looked at the gathered people, turning slowly as he spoke. "I am Ek-nar, Ra-ling of the Nikon Plains and brother to all weir in the Black Forest. I speak on behalf of the darklings in both lands and say that we do not accept Kalna as Ra-ling of the Black Forest, and that we do not consider him a legal candidate for Naming." His glance touched Kalna briefly, then he turned his back to him and faced three of the five elders who sat on the lower tier around the Naming Rock. "The words of power will not be sung this day," he declared loudly, his voice ringing clear and defiant. "The darklings will not accept a cripple, nor a lover of men, for their Ra-ling!"

Suddenly Thekis was there. Kalna hadn't seen him return for his full attention had been focused on Ek-nar. "You don't speak for all the weir, Ek-nar, only for the darklings, and you have badgered and frightened them until they don't know what to do! As for Kalna's friends, men or otherwise, that has nothing to do with the Naming, and you well know why they are here!"

"I only know that men are our enemies and that the crippled one gave them free passage onto our lands!" Ek-nar shouted, making sure the crowd heard him. "And why are they here? They come spreading lies about the Yorrga! They want war and would use the Yorrga as an excuse to cross our borders!"

"You're wrong!" Kalna yelled, furious. "They came to prevent the war, not start it!"

Ek-nar turned on Kalna, his wings out and cutting the air fiercely. He didn't step up on the Naming Rock, but so terrible was the look on his face that Kalna stepped backward on his bad leg and fell, one of Ek-nar's wings buffeting him in the face.

Believing Ek-nar meant to strike him, Kalna raised an arm to protect his head. He heard Ard shout something, then other voices were raised in anger. He looked past Ek-nar and Thekis and saw that Runner, Omecon, and another weir named Woodsrunner were struggling with Ard, trying to hold him back from attacking Ek-nar. Several other weir had started for Ek-nar; one was the elder Djan who was twice Ek-nar's size. But before anyone could reach the darkling lord, he straightened and raised his voice in a high-pitched warble that brought instant silence to the veld. Everyone stopped where they were and looked at the darkling lord, even Ard.

Ek-nar pointed down at Kalna. "Look you, weir of the Black Forest! Look on the cripple you would name Ra-ling! He can't even stand up! Look at him and tell me you would name this cowering whelp your Ra-ling!"

Ek-nar paused, giving everyone time to do as he bid. Kalna instantly found himself the focal point for doubting, questioning glances. He felt their misgiving, could almost touch their thoughts. They were all wondering if Ek-nar was right.

Uneasiness turned into anger and Kalna rolled over, got his good leg under him, and lunged toward Ek-nar, but he never reached his intended target for hands grabbed him from behind, twisting him around. He caught one brief glimpse of Jagivan's face, then the weir-man exerted certain pressure on one of Kalna's wings. Pain shot through him; it was so great that he couldn't even cry out. He fought to remain conscious as Jagivan lowered him to the rock.

Everything happened so quickly that no one was sure but that Jagivan was only trying to help Kalna up.

Ek-nar crossed his arms over his chest as he looked at the elders. "The Words of Power will not be sung this day, not for this weirling! I alone am fit for the title Ra-ling. Name me your Sun-child if you will, but not him! He is *not* fit!"

Thekis looked from Kalna to the elders. He was angry but also worried. If the darklings wouldn't sing the Words of Power, legally Kalna couldn't be accepted as either adult or Ra-ling.

A murmur of voices quickly filled the veld. Kalna drew a deep breath and opened his eyes. He saw Ard, Runner, and Omecon making their way toward the Naming Rock. Jylak had moved up beside Thekis and at that moment was glaring at Ek-nar.

The confusion among the weirfolk stilled suddenly as a single voice raised in a chanting melody. Every head turned as Glanna stood and approached the Naming Rock. She was fully Graya's equal in beauty; she was slender in build and she held her golden wings out to full span, her own anger mixed with determination to see her nephew named.

She stopped before the Naming Rock and inclined her head, first to the elders, then to Ek-nar. "The Words of Power will be sung," she stated firmly, her voice low and husky with emotion.

Kalna had argued with his aunt several times since her arrival at Galen Keep, but all disagreements were forgotten as each drew emotional support from the other.

Glanna's eyes were warm with sympathy and understanding as she looked down at Kalna. "Rise, Kalna, and accept your birthright."

"You dare defy me, Glanna?" Ek-nar growled.

"I do," she answered crisply.

"You are alone then. No one else will sing! There will be no one to answer your call. The Words of Power can't be sung by one alone and have any legal standing!"

"Perhaps my sisters will join me once I begin," she said.

"They won't!"

Glanna turned her shoulder to Ek-nar and looked at Kalna. Her presence gave him hope. He glanced once at Jagivan, who had moved a few steps away from the rock, distancing himself from the proceedings. Kalna pushed to his hands and knees. Glanna didn't offer him a hand for balance, but stood quietly waiting until he was ready; then raising her head, she began to sing.

The melody was strange yet it seemed to vibrate deep within him. The Words of Power concerned the concepts of love and tolerance and an inner knowing of self that would make the paths of life easier to walk.

As Glanna continued to sing, she turned to the line of darklings standing on the crest of the veld. Not one of them moved. She implored them to come and join her using both her mind and her voice. Still no one moved.

Her voice wavered as she looked at Ek-nar. The triumphant smile on his face promised retribution on the single darkling who had dared defy him.

Ek-nar turned and looked at Kalna. He knew he had won. Now he could claim the title of Ra-ling of the Black Forest as soon as he swept this cripple from the Naming Rock.

Ek-nar's thoughts were as clear to Kalna as if he'd spoken aloud. Kalna saw movement out of the corner of his eye as Ek-nar reached for him.

Ard couldn't touch Ek-nar's mind, but somehow he knew that Kalna was in danger. He jumped forward, stiff-armed Jagivan out of the way, and grabbed Ek-nar from behind, locking both arms and one wing down to his sides. As Ard struggled with Ek-nar, Runner and Omecon moved in on Jagivan; neither of them had missed the wierman's earlier actions.

Ek-nar, realizing that he was no physical match for the man who held him, began to sing. The eerie melody that escaped his lips made Kalna suddenly feel ill.

Ard had no idea what Ek-nar was doing, but he had instinct enough to know that whatever it was, it meant no good for anyone but Ek-nar. He held the darkling lord tighter and brought one hand up to cover his mouth, half strangling Ek-nar in the process.

The weirfolk were stunned by the fighting and didn't seem to know what to do. Some of those closest to the Naming Rock stood and moved closer to the combatants, but before any others became caught up in the fight, the bugling sound of a Narian horn was heard, its deep hollow tone capable of carrying for miles.

The Narian horns were few and were used only in times of celebration, war, or danger. Who had blown one of the honored horns and why? No one could tell from which direction the sound had come; it seemed to echo and reecho all around the veld.

There was movement in the ranks of the darklings near the crest of the rise. A path was being made. Suddenly out from behind the darklings strode a creature so beautiful that Kalna caught his breath. He had heard of kimmerlings but had never imagined that he would see one up close.

The kimmerling was manlike from the waist up, but from the hips down his body was that of a loper, four-legged, sleek, and powerful, and just behind his forelegs there stretched a pair of wings, larger and more powerful than those of a darkling. The beast half of the kimmerling was burnished bronze in color, as were his wings; the man half was a deep gold color and spoke of a body caressed daily by the sun.

There was a great stirring among the weirfolk as the kimmerling proceeded down the pathway toward the Naming Rock. Many stood so they might see better; others bowed their heads, honoring the coming of a time-runner few were ever lucky enough to see.

"It's Gamlyn," Thekis said softly, "but I've never known him to appear before so many."

As the kimmerling approached, he put his right arm through the coils of the Narian horn and rested it upon his shoulder. Ek-nar and Ard blocked Kalna's view for a moment, then suddenly the kimmerling stood near the rock no more than an arm's length away. He was a magnificent creature, his ethereal beauty causing tears of joy to spring to the eyes.

Gamlyn gently touched Ard's shoulder. "Ek-nar will behave himself now," he said, his voice soft and pleasing to the ear. "You may release him."

Ard looked into the kimmerling's amber eyes and obeyed without question. He, like everyone else, was spellbound by the great winged being who stood head and shoulders taller than anyone else there. Even the angry Ek-nar stood quietly, eyes wide in awe.

Gamlyn walked a circle around the rock, his glance searching for familiar faces in the crowd. He nodded to several people before returning to stop before Ek-nar and Thekis.

"Welcome to Pavion, Gamlyn," Thekis said, smiling. "You surprise us all with your coming, though, as always, it's a pleasant surprise."

Gamlyn looked down and returned the smile. "It's good to see you again, Thekis. It's been a long time." He turned and looked at Kalna. "I'd heard that a new Ra-ling was to be named this day. I've come to witness the Naming."

Thekis glanced around him and stopped when he reached Ek-nar. "There was to be a Naming, but we are having a slight problem," he began, "and were just about to decide what to do about it."

"There is no problem!" Ek-nar said, recovering his composure as well as his voice. "A Ra-ling will be named this day—but not the one the elders have chosen!"

Gamlyn looked at Ek-nar, now standing well out of Ard's reach. Ek-nar crossed his arms over his chest and stood proudly. "I am Ek-nar," he announced. "I am Ra-ling of the Nikon Plains and I have come here to—"

"You are known to me, Ek-nar," Gamlyn said, interrupting. "What I wish to know is why you have ordered the darklings to stand away and leave Glanna to sing alone."

Ek-nar's gaze shifted to those gathered around, as if daring any of them to refute what he would say. "The darklings won't sing because they don't accept Kalna as Ra-ling of the Black Forest. He is crippled and not fit to..."

Gamlyn took two steps toward Ek-nar. "Kalna is Graya's son and was not born crippled, therefore he has a rightful claim to the title of Ra-ling. The Words of Power will be sung for him today—have already been sung for him in a time where I have walked."

Ek-nar edged back a pace, staying out of the kimmerling's reach. "And I say that the darklings won't sing today!"

"Fool!" Thekis hissed at Ek-nar. "If Gamlyn says that Kalna was named, he means that—"

"The Words of Power need only two voices," Gamlyn said, interrupting Thekis. "If Glanna will sing again, I'll join her. We don't need any of our sister darklings today if it is their wish not to participate."

"That's against our laws!" Ek-nar cried angrily. "The Words of Power must be sung by darklings!"

Gamlyn shook his head. "There is no such law. They may be sung by any who know them!" He waved his hand at Ek-nar. "Go. Leave this place. You are not welcome here today if you cannot accept your brother darkling in love and honor."

The look on Gamlyn's face was too much for Ek-nar. Awed by the mere presence of the kimmerling and not a little frightened by the tone of his voice, he backed away, then turned and stalked up the pathway. When he reached the darklings, three followed him, the rest stayed where they were.

Gamlyn faced Glanna. "You may begin, sister."

Thekis motioned Ard and the others to sit as Glanna's voice rose high and sweet, her strength of purpose and confidence restored by the kimmerling. Gamlyn echoed each and every phrase sung, his voice lower and softer, but still carrying full and clear. It wasn't long before the other darklings on the crest joined in. With Ek-nar gone, they sang freely for Graya's son.

Kalna stood and listened as the Words of Power were

sung to him. He sensed their strength and wisdom and as the last notes faded away, he felt a mantle of peace fall over him.

Gamlyn reached out a hand to him. "From this day forward you shall be called Kalna, Black Fire, Strength of the Night. Come, the ceremony is finished, and you are now Ra-ling of the Black Forest."

Kalna stepped forward, forgetting his injured leg, but before he could stumble, Gamlyn caught him under the arms and lifted him to sit on his back. Thrilled beyond words, Kalna smiled down at Ard, who came to walk beside him as they made their way to the Garden of Eos just a short distance away. When they reached the garden, Kalna was given something warmer to wear, then food and wine were served and the introductions began. One by one each weir who had come to witness his Naming presented himself and welcomed Kalna to Pavion. Sometimes small gifts were offered. While all this was taking place, Thekis and Runner saw that Ard and Raney were fed and entertained at a table nearby. Both men were surprised and pleased by the number of weir who approached them to talk.

A few hours later Kalna saw Gamlyn motion to him. He excused himself from the small crowd gathered around him and went to the kimmerling.

"Walk with me awhile?" Gamlyn invited.

Kalna nodded. "You're going?"

"Yes. I have a friend waiting."

"Another kimmerling?"

"Yes, and she is very impatient sometimes."

Kalna's glance searched the bushes at the edge of the garden. "I would like to meet her."

"Another time perhaps, when there aren't so many people around. She's extremely shy." Gamlyn reached up into the tree and unhooked the Narian horn from a broken branch. He presented the horn to Kalna. "Before I go, I wanted to give you this. His name is Bomorro. It means Hill Sounder. He is very special; his sound literally reverberates through time. Whenever you are in danger or need, hold him high and blow with all your might. Those who are friends will come when you call."

"It's a beautiful gift, Gamlyn. I'll cherish it and guard it well." Kalna looked up at the kimmerling. "Gamlyn, may I ask you a question? Something personal?"

"Ask."

"Back in the veld you spoke of walking in another time where the Words of Power had already been sung for me. Is it true that your people can actually walk back and forth through time, or did you only foresee what was to be?"

Gamlyn smiled. "I can't foresee the future, Kalna, that is for seers to do, but I can go and visit there—not without cost though. A time-runner who overuses his talent ages very quickly because the energy drain is enormous, therefore we don't walk time without a good reason."

"But you were in our future and saw me named Raling?" Kalna pressed.

"I did . . . and saw myself there to sing for you."

"Tell me, what else have you seen?"

"I have seen you older, a leader among the weirfolk."

"What about the Yorrga? Are they in the future, too?"

"Yes."

Kalna's spirits sank. "I had hoped that we could somehow put an end to them. Tell me what they—"

Gamlyn shook his head. "No. If I have learned anything in my years of living, I've learned that it isn't wise for a person locked in time to know his own future—or ending. It destroys the challenge life presents and weakens the spirit to a point where nothing matters. Then, too, the future isn't stable; it's the first thing a time runner learns while traveling. Something I say to you today may actually change tomorrow, another reason why it isn't advisable for me to tell you too much—or anyone, for that matter. Believe me, it's a great temptation to meddle in the affairs of those locked in time."

"But what if you could save someone's life by. . ."

"If I saved one, soon I would try to save all, and life's balance would be lost. If life is to have meaning, death must be allowed its part, Kalna. We time-runners are few in number, and we've made it our policy not to interfere with those who are time locked unless we forgo our talent and take up residence in a certain time; then we are free to mingle and participate in the lives of those we would call friends."

"Does that mean you're going to stay here in our time?"

"My female friend likes this time and I have chosen to share it with her. I think we will be happy here. It is a good time to live."

"I wish I could believe that."

Gamlyn's eyes were soft with understanding. "You are bitter now because you have lost those most dear to you, but one day others will fill the emptiness you feel now. I promise you that. And I know that you'll make a good Ra-ling."

"I wish I had your confidence."

"That, too, will come in time. You have much to learn, Kalna, from weir and men alike. Learn all you can and never close your mind to a new concept or a teacher who doesn't look as others do. Be alert to all around you; even the wind has lessons to teach."

The nearby bushes moved ever so slightly. Gamlyn noticed and took a step away from Kalna. "I believe it's time for me to go now."

"Please, one more question?"

"Ask."

"Is Ek-nar my enemy?"

Gamlyn hesitated, then replied, "Ek-nar is a Ra-ling in his own right and in many eyes that means he can do no wrong, yet I sense a darkness in him. His is a spirit that will brook no interference, and he's not the kind to give up something that he wants, even if another has won it." Gamlyn started away.

"Will I see you again soon?" Kalna called after him.

"I won't be far away. If you need me, ask Thekis. He'll tell you where to find me."

Kalna thought of another question. "Gamlyn, do you know who's behind the killer Yorrga?"

"No, but I have a suspicion. A warning I give you. Neither you nor your new friends must wander the halls of Galen Keep alone. In the future I have seen, it could mean death to you all. Good-bye, Kalna."

Gamlyn was moving away as he spoke the last few words. As he disappeared in between the bushes just a short distance away, Kalna was sure he heard another voice, then all went silent.

He turned back to the garden and saw Ard and Raney walking toward him. Thekis and Runner trailed behind them. It looked as if the celebration was over. Time for him to shoulder new responsibilities, he thought, such as seeing that Ard and Raney were protected during their stay at the keep; and after his operation, he would take it upon himself to continue his battle against the false Yorrga.

Two weeks after Kalna's naming, the warm weather broke and winter arrived with a vengeance. Days of high winds and heavy snows effectively closed all of the mountain trails between Galen Keep and the Breedors.

Ard and Raney, who had been awaiting the Council's permission to leave, were told that they would have to remain at the keep until the spring meltoffs, which would be a good two months away. Neither man was happy with the news for both believed it was just another way to keep them prisoners a little longer.

Raney watched Ard pace the confines of their room. It was larger and more nicely furnished than the cell they'd shared upon their arrival at the keep; still, it seemed very much like their old cell, for there were guards stationed outside the room, guards who attended them wherever they happened to go.

"Ard," Raney said, "why don't we just leave? They keep telling us that we're not prisoners anymore, so let's get some things together and take off. It would be hard going, but not impossible."

"The snow is too deep for lopers," Ard said, coming back around to the right side of Raney's bed, "which means that we'd have to leave afoot and we'd have to carry all of our food and supplies with us. We'd be lucky if we made fifteen to twenty miles a day. It would take us a good month of travel—if we didn't lose our way."

"They might offer us a guide if we insisted upon leaving," Raney offered.

"No. They wouldn't give us anything, because what they really want is for us to stay here until they find these false Yorrga!"

Raney snorted. "If they had moved a little faster when we first told them about the Yorrga, they might have caught them at Rithe's Keep. Where do you suppose the Yorrga went?"

Ard shook his head. "There's no telling. All we can hope is that the snow has stoped them raiding into the Breedors. If it hasn't . . ." Ard left that thought dangling.

He's on edge, Raney thought, watching his friend move about the room. It's not just the Yorrga that has him like this, either. It's Kalna. Raney sipped at the cup of lukewarm tea he'd poured a short time ago and decided to broach the subject that was really bothering Ard.

"Do you think they might let us visit Kalna soon? It's been a full week since they operated."

Ard stopped his restless pacing and dropped into a chair on the other side of the room. His troubled glance touched Raney then slid away. "I spoke to Thekis several hours ago while you were napping. He said that we couldn't visit Ka for several weeks. Right now they're keeping him drugged in order to keep him quiet."

Coldness settled in Raney's stomach. "I thought the operation was successful."

"It was," Ard said. "His leg is not the problem. According to Thekis, Vidlar's work under the guidance of the Yorrga mask went beautifully, and Ka should be walking in six weeks' time."

"So what's wrong?" Raney asked, though he had a suspicion he already knew.

Ard's glance dropped to his clenched fists in his lap. Slowly he forced himself to relax. As he looked at Raney once more, he rubbed the palms of his hands against his thighs.

"Kalna isn't taking the darkling change-over as well as Thekis had hoped he would. He believes it has something to do with Kalna being male, some difference in body chemistry."

"How long will it be before they know . . . how it will be for Kalna?"

"Thekis said that the darkling change can last anywhere from several weeks to three or four months. The longer it takes, the greater the chance of mental damage."

And you? Raney thought, frowning as Ard stood up and began pacing again. What happens to you if Kalna doesn't make it through this crisis? Your linkage with him is stronger than blood, and it frightens you just as it frightens me, yet without it you probably would've died.

As he drank the last of his cold tea and set the cup aside, he couldn't help but reflect upon the Ancients and their creations, for what man could watch a bird dip and float on currents of air and not wonder what it would be like to fly? So one among the Ancients had dreamed of winged men, and darklings were born—but not without a price to pay.

# CHAPTER 20

Kalna swung his right leg back and forth while riding, exercising knee and calf muscles that had grown weak during the months he'd worn a cast of one kind, then another.

Twelve weeks had passed since the operation. Winter had slipped away and the spring sun was quickly melting the snow. The trails weren't clear by any means, but the snow had melted enough so the lopers could travel without too much trouble, and as they made their way down out of the high mountains toward the Lakeland Forests, signs of spring were even more noticeable, with some bushes and trees already showing their buds.

He was happy to be outside again and breathed deeply of the cool fresh air. He had spent many long, wearisome hours virtually a prisoner in his room during the last few months. The worst of that time he couldn't even remember, with bouts of fever and despondency so deep that many despaired of his recovery. Some, he knew, still doubted that he was well enough to be out and around, but Thekis had given in to his insistence that he was feeling well enough to ride with the escort taking Ard and Raney back to the edge of the Breedors.

Thinking back on the winter months he'd lived through, he knew that he might well have succumbed to darkling madness if not for Thekis, Glanna, Runner, Ard, and Raney. It had been Glanna's demand that he be taken off drugs that had been the first step to helping him regain his health; after that, Thekis and Runner had spent hours at his bedside reading and talking to him and telling him fabulous tales that drew his mind away from himself; and finally Ard and Raney had been allowed in to see him. Their mere presence had touched some strange chord within his being, especially Ard, whose piercing blue eyes had demanded he not lie abed like some frail old man but get up and move around and fight the lethargy that seemed to claim his every thought and action. Ard had stirred his pride with a single look and had offered help with a smile and an open hand.

He remembered that moment of reaching out, of catching Ard's hand in his own. A tingle of power and a strength of purpose had coursed through him the moment their hands touched. One week later he was on his feet using crutches again; three weeks later his cast had come off and he was taking his first pain-free steps under Ard's watchful eyes. The weeks that had followed had been good ones as spirit and body regained balance.

He slipped his right foot back into his stirrup and looked ahead to where Thekis and Jylak were breaking trail with their mounts. Ard, Raney, Runner, and Omecon rode behind him.

They had been on the trail for four days and were nearing the northern tip of the Black Lake. They would camp on the border of Bree lands that night and in the morning bid Ard and Raney farewell. The High Council had decided that a small escort would be the best way to ensure the men's safe return to Bree territory. They had left the keep late one night after everyone was abed and had kept to trails that would avoid curious eyes, figuring that the fewer who knew who they were and where they were going, the less chance of anyone connected with the killer Yorrga learning of their plans.

Up until the last week or so, Ard and Raney had shown great patience in the delay of their return home, but as the trails had begun to open up, they had become restless and had finally decided that they couldn't wait any longer. It was everyone's hope that the message Ard and Raney carried to Lord Drian would forestall any open declaration of war that spring. Ard was sure that once he fully explained the situation to his father and the other men who spoke for the Sister Houses, his people would ally themselves with the weirfolk against the killer Yorrga.

During the past few weeks, several of the loo woods wachters had managed to make their way down out of the mountians and into Bree territory, but all had returned to report no news or signs of the killer Yorrga in or around Rithe's Keep or Dar-rel lands.

So where are they? Kalna wondered. Had Alfar sent them deeper into the Lakeland Forests to wreak havoc on more unsuspecting Bree? Or had they gone farther north into unexplored territories? Or worse yet, were they hiding among the Black Forest weir? Thekis had told him that several on the Council were of the opinion that the killer Yorrga had to come from among their own people, but until several were captured, it was mere speculation.

He turned in his saddle and glanced behind him. Ard waved a hand and rode up alongside as the trail widened a little. "Everything all right, Ka?"

Kalna smiled. "Just checking to see that we hadn't lost anyone."

"Not so far," Ard responded cheerily, "though I'd hate to try to get back to Pavion by the trails we've been following. I'm so turned around now that I'm not sure what direction we're headed."

"We're still headed west. We should be at Black Lake in a few hours. Thekis said we would camp on the edge of Bree lands tonight. A three-hour ride tomorrow will bring you to the House of Granfiel."

"We should be safe enough from that point on."

"We could come with you further," Kalna offered.

"No, that isn't necessary. We'll be all right."

"What if Lord Alfar still has men out looking for you?"

"We'll keep our eyes open and we won't linger, I promise.

"Do you think your father will believe the news you carry about Alfar and the killer Yorrga?" he asked, changing the subject. He didn't want to think about Ard leaving.

"I'll make him believe me, Ka! And together your people and mine will track down these killer Yorrga!"

Kalna woke the following morning feeling depressed. Part of it was the cold damp air; part of it was knowing he'd be saying farewell to Ard and Raney. He was going to miss them. Raney had become a good friend, and Ard had become the brother he'd never had.

During and after breakfast, Ard spoke chiefly to Thekis; his tone of voice was brisk as if he was anxious to be on his way. After one or two feeble attempts to be included in the conversation, Kalna went to help Raney and Omecon with the mounts, leaving Jylak and Runner to clean up camp.

A little while later they returned to camp leading the lopers. Raney saw the look on Kalna's face and believed he knew what was wrong. "I'm going to miss you," he said, dropping a hand to Kalna's shoulder, "but we'll be seeing each other again. We aren't going to let any treaty keep us from visiting each other, are we?"

Kalna looked into Raney's eyes and realized the man was trying to cheer him up. "No. We aren't," he said firmly.

Raney mounted, took the food pouch Runner gave him, and fastened it to his saddle. Ard said his good-byes to Thekis and the others and turned to his mount. He paused as he took the reins from Kalna.

"It's been a strange time these past few months," Ard said, "and I've gotten used to having you around. Perhaps when all this is over, we can get together again. I'd like to know more about your people, Ka, and have you get to know mine."

"I'd like that, too. I wish I could come with you now."

Ard's look softened. He reached out and ran a hand down along Kalna's cheek. "You've been more than a good friend to me, Ka. I'll never forget you."

"Nor I you."

Ard leaned forward; his lips brushed Kalnà's forehead, then he turned and mounted. Kalna felt the pressure of tears but somehow managed to hold them back as the two men rode away, their trail south along the edge of the lake.

"Ready to go?" Thekis asked Kalna a few moments later.

Kalna looked down at the dweorg. "It's a mistake, letting them go on alone," he said softly. "We should ride with them."

"All the way to the House of Char?"

"Yes!"

"If what Ard says about his father is true, I doubt we'd be received with open arms."

"No, I suppose not."

"Better for Ard to do some explaining first, I think," Thekis said, catching Kalna's arm. "Come, let's start back. We have a lot to do if we're to going to stop these killer Yorrga."

Kalna resisted the pull on his arm to gaze one last moment at the backs of his friends as they moved into the shelter of some trees. "Thekis?"

"What?"

"I fear for them."

"They'll be safe enough as soon as they reach the House of Granfiel."

Kalna tried to shake off the cold feeling in his gut but

it wouldn't go away. "I feel as if I'm never going to see them again," he said softly, but Thekis didn't hear, for he had gone to mount his loper. Kalna looked one last time to the south, then turned and mounted, knowing the others were waiting for him.

Thekis gave the signal and they started out, Kalna a silent figure riding in the middle, his thoughts on his friends.

They had been several hours on the trail before Kalna broke his silence. "Thekis? What do you think of lahal?"

Thekis turned to look at Kalna, who rode to his right. He had been worried about his silence and was relieved to hear him speak. "It's a talent, Ka, just like any other. I've heard it described as receiving visual premonitions. Is that how it is with you?"

"You know?" Kalna asked, surprised.

Thekis smiled. "Dari told me a year ago. He said it had been giving you some trouble. I told him not to worry, that your control would develop in time."

"I don't feel that I'm in control of anything right now!"

"It's the darkling change, Ka. It will pass. As for lahal, you must always remember that premonitions, visual or otherwise, are always open to interpretation. Why all this about lahal right now? Have you *seen* something?"

"Yes, I think so. Just before Ard and Raney rode out of sight, I saw them entering a dark cave. There was something in the dark with them. It struck them and they fell. Then I'm there, in the dark, and I run. Something follows me. There's blood everywhere and I'm afraid. I hear laughter, insane laughter. Something reaches for me and . . ." Kalna shook himself, as if warding off cold.

"Kalna? Are you all right?"

Kalna nodded. "The *seeing* was like a dream that has haunted me since my parents died, the running in darkness with something behind me. In my dream I'm always looking for Ard and Raney, though I didn't know that at first. Each time I dream the same dream, it becomes a little clearer."

"Everyone dreams, Ka. Dreams are not lahal. It's possible that certain images might cross over from one to the other, I suppose, but..."

Kalna suddenly jerked back on the reins, drawing his loper back on its hind legs. It woofed in pain as Kalna pulled its head around and kicked it in the sides. Runner, who had taken the rear position, reached out and tried to catch the reins to Kalna's mount as he dashed by, but he missed.

"Ka! Stop!" Thekis yelled, turning his mount to follow. "Jylak! Omecon! This way!"

Fearing that darkling madness had once again overtaken Kalna, Runner almost lost his seat as he spun his loper around and started off in pursuit, the other three weir pounding madly after him.

Kalna rode as one possessed. He rode low in the saddle, wings held tight to his back, ducking branches or knocking them aside with arm or shoulder.

Runner was in the lead, but Thekis and Jylak were both much lighter in their saddles and they soon passed the beran and closed on Kalna's mount. Twice, narrow places in the trail forced them to go single file, slowing their headlong rush.

Thekis clenched his teeth in frustration and fear for his nephew. If Kalna's mount slipped...no, he wouldn't let himself think of that! As branches whipped by his face, arms, and shoulders, he prayed to Yaril that Ka would keep his wings tucked. He cursed aloud as visions of tattered, bloody wings caught at him. *Hang on, Ka! Hang on!*

"Kalna, stop!" Jylak yelled. He rode right behind Kalna now but the trail was too narrow for him to pull up alongside without endangering Kalna.

The chase seemed to go on forever, but even the strongest of lopers can't run at top speed for long. Finally the trail widened and Jylak was able to push his mount that extra bit. He reached out and grabbed at the reins to Kalna's mount as he came abreast and pulled back. Kalna hardly seemed aware of what was happening.

The two lopers were brought to a halt and seconds later the others caught up.

"Is he all right?" Runner demanded of Jylak.

"Ka? What happened?" Thekis asked sharply.

There was a dazed, faraway look in Kalna's eyes. It faded slowly, as full awareness returned. Kalna looked at Thekis. "We shouldn't have let them go alone! They've been taken! The Yorrga have them!"

"Ard and Raney?"

"Yes!" Kalna turned to the side and spat, unable to swallow the sour-tasting spittle that filled his mouth. He had known it was a mistake to let them ride off alone. He had known it!

Thekis glanced at the others. It was obvious from their looks that they thought Kalna had been taken by another fit of darkling madness. His glance returned to Kalna. "What do you want us to do, Ka?" he asked, trying to sound calm.

"We have to go after them."

"We've come a long way, Ka. There's a good chance we might not be able to catch up with them now."

"Thekis," Omecon exclaimed. "You're not seriously thinking of going back?"

"They are my friends!" Kalna cried, glaring at the weirman. Omecon shrank back from the blaze of anger he saw in Kalna's eyes.

Kalna had no need to touch the emotions of those around him. The truth was in their faces; they believed him darkling mad. He turned and concentrated on Thekis. "I know what I'm saying, Thekis! I saw it happen. Ard and Raney were attacked by Yorrga."

"Then they are probably dead, Ka," Thekis said gently.

"No! They live. I can feel it!" Kalna grabbed at the dweorg's arm. "You wanted to know who's behind the

Yorrga. Well, this is our chance to find out! Help me rescue Ard and Raney and we'll have our answer!"

"We are too few!" Omecon protested.

"Perhaps," Thekis admitted, "perhaps not." He saw that Kalna was not going to be turned away from this. The others saw it, too. "We could go carefully and at least find out where they're taking Ard and Raney. It may bring us to their leader."

"It would be wise for one of us to go for help," Jylak said. "We could leave a trail for those who follow."

"A good idea." Thekis chose quickly. "Omecon, ride to Gabison and bring back as many as will come. We'll leave a trail but you'll be almost a day behind us at best; it can't be helped. We won't do anything on our own unless we can see our way clear."

"I'll stay," Omecon said. "Send Runner."

"I go where Kalna goes," Runner said firmly.

"No arguments," Thekis said. "You are more familiar with the trails, Omecon. Go now, we'll see you soon."

Omecon nodded; grim-faced, he turned and started back uptrail. They watched him out of sight, each knowing that the chances of his catching up with them before they found the Yorrga were slim.

"All right, Ka," Thekis said. "You take the lead; and let's all pray that when we find these killer Yorrga, they aren't more then we can handle."

# CHAPTER 21

It was late afternoon when they found the place where Ard and Raney had been intercepted. Jylak finished inspecting the hoofprints on the muddy trail and came to stand beside Thekis.

"From all I can tell, Ard and Raney were met by six or seven riders coming from the west. There's no sign of a fight, but that doesn't mean there wasn't one. They may or may not have ridden off willingly. I can't tell."

"Not willingly," Kalna said firmly.

Thekis looked up at Kalna, who had stayed in the saddle. It was obvious from the look on his face that he resented the delay and was ready to push on. "Are you sure it was Yorrga you saw in your sending?"

"Yes!"

"He was right about the two men being stopped by someone," Runner said. "If he says it was Yorrga, I believe him."

"And what if he read the sending wrong?" Jylak asked the beran. "What if they were met by other Bree from

242

the House of Granfiel? If we follow them, we might be walking into a lot of trouble."

"Yorrga or Bree," Thekis said, "I think we'd better make sure, if only for Kalna's peace of mind."

"But what if—"

"We'll go carefully," Thekis said, "and we'll leave trail markers. Omecon will be along as quickly as he can gather help."

The trail led west away from the House of Granfiel, and it continued in the same direction for several hours. That more than anything proved that Ard and Raney had been pulled away from their intended course. Twice the trail ended at the edge of a river. It became clear that the riders were trying to hide their trail. But each time the trail disappeared, Kalna unerringly led them forward, picking up the trail some distance on.

Jylak dropped back to ride beside Thekis. "How does he know where he's going?" he said softly. "Is he using lahal?"

"No. Not right now. I believe he's following something a lot deeper than lahal. It has something to do with the joining he and Ard shared. It's linked them in a way that allows him to sense where Ard is. I've heard of such bondings before but never between man and weir."

Jylak looked ahead to where Kalna and Runner rode side by side. "I hadn't known about the joining. It explains a lot." He turned and looked at Thekis. "Does Kalna understand the full consequences of a joining?"

"Consciously, no, I don't think so. Graya once told me that she and Ka had joined several times, but she had always maintained control and was careful not to let the bonding become too strong. Even so, Kalna's grief over his mother's death might well have caused his own if not for Ard's interference. Such is the risk if the bonding is too firmly entrenched."

"You think that Ard and Kalna might be . . ."

"I don't know, Jylak. I hope not."

"But it is possible."

Thekis frowned at his friend. "All too possible. That's

why we must find Ard before anything happens to him. If he's in the hands of the killer Yorrga and they decide to execute him rather than keep him as a hostage, Kalna might not be able to withstand the emotional shock of his death."

"Is there no way such a bonding can be broken?"

"Not that I know of. Distance at the time of death might help, but I'm not even sure of that. Our best chance of keeping Ka whole and sane is to make sure Ard stays alive."

"If you knew that, why did you let him go back to the Breedors?"

"The Council thought we had to take a chance. Ard is Lord Drian's son and the only one right now who might be able to keep the Bree from declaring war against us, if it isn't too late already."

The ruins of Rithe's Keep looked different in the morning light. Kalna and the others had arrived there late the night before and had sheltered north of the ruins in a heavy copse of pine trees. Here the snow was almost gone, but the ground was still saturated with runoff and squished at every step.

Kalna looked down at the plumes of smoke rising about the ruins, his face grim. Either the Yorrga had just recently returned, or the loo woods wachters sent to investigate had lied to the Council.

He sensed someone behind him. His special awareness told him that it was Runner. He turned. "Anything wrong?"

The beran shook his head. "Thekis sent me to find you."

"And to make sure I wasn't doing something foolish, like scouting the Yorrga camp," Kalna finished for him. He raised a hand as Runner opened his mouth to reply. "Don't deny it," Kalna said ruefully. "I know my uncle too well."

Runner smiled. "As he knows you." He glanced down at the encampment. "Is your friend still there?"

"Yes. I can feel him. Raney must be there, too. I'd like to get a little closer to make sure though."

"Thekis wouldn't like that."

"I know."

Runner caught Kalna by the arm. "Come, let's go back and find something to eat. Maybe Thekis has some plan we don't know about."

Reluctantly Kalna stepped back into cover and turned and followed the beran back to their secluded camp. Both Thekis and Jylak were awake and angry that Kalna had slipped away without telling someone.

"We can't chance being seen," Thekis admonished him, "not if we want to end this thing once and for all. If the killer Yorrga are alerted, they'll only scatter and re-assemble somewhere else, and at the moment we are too few to prevent it. We have to wait for Omecon. I'm sending Jylak back to meet him and warn him about what we've found here."

"And the three of us just sit and wait," Kalna muttered.

"Yes," Thekis said firmly.

"And what about Ard and Raney?" Kalna demanded, his wings vibrating slightly beneath his cloak. "What if Lord Tennebar is doing to them what he did to me?"

"Ka, stop and think a moment," Thekis said. "You've been telling us that you can feel Ard. If they were doing anything to him, wouldn't you feel it?"

"Yes, I think so," Kalna agreed, sitting down on a log next to Jylak, "but I don't like the thought of waiting here until it's too late. I'd at least like to know where they're keeping Ard and Raney before any fighting starts."

"We'll try to locate them, Ka, I promise," Thekis said, "but we must be careful. Jylak, why don't you get started? Find Omecon and those he gathered and bring them here as quickly and quietly as you can. While you're gone, we'll do some scouting around."

* * *

The air was cold and the sky clear as night fell over the ruins. A full moon lay low in the southern sky giving light where it wasn't wanted.

Kalna moved carefully step by step along one of the inside walls, staying to the shadows wherever possible. He had passed close to three of the enemy campfires searching for hints of Ard's or Raney's aura, but had not as yet been successful in finding them. He could feel Ard in the vicinity but couldn't seem to locate him precisely.

Suddenly a form loomed out of the darkness in front of him. He dropped silently to the ground and remained motionless. Moonlight touched a Yorrga mask; it was a long-tongue, alone and wary.

Suddenly another Yorrga appeared; it was a crooked-mouth. "What's wrong?" he asked.

Kalna held his breath as Long-tongue took another step closer. If he looked down . . .

The Yorrga stood quietly listening and watching the movements of the weirmen in and around the shelters. Some were masked, others not. "I thought I saw something moving out here."

"I don't see anything," Crooked-mouth said. "Maybe it was a bird."

"Not a bird," Long-tongue said. "It was bigger than a bird."

"A wild velhund perhaps."

"I don't know, but whatever it was, I think it's still near."

Puddles of snow-melt quickly penetrated Kalna's clothes, and silently he cursed his own stubbornness in getting so close. If he was caught, the Yorrga would be alerted and whatever advantage they'd have gained by a surprise attack would be lost.

Crooked-mouth turned around. "Well, whatever you saw has gone now. Come back to the fire and finish our game."

"I think the Master should be told."

"What? That you saw a shadow? Don't be a fool!

He's busy making plans with Alfar. He wouldn't like to be interrupted."

"Maybe not, but I'm going to tell him that I saw some-*thing* or some*one* skulking in the ruins. It could be that someone was following the Bree."

"We covered our trail!"

"You've grown overconfident. The Master would not approve."

Crooked-mouth grabbed at Long-toungue's shirt. "And you'll tell him, I suppose?"

Long-tongue knocked the hand away. "Perhaps I will! Get out of my way!"

Kalna froze as Long-tongue started toward him. Three more steps and ...

"Wait!" Crooked-mouth cried. He grabbed Long-tongue's arm and turned him around. "I didn't mean that you shouldn't tell him what you saw. I was just trying to save you from bothering the Master with something you weren't sure about."

Kalna raised his head slightly and slowly wormed his way back into deeper shadow. The two Yorrga argued a moment longer, then both passed by Kalna, heading straight for the tower that stood in the center of the ruins. Kalna watched them enter the door at the base of the tower, then he stood and moved back around the end of the wall. Minutes later he was back in the safety of the forest heading for camp.

Thekis literally pounced on Kalna when he returned to their camp. "Where have you been?" he demanded angrily, spacing his words. "We were to have met back here over two hours ago! We were sure you'd been captured by the Yorrga!"

Kalna pulled his arm out of Thekis's grasp and untied the sash holding his cloak around him. One glance at the empty camp had told him that Jylak hadn't returned with Omecon and the others. He had hoped they might be there.

"I got too close to one of their campfires and had to stay put for a little while or risk being seen," he said, as he took his cloak off and hung it over a nearby branch.

Once free of the cloak he was able to stretch his wings. They were already a half arm's length long and growing stronger by the day.

"I warned you about getting too close," Thekis growled.

"I know and I didn't listen," Kalna admitted. "I'm sorry, but I had to find out where Ard and Raney are being held."

"Did you?"

"Not exactly, but I think they may be somewhere in the tower because that's where Alfar and Lord Tennebar were meeting, according to two Yorrga I overheard talking."

Thekis looked at his nephew and shook his head. "Too young for caution, too old to scold" was the saying, and at that moment it fit Kalna perfectly. For the hundredth time in the past few months he wished that Dari and Graya still lived and that he didn't have responsibility for this young, impulsive darkling whom he loved as much as one of his own children. He was getting too old to play the role of teacher and father; but if he didn't do it, who would? Jarad perhaps with Glanna's help. No, that wouldn't work. Kalna was too old to accept Glanna's mothering and Jarad was too weak to control and guide the impetuous and talented spirit that could one day make Kalna a leader among the weirfolk. "If he lives long enough," he said softly.

Kalna looked at Runner, who was chewing contentedly on a piece of dried meat. "Did you see anything of Ard or Raney?"

The beran shook his head, the moonlight glinting off his horns. "No, but I did see a contingent of men arriving."

"Lord Alfar and his men."

"Probably," Runner said. "I also found out where they're keeping their mounts."

"Good," Thekis said. "We'll have to loose and scatter them when we attack. The ruins are too open to try to surround them, so when we move in, it will have to be fast. Let's just hope that Omecon found enough weir to do this right."

Kalna unrolled his blanket and sat down. He couldn't see Thekis under the shadow of the pine he'd chosen for his shelter, but he could feel him. Thekis was worried and his body ached, old muscles protesting abuse. Kalna had to admit that he, too, was worried, for them as well as Ard and Raney.

"Thekis, how many of us do you think it will take?" he asked.

"To disrupt the Yorrga, or to stop them?"

"Either. Both."

"Well, we've counted approximately forty-five men and weir down in the Yorrga camp, but we have no way of knowing if this is their only camp. Alfar must have a couple of hundred more men at his command, but he has to keep some of them at the House of Dar-rel to maintain the facade of being on the Bree's side." Thekis hesitated a moment before continuing. "I think we could disrupt things here with thirty or so. By that I mean kill and scatter those down in the ruins and rescue Ard so he can carry the truth back to his father and end Lord Alfar's end in this business. As for stopping the Yorrga completely, that isn't going to be as easy, because before we stop them, we're going to have to find out precisely who they are and what they want—besides war with the Bree—and that means that we have to capture some of them alive."

"How many of us would that take?"

"Fifty, sixty, maybe a hundred."

"Will Omecon be able to gather that many?"

"I doubt it, especially this time of year when so many migrate to Galen Keep or Endwall. We'll be lucky if he turns up with thirty or forty."

Kalna had never been in a battle before, had never used a knife or weapon of any kind in other than his own defense. The thought of going up against men, weir, and Yorrga who seemingly killed without compunction made him feel sick inside. Then a scene came to mind: his father sprawled in death, his mother dying, his home burning, and the Yorrga leering at him from the doorway. Slowly the sickness dissolved leaving anger in its place. He hadn't sorted out in his mind how one Yorrga mask could heal while another could kill, but he was determined to know the truth, and if knowing the truth meant that he would have to become a killer also, then so be it!

# CHAPTER 22

They came early the next afternoon, filtering in under the trees like shadows, moving quietly as they entered camp. Thekis and Kalna met Jylak and Omecon first, then greeted the others, thanking them for coming. Kalna counted twenty-four weir. Jylak said there were three more staying with the mounts a short distance away. Not as many as they had hoped for.

Kalna looked down at Thekis and read the concern in his eyes. "We'll just have to do the best we can, Ka. Go find Runner. We'll have to begin making plans."

Several hours passed. The watches were changed. Food was brought out and eaten as plans were laid. Kalna marveled at the quiet efficiency of the weir who had answered Omecon's call. Seven were beran; three were faun; three were dweorg; one was leondar; and the rest were weirmen and weirwomen. Kalna was startled for a moment when he first saw the two female beran and the three weirwomen enter camp, but acceptance came quickly, for he knew none of them would be there if they didn't understand exactly what was going on and weren't prepared to fight.

He remained silent during most of the discussions, leaving Thekis, Jylak, and Omecon to do the planning. When all was said and done, the final plan was simple: They would divide into three groups; one group would circle around to the west, scatter the Yorrga's mounts, and enter the ruins from what once had been the main courtyard; the second and third groups would enter the ruins from the east and south and strike at the small camps on the perimeter of what was left of the main keep and then make for the center of the ruins and the tower where it was believed that Ard and Raney were being held.

Thekis stressed the importance of taking prisoners but cautioned against leaving too many alive. "We're outnumbered and we'll have to move quickly. We need a few prisoners alive to give us information on just how big this Yorrga thing has become, but guard yourself first and don't hesitate to kill if you can't capture. The enemy is in greatest strength around the tower."

"Once we hit the outer camps, those near the tower will be ready for us," the leondar said.

"All the more reason not to worry about prisoners until we hit the center," Thekis said. "As it is, we're apt to be jumping into a nest of spitter snakes that will eat us alive if they get the chance. There are four among us authorized to signal a retreat. Listen hard and move quickly if you hear the nalcra's cry. If there's no chance of finishing what we start here, we'll have to regroup and decide what to do next."

"What happens if the two we're trying to rescue are dead already?" A beran asked.

Thekis turned to Kalna, who stood to answer, his cloak slipping off his shoulders. "They live," he said firmly.

"You saw them?" the beran pressed.

Kalna took the question as a challenge and unconsciously his wings opened wide. "I felt them!"

Not until that moment had any of the weirfolk realized just who the handsome youth was. The whispered words "Ra-ling" and "empath" could be heard passing from mouth to mouth as the weir looked at Kalna. There was awe on some faces, excitement on others; before them stood their new Ra-ling—one day, perhaps, their leader.

Kalna took two steps backward, overwhelmed by the magnitude of the emotional surge pouring toward him, for it was like a great wall of water washing up against his face and leaving him breathless.

A strong hand caught at his arm, giving him support. "Kalna, are you ill?"

Kalna recognized Runner's voice. He shook his head and tried to breathe deeply, pushing back at the cloud of joy, reverence, and awe that had all but engulfed him. Moments later he managed to regain his equilibrium by concentrating on his uncle's face.

Thekis saw the dazed look in Kalna's eyes and realized what was wrong. He stood up and clapped his hands softly for attention. "We all know what we are to do. Prepare your weapons and make sure you know who runs at your side, so that when the fighting begins, you know friend from enemy, for not all of the Yorrga go masked. We'll move when it begins to grow dark and try to catch them at their suppers. Go quickly and quietly and listen for the battle cry from the west. That will be the signal for everyone to move in."

Thekis took Kalna off to one side as the weirfolk began to divide into groups. There was a worried look on his face. "Are you all right, Kalna?"

"I am now," Kalna replied, keeping his glance fixed on Thekis.

The dweorg looked up knowingly. "Your gift is growing stronger, isn't it?"

"I don't know that I'd call it a *gift*," Kalna mumbled. "That last surge almost smothered me!"

"You're maturing physically and mentally, Ka, and your gifts, whatever they are, are also growing. Being an empath isn't easy, but there are ways to protect yourself. When all of this is over, I'm sending you to a special teacher, one who'll help you cope with what you are becoming; but for now, you'll just have to do the best you can. I think it might be best if you stay behind and leave the fighting to us. The forces within you are all peaking now and—"

"No! I'll not be left behind! We are too few in number. I know I'm not seasoned in battle, but I can follow orders and I know how to use a knife—and if anyone can find Ard and Raney in that tower, it's me!"

"Ka," Thekis said gently, "you are our Ra-ling now. If anything should happen to you, I—we would never forgive ourselves, nor would anyone forgive us."

Kalna glanced at Runner, who stood to one side listening quietly. The beran's eyes were steady. Almost as if he could touch Kalna's thoughts, he gave him a quick tip of the head.

Kalna took the nod as a signal not to give up. He turned back to Thekis, his wings stretched out as if for battle. "Uncle, you once told me that Ra-lings were leaders. Leaders don't stay behind. I *am* going with you and I *will* fight!"

Thekis shook his head in defeat, then glanced at Runner. "You were a big help!"

Runner's eyebrows raised in dismay. "I didn't say a word!"

"Take that offended look off your face," Thekis growled. "You know exactly what I mean. And just for being so supportive of Kalna's position, I'm making him your responsibility! When the fighting starts, you'll guard him with your life; if he comes to any harm, you may be sure that you'll answer to me *personally*! Understood?"

"I would have it no other way," Runner answered proudly.

"And you!" Thekis snapped, pointing a finger at Kalna. "You will not take any chances down there!

You'll keep your wits about you and you'll follow my orders!"

"Agreed," Kalna said meekly.

Thekis gave the two a look, then stalked off, muttering to himself.

"He's a crusty old terrapin," Runner observed, smiling at Thekis's back, "but I like him."

"So do I," Kalna said. "He reminds me of my father."

The shadows were growing deep around the ruins as the weirfolk moved into position. The smell of woodsmoke from cooking fires was pungent on the air. The sky was clear, its dark blue promising a cold night.

Kalna crouched nervously between Thekis and Runner behind the cover of an overgrown hedge only twenty paces away from a crumbling wall. He peered around behind him and was amazed to see only two of the nine in his group. The others had all disappeared, working their way closer to their targets. The soft rustle of the wind stirring the dry leaves on the trees helped to cover their movements.

The flutter in Kalna's stomach had worked its way up to his throat. He checked his knife for the fiftieth time and hefted the short sword one of the weir had given him. In the past two days Runner had shown him how to parry and block a sword thrust and how to attack up under another's guard, but there had been little time for practicing such maneuvers.

Thekis watched Kalna out of the corner of one eye and tried not to look worried. This was no place for the untried, he thought. Kalna had proved to be a survivor and a tenacious one at that; but all it would take was one small mistake and the life he held so dear would be lost.

Kalna felt Runner's hand on his arm. The beran was pointing off to their right. Someone from the ruins had stepped out to answer nature's call. The man or weir, it was too far to tell which, stopped near a bush. He started to undo his belt, then froze. A second later he spun around and darted back toward the ruins; but before he could open his mouth to yell a warning, an arrow drove into his back, flinging him forward to the ground.

Kalna braced himself against the wave of pain coming from the enemy who was down but not dead. It was a man; he was sure now. He shuddered as the man tried to crawl toward safety, terrible mewling sounds escaping his lips.

Someone among the weir darted out from behind the bushes toward the downed enemy. It was the leondar. He reached the man, lifted his head, and made one deft stroke across his neck. Seconds later the leondar was back among the bushes and the enemy's body lay still in the grass.

Kalna drew a deep breath and released it slowly, free of the man's pain but now fully aware of how vulnerable he was. There had to be a way for him to shut off the emotions of others. If he couldn't . . .

He was startled out of his thoughts by a surge of excitement coming from all those around him. A weir battle cry cut the air, and suddenly his comrades burst from their hiding places and raced across the open ground into the ruins.

"Stay close to me, Ka!" Thekis yelled, as he slipped through the bush barrier. "Runner?"

"Right beside him!" the beran answered, pushing through the bushes in Kalna's wake.

Kalna remembered little of that run through the ruins or the frantic scrambling climb over the grass-covered hill of rubble protecting the southernmost camp of the enemy. It was all a blur of weir bodies hurtling ahead of him, and uneven ground, and treacherous pits that had once been cellars. He slipped and felt someone catch his arm, lift him up, and push him onward. It had to be Runner, though he didn't turn to check.

As he crested the rise, he saw two things: the battle raging off to his left near the courtyard, and his comrades running silently downslope into the enemy camp where men, Yorrga, and enemy weir were milling around, some searching for weapons, others starting for the courtyard not realizing that they were being attacked on more than one front. By the time they did see their danger, it was too late for them.

The weirfolk who ran with Kalna were in among the enemy so swiftly, cutting and slashing, that few of the enemy managed to survive the initial attack; those who did, fought back fiercely. Two wore Yorrga masks.

Kalna followed Thekis down into the battle, his own emotions now running so high that, for the moment, they effectively blocked the barrage of emotions coming from those around him. He saw one of his comrades go down, his head nearly cleft from his shoulders by a slashing stroke of a sword. The Yorrga who wielded the sword gave a triumphant cry and turned, his glance catching Kalna, who hurtled toward him.

Kalna saw the Yorrga shift his stance but never broke stride. The Yorrga threw himself to the left to avoid Kalna's blade as he darted past; then he recovered and met Kalna face to face as Kalna turned. Kalna ducked and heard the enemy's sword whistle past his head. He lunged in under the Yorrga's arm as Runner had taught him, his knife thunking solidly into flesh. The Yorrga screamed defiance and brought his sword back around, catching Kalna with the flat of it on the shoulder; but Kalna was moving away and the glancing blow did little more than throw him off stride. He stumbled, went to his knees, and was up again as Runner appeared beside him.

"Well done!" the beran cried, as they ran after the rest of their group who were headed toward the center of the ruins and the tower. "Remember! In and out quickly! Don't stand and trade blows with them!"

"I remember," Kalna answered, as he glanced back and saw the Yorrga down on his knees clutching his stomach. Other bodies lay scattered around. He looked forward and counted six left in his group not counting himself. He saw the leondar, Jylak, Runner, and two others he recognized, one a female beran, one a faun. Where was Thekis?

Then there was no time to wonder where anyone was

for they hit another of the enemy camps. Their momentum carried them halfway through the enemy line before they were stopped. There were three Yorrga in this camp and a good dozen weirmen, all waiting and ready for them. The fighting was vicious and deadly; two more of their number fell—Jylak and the faun.

Kalna heard Runner shout something, then found himself locked in combat with a weirman who attacked him from the side. He received a bad cut on his left arm and lost his sword. He parried another blow with his knife and as pain ate into the frenzy of battle madness, he began to feel the anger, hate, fear, and pain of those around him. He faltered and went to a knee.

The weirman moved in. Kalna saw his danger and acted without thinking. He lunged upward as the weirman began to bring his sword down in a two-fisted hold. Kalna's shoulder slammed into the weirman's stomach and they fell together. The weirman's head slammed back against a broken wall of the ruins; the sound of his head cracking against stone made Kalna's stomach twist. The weirman shuddered and went still.

Kalna pushed away from the body and staggered to his feet. He turned and saw a long-tongue Yorrga coming toward him. He felt his death in the other's elation, and dropped back as the Yorrga's sword whistled past his face. That move brought disaster, for he tripped over the body of the weirman he'd just killed.

Long-tongue brought his sword around, raised it once more—then suddenly Runner struck him from behind, his sword driving into the Yorrga's back. The Yorrga turned halfway around, tried to lift his sword, then crumbled.

Runner saw the blood on Kalna's tunic and leaped the Yorrga's body. "Are you all right?" he demanded harshly.

Kalna tried to answer, but the overload of pain and hate coming from the still-living Yorrga and Runner's own anxiety and fear for him was pushing him to the brink of unconsciousness.

"Kalna!"

Kalna gritted his teeth against the conflicting emotions and opened his eyes. "Arm wound—not bad," he gasped. "Other's pain—hate—can't think—can't breathe!"

The beran looked around, searching for a safe place to hide Kalna. The fighting was at its worst near the main tower doors where men, weir, and Yorrga had all come together, but things were quieter over near a crumbled opening in a wall connected to the tower. Runner caught Kalna up and pushed him over his shoulder. He strode over dying men and weir and worked his way around several combatants until he found what looked like a safe place and let Kalna down from his shoulder. He didn't like the whiteness of Kalna's face nor the look of his bloodied arm, but there wasn't time to do anything about either. He caught at a piece of Kalna's tunic, ripped it apart, wrapped it twice about Kalna's arm, and told him to hold it tight.

"Here's my extra knife," he growled. "Now stay here out of the way and don't move. No one will see you if you stay quiet. I'll be back as soon as I can!"

Kalna felt Runner's conflicting loyalties, one to him, the other to his friends who looked to be fighting a losing battle. "Go!" he said, pushing Runner's hands away. "I'll be all right!"

Runner hesitated, then glanced out to where most of the fighting was taking place. He turned back. "Promise you'll stay here?"

Kalna winced at the thrust of compulsion Runner aimed at him and nodded. The beran gave one last glance at him and then was running across open ground, throwing himself back into the battle.

Kalna began to breathe a little freer with Runner gone. He still tasted the conflicting emotions of those doing battle and those who lay dying, but none were so close that he was overwhelmed by them. He looked down at his arm; it throbbed with the beat of his blood but at that moment it was a little hurt compared to the hurts of those dying in the ruins.

He watched the fighting and saw both men and weir fall. Thoughts of cowardice entered his mind as he realized that he didn't want to go back out and fight. He remembered the feel of his knife sinking into living flesh and again felt the pain he had caused in his few brief minutes of fighting. Tears welled in his eyes and trickled down his cheeks as he wept for those whom he would never know, for those whom he might have called friend had he a chance to know them better.

Sick with the sight of killing, he looked away and, in turning, saw that the hole where he sat opened out into a partially destroyed hall. A moment later he realized that the hall had to lead directly into the tower unless it was blocked by fallen rubble. Thoughts of the tower reminded him of why they all were there.

He closed his eyes and sent his awareness outward, searching for signs of Ard or Raney. He was closer now. Perhaps he could—He recoiled as he touched pain; he shifted his focus off to one side and continued his search, weaving a pattern through the emotional surges given off by those standing in his path.

Suddenly he felt Ard...it was one aura he would never mistake! He stood and stepped through the wall and moved left down the hall. The battle outside slowly dimmed, but within the ruined keep and its tower there was pain and death aplenty as the wounded enemy tried to find safety behind walls of stone.

He went forward keeping to the side of the wall where the shadows mirrored night.

Runner heard the weirfolk call for retreat. Several small wounds bled freely down his fur; none were life-threatening. He backed away from the weirman he'd just stabbed and turned, darting back to the place where he'd left Kalna. Searching along the wall as he ran, he sighted the hole in the wall and saw something moving. He ran faster, afraid someone had found Kalna. When he reached the hole he found it empty. He saw the darkness beyond and plunged into it, ready to do battle. No one was there; then something moved in the shadows.

"Kalna!" he hissed softly.

"Runner?"

Runner shot down the hall and caught Kalna by his arms. "Come! They've called us to retreat!"

"But Ard's here! I can feel him!"

"No matter. We have to go back!"

Suddenly Kalna stiffened, his hands clamping tight on Runner's arms.

Runner saw Kalna's teeth flash in the semilight; it was a grimace of pain. "Kalna! What's wrong?"

"Ard!" Kalna gasped. "They're hurting him!" He tore from Runner's grip and ran down the hall toward the center tower. "This way!"

"No, Kalna! No!" Runner cried, darting after him. He was only a step or two away from Kalna as they reached the central tower. One glance at the large open doors and the confusion of men and weir still fighting there and he realized that some had not heard the signal for retreat.

Runner looked down at the weapon in his hand and realized the havoc he could wreak on the enemy from behind, but he also knew he would die doing it; then he saw Kalna darting from pillar to pillar along the back half of the hall, unarmed but for a knife and all but helpless when struck by close emotional surges. He cursed under his breath and started after him, imitating his progress behind enemy lines and praying that Yaril would protect them both. He was halfway across the back hall when he saw Kalna dart down a stairway that led below ground. He reached the stairway moments later and plunged down into the darkness after Kalna. He smelled smoke and went on more quickly, using the wall for a guide. He was sure he heard the sound of Kalna's booted feet ahead.

Twice he smelled fresh air and saw the glimmer of a darkening sky above. He bypassed a dozen open doorways that had to lead to underground rooms throughout the ruins. He ignored them all and continued on down the main corridor. Suddenly the sound of Kalna's footsteps ceased.

He hurried forward. "Kalna?" he whispered.

There was no reply, then Kalna's voice came out of the darkness. "Here, Runner."

"Here where?"

"Straight ahead."

Runner walked forward ten or so steps and felt something brush his arm. He caught at Kalna's hand. Relief and anger mixed as he demanded, "How did you know it was me?"

"I *felt* you. Your aura is almost as easy for me to read as Ard's and Raney's."

"Is that what you're doing? Following Ard's aura?"

"Something like that. He's close. I can feel him."

"You said he was hurt? Can you tell how badly?"

"No. All I know is that he's in pain. We've got to find him!"

"All right. We can try. We certainly can't go back the way we came. Lead on."

"I can't," Kalna cried. "There's something in the way. I get the impression of a door, but it doesn't feel like a door and I can't find any handle or hinge."

"We need light. Have you any matches?"

"No, but maybe we don't need them. Help me out of my tunic," Kalna said. "I can give us light but I need something to burn."

"Darkling fire? No, Kalna, not while you're in darkling change!"

"Why not?" Kalna snapped, dropping his tunic at his feet.

"You could hurt yourself—the stress, the use of darkling energy—it might do you permanent harm!"

"No more harm than Ard's death!" Kalna shot back. "I can feel him, Runner—more than anyone I've ever felt before. If he dies, I don't think I could stand it. We have to reach him! We have to!"

Runner heard the desperation in Kalna's voice. "All right, go ahead, but please be careful."

Kalna hardly waited for the words to leave Runner's mouth. He dropped to his knees before the small pile of cloth and concentrated, drawing on his inner energy. He felt it course up and down his spine; then it moved to his arms and fingertips. No spark this time, but a gout of flame that ignited the tunic in a flash fire and lighted the small chamber they were in. It looked to have been used as some kind of a wine cellar; old racks lay propped against the side walls and off to one side was a series of five large vats turned on their sides; all were green with moss.

Kalna pointed to one of the side walls. "Look there."

Runner went to the stone wall and quickly searched for seams. He found several but nothing that looked like a door; then he saw a slight out-jutting of rock like a narrow lintel. He reached up and ran his fingers along the rock.

The light began to dim. "Find anything?" Kalna asked softly. Suddenly he felt light-headed and very tired.

"No," Runner answered without turning. "Wait! I found something, a lever I think." He pushed the small lever to the right but nothing happened. He tried the left. There was an audible clicking sound and a section of the stone wall turned on a central pivot.

Runner peered into the passage beyond.

"It looks like some kind of an escape route."

# CHAPTER 23

"I smell blood," Runner whispered, as they reached a bend in the dark underground tunnel. "Keep your knife handy and be ready to use it."

Kalna also smelled blood and it made him sick inside, for he knew it was Ard's blood. He could feel him somewhere ahead; he was in pain and teetering on the brink of unconsciousness, yet he held on, suffering in silence and searching desperately for a way to escape. Raney was there, too, though his aura wasn't as strong. Like Ard, he projected pain but not on the same level as Ard.

"Both men are hurt," he told Runner softly. "Ard worse than Raney. They search for a way out."

"Which could mean they're locked away somewhere or still in the hands of the Yorrga. If we corner whoever has them, they'll probably try to use them as hostages."

"Do you think it's Alfar who has them?"

"It's possible. Judging from what you've said about him, I wouldn't put it past him to leave his men to fight while he slips away to safety. We'd better go slowly from this point on."

Runner kept a hand on Kalna's shoulder as they continued on, trusting Kalna's uncanny ability to keep to a trail he couldn't see. They turned another corner and suddenly he felt a cool draft of air on his face. Ahead he could see a break in the darkness. When they reached the light, it showed them a stone stairway that led upward. Runner stepped around Kalna and started up the steps.

"Not that way," Kalna said. "This way." He pointed down the tunnel winding its way farther and farther from the ruins.

"Are you sure, Kalna?"

"Yes. Some may have escaped that way, but Ard and Raney were taken this way."

Runner hesitated, torn between following Kalna back into the darkness and taking him to safety—by force if necessary. But before he could decide, Kalna turned and moved down the tunnel. Runner cursed under his breath and went after him, catching up a few running strides later.

"Kalna, this isn't wise. We should get out while we have the chance. Go for help and ..."

"There isn't time!" Kalna hissed softly. "Leave if you want, but I'm going on. Ard needs me!"

"All right," Runner said, surrendering. "I'll come, but if anything happens to you..."

"It's on my own head! Now be quiet. I think I see light ahead!"

The tunnel ended at an open doorway similar in design to the one that hid the upper section of the passageway. They crouched at the doorway and peered inside. The room beyond was long and dark with shadows. The only light came from the far end where several torches burned brightly. Thick pillars of stone upheld interlocking stone arches that went the full length of the cavernlike room. To the right there were what looked like storage shelves and long tables attached to the walls. On the tables stood bottles and wooden boxes and strange-looking glass shapes that defied naming. To the left there was an area that held chairs, a table, and a bed; living quarters for someone.

Kalna sensed great age in the room and an alienness that set the hairs on the back of his neck upright. Unlike the rest of the tunnelway, the room did not feel damp. What was this place? he wondered. Who had lived here?

Runner slipped past Kalna and moved into the room, stopping behind one of the pillars. He signaled Kalna to stay where he was then he sidled on to the next pillar, slowly working his way toward the far side of the room.

Kalna hesitated, then followed. Ard's need drew him as surely as sun drew water.

Runner glanced back, frowning when he saw Kalna coming up behind him. He waited until Kalna reached his side and caught at his arm. "Stay here!" he commanded softly.

Kalna shook his head. He felt Runner's frustration as a deep thrumbing resonance within his mind and knew that the beran wanted nothing more than to get them both out of there. But he wasn't about to go, not without Ard and Raney.

His glance went past Runner. There was something on one of the tables along the wall; it was a head—no, not a head, a mask—a Yorrga mask! And there was another and another, all standing in a row. He pointed and Runner turned to look.

It suddenly dawned on Kalna where they were. "Yaril's Grotto!" he hissed softly. "Runner, it's—"

Runner turned and quickly put his hand across Kalna's mouth, for suddenly voices could be heard coming from the far end of the room. There was a moment of silence, then the voices were raised again. It sounded like some kind of an argument.

Runner hefted his sword, looked once more at Kalna, then silently glided out toward the next pillar. Kalna followed. Two more pillars closer and they were able to see the other occupants of the room. One was Raney, who stood next to a table, his arms lashed to his sides. Ard lay at his feet, untied but in no condition to cause any trouble; his eyes were closed and his tunic front was dark with blood. Near them stood one of Alfar's men, a burly, dark-haired man with a bloody rag tied around his upper arm. Beyond him, standing near another dark doorway, were a Yorrga, Lord Alfar, and Jagivan, a golden mask dangling from his right hand. In his left hand he held a book that seemed to be what he and Lord Alfar were arguing about.

Jagivan was Gold-mask, who was also Lord Tennebar! Queasiness crept up from the pit of Kalna's stomach as he realized the full implications of Jagivan's role in the Yorrga uprising. He shook his head, unable to understand what would drive the weirman to claim the name of Darkness and jeopardize the very existence of the weirfolk with war. Fast on the heels of that thought was another that was equally disturbing: Was Ek-nar involved in his brother's plotting and bid for power? If so, it might explain why he had tried to have himself named Ra-ling of the Black Forest.

Lord Alfar's voice suddenly rose in anger. "And I say that what you hold will be safer with me! This place is lost to us now! We must hide the master control and all pertaining to it somewhere where no one will look. And I know a place!"

"No!" Jagivan snapped. "It stays with me! I'm now Guardian of Yaril's knowledge!"

"You'll be guardian of nothing once your people find this place and take it back!"

"This place is nothing without this!" Jagivan cried, holding the book out. "Here lies the power of the Ancients, and I alone know how to use it!"

"Enough!" Lord Alfar shouted. "Keep the mask and the book, but come with me now before the weirfolk find us!"

"You fear them!" Jagivan gloated. "You who said they were nothing more than misshapen animals!"

"Never mind what I fear! Let's go! If we take the escape route, we can circle around and see what's happening back at the tower without exposing ourselves. Who knows, we may even be winning."

Jagivan raised the gold mask and placed it on his face. "It's entirely possible. The Yorrga I've trained will fight until they die."

Lord Alfar turned and looked at Ard and Raney. "What about them?"

"I had hoped to use them, but Ard is dying and the other is of little account," Jagivan said, his voice deeper and hollow sounding with the mask on. He turned to the Yorrga standing nearby. "Kill them!"

Raney heard the order and stepped forward over Ard's body, intent upon defending him in any way he could.

As the Yorrga drew his sword and started toward the condemned men, Kalna sprang up and raced across the floor. Runner gasped in surprise and darted out after him.

Lord Alfar's man had stepped back a pace to give the Yorrga room, then he turned at the sound of Kalna's footsteps and saw someone hurtling toward him out of the shadowed part of the room. He reached for his sword but never got it free. The momentum of Kalna's charge carried him straight into the man, his knife thrust deep and clean.

The Yorrga spun around and saw Kalna and the man fall together. Before he could react, he caught movement out of the corner of his eye and brought his sword up and around just in time to meet Runner's attack.

Both Alfar and Jagivan spun around. Alfar hesitated a moment, then seeing that it was only two who had attacked them, he ran toward the battle, drawing his sword. Jagivan slipped his precious book into a pouch at his belt and followed Alfar.

Kalna saw them coming and tried to jerk his knife free, but the blade was wedged in between the man's ribs. His hands grew slick with blood. Desperate, he gave up and reached for the man's sword, still in its sheath.

"Kalna! Look out!" Raney cried, as Lord Alfar slid to a halt and brought his sword around in a blow meant to decapitate him.

Kalna rolled over just in time to see Raney block Alfar's blade with his body. He froze, eyes wide in horror, as Raney toppled, blood spurting all over.

Runner disentangled himself from the body of the Yorrga he'd killed. His fur was matted with blood, his own and the Yorrga's. He saw Alfar raise his sword again.

"You were a fool to come back into the Breedors, weirling!" Alfar cried, positioning his blade. "Now join your friends in death!"

Kalna raised his hands in a last desperate attempt to save himself, but this time his power failed and he crouched defenseless as Alfar laughed.

Suddenly Alfar rose upward slightly, eyes wide in shock as Runner's horns drove into his back, tearing through skin and muscle and into the heart. The two fell together, landing on top of Ard and the man Kalna had killed.

Runner jerked back, pulling free, gouts of blood and skin dripping from his horns. "Run, Kalna!" he yelled, whirling around to face Jagivan, who himself seemed stunned by Lord Alfar's fall.

Kalna pushed to his feet, his stomach churning with revulsion and the heavy odor of blood in his nostrils. He saw Jagivan lunge at Runner. The beran sidestepped Jagivan's blade, then suddenly he slipped in a puddle of blood. Jagivan darted forward and brought his sword around, catching Runner in the side. The force of the blow threw Runner up against the nearby table. The table gave way under his weight, throwing him headfirst against the stone wall.

Jagivan turned and saw Kalna backing away. "Oh, no you don't," he growled. "You don't escape me a second time." He advanced a step, then another. "I have need of you, darkling, just for a little while, for where two have come, others are sure to follow, and you'll make an excellent shield."

The madness emanating from Jagivan drove Kalna into a madness of his own. Panic-stricken, he turned and ran as Jagivan lunged for him. Darkness closed around him as he fled blood and death and the thunderous beat of rage that followed him.

He heard Jagivan's booted feet closing on him as maniacal laughter echoed through the room. Suddenly Jagivan was there catching at his tunic and swinging him into one of the pillars. Cloth gave and his wings were free. He pushed himself off from the pillar with his outstretched hands, but before he could recover, taloned fingers grabbed his right wing.

Kalna cried out in pain and suddenly remembered the dream that had haunted him for so long: running in darkness, someone following him, terrible mad laughter, then being caught. And that is where his dream had always ended. The thought of death flickered through his mind. Was that why he'd never finished the dream?

Jagivan laughed at Kalna's pain. "Wing hurts, does it? One quick cut of my knife and it would trouble you no longer—then you'd be like the rest of us, weir in blood but not in power!"

When Kalna failed to respond, the weirman readjusted his hold once again and began pulling Kalna toward the tunnelway. "We've got to get out of here before someone else finds us," he mumbled to himself.

Go with him and you're dead, Kalna thought. He clenched his hands, still sticky with blood. He's killed everyone you know! Let him live and you betray them all!

He sensed Jagivan's rage subsiding as he concentrated on escape. Believing this was his only chance, Kalna twisted around and drove his left fist into Jagivan's stomach, then tore from his hold and darted back around one of the pillars.

"Damn you, darkling!" Jagivan raged, "I'll kill you when I get my hands on you again!"

Kalna sidled around the pillar as Jagivan started after him. He couldn't see the weirman, but he could feel him. He licked at dry lips and concentrated on the words his mother had taught him. The tingle of power was there, all he had to do was focus it. It had failed him just a short time ago. If it failed him again . . .

Suddenly Jagivan appeared, stepping out of the shadows. "I've got you, darkling! No more games!"

Kalna raised his hands as the power built within him.

Jagivan took another step closer, his sword only inches from Kalna's hands. His gold mask seemed to glow in the light from the far side of the room.

Jagivan laughed at Kalna's stance. "Threats, darkling? Your power is erratic. You need time to hone your skills, time I'm not about to give you. Come with me now, and perhaps I'll let you live."

"No!" Kalna yelled, pushing the power outward—but again it failed.

"Full in the throes of darkling change and unable to call up a single spark!" Jagivan crowed. "I don't know why I let you scare me that night in your room. Enough delays! You're coming with me. *Now!*"

Suddenly something rose up behind Jagivan as he reached for Kalna. Kalna saw a blotch of white, then a face, haggard and scarred. It was Ard—burning with pain and anger as he drove a knife into Jagivan's back.

Jagivan cried out as he spun around, the knife sticking out of his lower back. Ard stood braced against the pillar, the pain of defeat slowly filling his eyes as Jagivan lifted his sword for a death thrust.

Kalna reacted without thinking and threw himself bodily at Jagivan, pulling the weirman's arm down as they fell together. Jagivan's scream reverberated around the room as they rolled over, the knife in his back driving deeper.

The shock of Jagivan's pain was like an explosion behind Kalna's eyes. He rolled free and pushed to his feet, backing away as quickly as he could.

Jagivan raised himself up partway, then fell back to the floor stomach down, groaning in pain.

Kalna trembled, caught between the two fields of pain and aware that only death would free him—Jagivan's death—and Ard's. One he could kill. The other—never!

Suddenly Ard's knees gave away. Clenching his teeth against the twisting pain, Kalna darted forward and caught Ard as he slid down the pillar, and lowered him gently to the floor.

"Is he dead?" Ard gasped.

"No, not yet."

Ard clasped Kalna's arm tightly as a spasm of pain shook him. Kalna grew faint and had to fight to stay conscious. Gradually the pain subsided and Ard's hand loosened its grip.

"Ard?" Kalna cried.

Ard opened his eyes. "I really hurt, Ka."

"I know." Kalna tried to ease the bloody tunic away from Ard's chest.

"No, Ka," Ard said, a catch in his breath. "Don't."

"You're going to live, Ard! I won't let you die. I'm going for help."

"Who?"

"Thekis. Omecon."

Ard tried to smile. "I knew you'd come, Ka. I told Raney—you'd find us. I saw part of the fight. Raney's dead."

"Yes, I know." Kalna leaned over and kissed Ard's forehead. "I'll be back as soon as I can, Ard."

He stood up and turned and was startled not to find Jagivan's body. In the semidark all he could see was a trail of darkness on the stone floor. In that same moment he realized that the pain he'd felt emanating from Jagivan was gone. All he felt now was Ard's pain. There was no time to make sure of his enemy, not with Ard's life hanging in the balance. He picked up Jagivan's sword and handed it to Ard, who summoned the strength to take it.

"Just in case Jagivan's still alive, Ard. I'll be back as quickly as I can! I swear!"

Ard watched Kalna disappear into the darkness. Hurry, brother, he thought. If you love me, hurry.

Four days had passed since the attack on the Yorrga camp. The day had started out cool and wet, but the sun had finally broken through the clouds and the air was warming up.

Thekis limped toward the lean-to where Prince Ard lay resting. He peered inside and found Kalna tending a small fire.

Kalna looked up, sensing another's presence. He smiled tiredly when he saw his uncle. "I thought you were supposed to be resting."

"I've been resting, but it doesn't look as if you have," Thekis responded good-naturedly. He glanced at Ard, who was still sleeping. "How is he?"

"He's breathing easier now. Whatever it was that you gave him seems to be working."

"I'm a fair physician even without a Yorrga mask. The wound was deep and he'd lost a lot of blood, but luckily no vital organs were damaged. He'll be all right if we can avoid his getting an infection."

Kalna glanced at his uncle's leg, which was bandaged from knee to thigh. "And how are you doing?"

"I'll live. Come out with me a moment where we can talk without disturbing Ard."

Kalna stood and followed Thekis. They crossed the camp and came to stand at the edge of the hill overlooking the ruins. There was a lot of movement below as the survivors of the battle saw to the dead.

Kalna was startled by the numbers of weir he saw. "You told me only thirteen had survived the battle. Where did all the others come from?"

"They've been arriving all morning," Thekis answered. "The news that we'd found Yaril's Grotto brought them. We're stripping the grotto now and sending everything we find on to Galen Keep. I'd like to have left everything where it was, but now that others know how to find the grotto, it wouldn't be wise."

"Has Jagivan's body been found yet?"

"No. All we found was the mask."

"Then he escaped."

"It's possible, or he may be out lying in the woods somewhere, dead or alive—there's no telling. We're still looking."

"Have you got anything out of any of the prisoners?"

Thekis looked up at Kalna, pleased by the questions, for it proved that his nephew was far stronger than he looked; it also bode well for his chances of living through darkling change without any mental damage.

He turned and looked down at the ruins as he answered Kalna's question. "Three of the four prisoners have died. The one who still lives is known to several of the weir who helped us fight the Yorrga. His name is Avar; he has no weir talents. That seems to be the one thing all four prisoners had in common—they were weirmen with nothing to mark them as weir. Avar spoke of never being accepted among his own kind; he claims that he and Jagivan and the others like them were tired of being neither men nor weir and they decided to exact some revenge by starting a war and letting their enemies destroy each other; then, when the time was ripe, they would step in and take over; on which side, he didn't make clear."

Kalna stood quietly studying the ruins and thinking. "Thekis, when Runner and I came upon Jagivan and Lord Alfar arguing, Jagivan said something about a master control. Do you think he could've meant the gold mask?"

"Yes. It's like none other I've ever seen. It wouldn't surprise me if it actually came from the Ancients' home world, wherever that was. Avar said that Jagivan used the gold mask to create a type of Yorrga that would kill upon command. He also spoke about the book you saw in Jagivan's hands. He claims that it's more than a book. He says it contains hundreds of small metal bands similar to those we implant in the Yorrga healing masks, each band containing information on any subject you'd care to name, from history to philosophy, from war to surgery."

"Do you think he's telling the truth?"

Thekis rubbed his jaw with the back of his hand. "Those who've been asking him questions have not been gentle. Yes, I'd say he was telling the truth."

"So, some time ago, Jagivan was poking about the ruins and he found Yaril's Grotto, the mask, and the book," Kalna said, summing it up. "He studied them and decided that there was more than one way to become important in the eyes of his people. And so he created the killer Yorrga, and loosed them on Ard—and my family."

"If only it had been someone else who'd found the grotto," Thekis said, "someone who wasn't hurting or unhappy with his life. When I think of all the Guardians down through the ages who must have used the mask and the book whenever the weirfolk were in trouble or in need of some special knowledge, I can't help but wonder what happened to the last one."

"What bothers me," Kalna said, looking down at the dweorg, "is why anyone would hide such knowledge. Why didn't the Guardians share Yaril's book with everyone?"

"Only they could answer that, Ka. Who knows, perhaps Yaril wanted us to be something different—or more than the Ancients had planned for us. Some kinds of knowledge do tend to limit the imagination—and isn't that what makes us more than the other animals?"

Kalna smiled. "You would've made an excellent Guardian, Thekis. Are you volunteering for the job?"

Thekis slapped Kalna's leg. "Not yet, but who knows?"

"So what do we do now? We have the mask and Jagivan has the book."

"Perhaps we'll find his body yet. He couldn't have gone far, wounded as he was. And if we don't find him, it's just possible we'll still be able to create other healing Yorrga by using the gold mask and a still-working band from one of the functioning masks we have. At least, that's my hope."

"Do you think Ek-nar had any part in all this?"

"You'd never get him to admit it if it's so, and we'd have to be damned careful with our accusations until we had proof."

Kalna looked back toward the lean-to. "What about Ard?"

"As soon as he's well enough to be moved, we'll take him to the House of Char—with a large escort this time. We still don't know how many killer Yorrga escaped or how many more were involved in this plot, and with Ja-givan still unaccounted for, we'll take no more chances. Ard still is the only man capable of ending the threat of war between our two people."

Kalna nodded, then his thoughts turned to another matter. "Where are they burying the dead?"

"The bodies of Lord Alfar and his men are being laid out in one of the tower rooms. Jylak's and Omecon's bodies are being taken back to Pavion for burial. The enemy weir are to be buried south of the ruins; those who fought with us and died will be taken back to their homes."

Kalna thought about one not named. "What about Raney?"

"He's been buried already, in a specal place," another voice answered.

Kalna turned to find Runner standing behind him. "How long have you been there?"

"Just a few seconds," the beran replied. "Didn't you feel me?"

"Not this time," Kalna answered, smiling. "I guess my mind was elsewhere. You said you'd buried Raney. Where?"

"Come. I'll show you."

Runner led Thekis and Kalna down the hill toward the north side of the ruins and into what had once been a garden, now overgrown with trees and old, dried vines. "It will be beautiful here in the spring, I think," Runner said, coming to a mound of fresh dirt. "And I've marked the place just in case someone from the House of Char wants his body returned."

Kalna had been much relieved to learn that Runner was not among the dead when he had returned to the grotto with help for Ard. Other than a few patches of bandaging, the beran looked little different from the day he'd first met him, except perhaps in the eyes, where death had left its shadow.

Kalna looked down at the marker and read the inscription there. Tears blurred his vision as he looked away.

No Greater Gift

It was a fitting epitaph for a valiant friend, he thought. Ard will be pleased.

# ABOUT THE AUTHOR

Marcia Joanne Bennett was born on June 9, 1945. Raised in a rural community, she has spent all but a few of her working years in central New York State.

After graduating from Albany Business College in 1965, she spent the next seven years in banking.

Several years ago she established a small craft shop in her hometown. While running the shop she began writing, a hobby that quickly became an addiction. Her other interests range from reading, painting, and basketry to astrology and parapsychology.